BREATHLESS

DEAN KOONTZ

RANDOM HOUSE
LARGE PRINT

BREATHLESS

A Novel

Copyright © 2009 by Dean Koontz
Title page art from an original photograph by Thomas Buttler

Published in the United States of America by Random House Large Print in association with The Random House Publishing Group, New York. Distributed by Random House, Inc., New York.

A signed, limited edition of the original trade hardcover has been privately printed by Charnel House. Charnelhouse.com

Cover design: Carlos Beltran

The Library of Congress has established a cataloging-in-publication record for this title.

ISBN: 978-0-7393-2865-1

www.randomhouse.com/largeprint

FIRST LARGE PRINT EDITION

10 9 8 7 6 5 4 3 2 1

This Large Print Edition published in accord with the standards of the N.A.V.H.

To Aesop, twenty-six centuries
late and with apologies
for the length.

✳

And as always and forever
to Gerda

Science must not impose any philosophy,
any more than the telephone must tell
us what to say.
                    —G. K. CHESTERTON

BREATHLESS

PART ONE

Life and Death

One

A moment before the encounter, a strange expectancy overcame Grady Adams, a sense that he and Merlin were not alone.

In good weather and bad, Grady and the dog walked the woods and the meadows for two hours every day. In the wilderness, he was relieved of the need to think about anything other than the smells and sounds and textures of nature, the play of light and shadow, the way ahead, and the way home.

Generations of deer had made this path through the forest, toward a meadow of grass and fragrant clover.

Merlin led the way, seemingly indifferent to the spoor of the deer and the possibility of glimpsing the white flags of their tails ahead of him. He was a three-year-old, 160-pound Irish wolfhound, thirty-six inches tall, measured from his withers to the ground, his head higher on a muscular neck.

The dog's rough coat was a mix of ash-gray and darker charcoal. In the evergreen shadows, he sometimes seemed to be a shadow, too, but one not tethered to its source.

As the path approached the edge of the woods, the sunshine beyond the trees suddenly looked peculiar. The light turned coppery, as if the world, bewitched, had revolved toward sunset hours ahead of schedule. With a sequined glimmer, afternoon sun shimmered down upon the meadow.

As Merlin passed between two pines, stepping onto open ground, a vague apprehension—a presentiment of pending contact—gripped Grady. He hesitated in the woodland gloom before following the dog.

In the open, the light was neither coppery nor glimmering, as it had appeared from among the trees. The pale-blue arch of sky and emerald arms of forest embraced the meadow.

No breeze stirred the golden grass, and the late-September day was as hushed as any vault deep in the earth.

Merlin stood motionless, head raised, alert, eyes fixed intently on something distant in the meadow. Wolfhounds were thought to have the keenest eyesight of all breeds of dogs.

The back of Grady's neck still prickled. The perception lingered that something uncanny would occur. He wondered if this feeling arose from his own intuition or might be inspired by the dog's tension.

Standing beside the immense hound, seeking what his companion saw, Grady studied the field, which gently descended southward to another vastness of forest. Nothing moved . . . until something did.

A white form, supple and swift. And then another.

The pair of animals appeared to be ascending the meadow less by intention than by the consequence of their play. They chased each other, tumbled, rolled, sprang up, and challenged each other again in a frolicsome spirit that could not be mistaken for fighting.

Where the grass stood tallest, they almost vanished, but often they were fully visible. Because they remained in motion, however, their precise nature was difficult to define.

Their fur was uniformly white. They weighed perhaps fifty or sixty pounds, as large as midsize dogs. But they were not dogs.

They appeared to be as limber and quick as cats. But they were not cats.

Although he'd lived in these mountains until he

was seventeen, though he had returned four years previously, at the age of thirty-two, Grady had never before seen creatures like these.

Powerful body tense, Merlin watched the playful pair.

Having raised him from a pup, having spent the past three years with little company other than the dog, Grady knew him well enough to read his emotions and his state of mind. Merlin was intrigued but puzzled, and his puzzlement made him wary.

The unknown animals were large enough to be formidable predators if they had claws and sharp teeth. At this distance, Grady could not determine if they were carnivores, omnivores, or herbivores, though the last classification was the least likely.

Merlin seemed to be unafraid. Because of their great size, strength, and history as hunters, Irish wolfhounds were all but fearless. Although their disposition was peaceable and their nature affectionate, they had been known to stand off packs of wolves and to kill an attacking pit bull with one bite and a violent shake.

When the white-furred creatures were sixty or seventy feet away, they became aware of being watched. They halted, raised their heads.

The birdless sky, the shadowy woods, and the meadow remained under a spell of eerie silence. Grady had the peculiar notion that if he moved, his boots would press no sound from the ground under him, and that if he shouted, he would have no voice.

To get a better view of man and dog, one of the white creatures rose, sitting on its haunches in the manner of a squirrel.

Grady wished he had brought binoculars. As far as he could tell, the animal had no projecting muzzle; its black nose lay in nearly the same plane as its eyes. Distance foiled further analysis.

Abruptly the day exhaled. A breeze sighed in the trees behind Grady.

In the meadow, the risen creature dropped back onto all fours, and the pair raced away, seeming to glide more than sprint. Their sleek white forms soon vanished into the golden grass.

The dog looked up inquiringly. Grady said, "Let's have a look."

Where the mysterious animals had gamboled, the grass was bent and tramped. No bare earth meant no paw prints.

Merlin led his master along the trail until the meadow ended where the woods resumed.

A cloud shadow passed over them and seemed to be drawn into the forest as a draft draws smoke.

Gazing through the serried trees into the gloom, Grady felt watched. If the white-furred pair could climb, they might be in a high green bower, cloaked in pine boughs and not easily spotted.

Although he was a hunter by breed and blood, with a Sherlockian sense of smell that could follow the thinnest thread of unraveled scent, Merlin showed no interest in further pursuit.

They followed the tree line west, then northwest, along the curve of meadow, circling toward home as the quickening air whispered through the grass. They returned to the north woods.

Around them, the soft chorus of nature arose once more: birds in song, the drone of insects, the arthritic creak of heavy evergreen boughs troubled by their own weight.

Although the unnatural hush had relented, Grady remained disturbed by a sense of the uncanny. Every time he glanced back, no stalker was apparent, yet he felt that he and Merlin were not alone.

On a long rise, they came to a stream that slithered down well-worn shelves of rock. Where the trees parted, the sun revealed silver scales on the water, which was elsewhere dark and smooth.

With other sounds masked by the hiss and gurgle of the stream, Grady wanted more than ever to look back. He resisted the paranoid urge until his companion halted, turned, and stared downhill.

He did not have to crouch in order to rest one hand on the wolfhound's back. Merlin's body was tight with tension.

The big dog scanned the woods. His high-set

ears tipped forward slightly. His nostrils flared and quivered.

Merlin held that posture for so long, Grady began to think the dog was not so much searching for anything as he was warning away a pursuer. Yet he did not growl.

When at last the wolfhound set off toward home once more, he moved faster than before, and Grady Adams matched the dog's pace.

Two

Authorities raided the illegal puppy mill late Saturday afternoon. Saturday night, Rocky Mountain Gold, an all-volunteer golden-retriever rescue group, took custody of twenty-four breeder dogs that were filthy, malnourished, infested with ticks, crawling with fleas, and suffering an array of untreated infections.

Dr. Camillia Rivers was awakened by a call on her emergency line at 5:05 Sunday morning. Rebecca Cleary, president of Rocky Mountain Gold, asked how many of the twenty-four Cammy might treat in return for nothing but the wholesale cost of what drugs were used.

After looking at the nightstand photo of her golden, Tessa, who had died only six weeks earlier, Cammy said, "Bring 'em all."

Her business partner and fellow vet, Donna Corbett, was in the middle of a one-week vacation. Their senior vet tech, Cory Hern, had gone to visit relatives in Denver for the weekend. When she called the junior tech, Ben Aikens, he agreed to donate his Sunday to the cause.

At 6:20 A.M., a Rocky Mountain Gold caravan of SUVs arrived at the modest Corbett Veterinary Clinic with twenty-four goldens in as desperate condition as any Cammy had ever seen. Every one was potentially a beautiful dog, but at the moment they looked like the harbingers of Armageddon.

Having endured their entire lives in cramped cages, not merely neglected but also abused, having been forced without vet care to bear litter after litter to the point of exhaustion, they were timid, trembling, vomiting in fear, frightened of everyone they encountered. In their experience, human beings were cruel or at best indifferent to them, and they expected to be struck.

Eight members of the rescue group assisted with bathing, shaving fur away from hot spots and other sores, clipping knots out of coats, deticking, and other tasks, all of which were complicated by the need continually to calm and reassure the dogs.

Cammy was unaware that the morning had passed until she checked her wristwatch at 2:17 in the afternoon. Having skipped breakfast, she took a fifteen-minute break and retreated to her apartment above the veterinary facility, to have a bite of lunch.

For a long time, Donna Corbett had run the practice with her husband, John, who was also a veterinarian. When John died of a heart attack four years earlier, Donna divided their large apartment into two units and sought a partner who would be as committed to animals as she was and as John had been, who was willing to **live** the work.

The Corbetts viewed veterinary medicine less as a profession than as a calling, which was why Cammy didn't need to consult with her partner when agreeing to treat the puppy-mill dogs pro bono.

After quickly putting together a cheese sandwich, she opened a cold bottle of tea sweetened with peach nectar. She ate lunch while standing at her kitchen sink.

As she'd been working with the folks from Rocky Mountain Gold, two calls had come in, one regarding a sick cow. She referred the caller to Dr. Amos Renfrew, who was the best cow doc in the county.

The second inquiry came from Nash Franklin, regarding a horse at High Meadows Farm. Because the situation wasn't urgent, Cammy would pay Nash a visit later in the afternoon.

She had nearly finished the cheese sandwich

when Ben Aikens, her vet tech, rang her from downstairs. "Cammy, you've got to see this."

"What's wrong?"

"These dogs. I've never seen anything like it."

"Be right there." She shoved the last piece of the sandwich into her mouth and chewed it on the run.

Puppy-mill breeders were routinely so physically and emotionally traumatized by their abuse that the new experiences of freedom—open spaces; cars; steps, which they never before climbed or descended; strange noises; soap and water; even kind words and gentle touching—could induce a dangerous state of shock. Most often, the cause of shock was chronic dehydration or untreated infections, but there were times when Cammy could attribute it to nothing else but the impact of the new, of change.

If they could be cured of their diseases and conditions, the dogs would need months of socializing, but in time they would find their courage, regain the joyful spirit that defined a golden, and learn to trust, to love, to be loved.

Descending the exterior stairs from her apartment, she prayed that all these dogs might survive and thrive, that not one of them would be lost to infection or disease, or shock.

Cammy entered the clinic by the front door. She hurried through the small waiting room, along a hallway flanked by four examination cubicles, and through a swinging door into the large, tile-floored open space that included treatment stations and grooming facilities.

Awaiting her was a sight far different from the crisis she had anticipated. Every one of these brutalized dogs appeared to have shed its anxiety, to have suppressed already the memories of torment in favor of embracing a new life. Tails wagging, eyes bright, grinning that fabled golden grin, they submitted happily to belly rubs and ear scratches from the Rocky Mountain Gold volunteers. They nuzzled one another and explored the room, sniffing this and that, curious about things that a short while ago frightened them. None lay in cataplexic collapse or hid its face, or cowered, or trembled.

This unlikely sight had startled Cammy to a stop. Now, as she moved farther into the room, Ben Aikens hurried to her.

Ben, twenty-seven, had a perpetually sunny disposition, but even for him, his current mood seemed unusually buoyant. He was virtually shining with delight. "Isn't it fantastic? You ever seen anything like it? Have you, Cammy?"

"No. Never. What happened here?"

"We don't know. The dogs were like before, anxious, distressed, so pitiful. Then they—Well, they— They went still and quiet, all of them at once. They lifted their ears, all of them listening, and they heard something."

"Heard what?"

"I don't know. We didn't hear it. They raised their heads. They all stood up. They stood so still, motionless, they heard something."

"What were they looking at?"

"Nothing. Everything. I don't know. But look at them now."

Cammy reached the center of the room. The rescued animals were everywhere engaged in the spirited behavior of ordinary dogs.

When she knelt, two goldens came to her, tails wagging, seeking affection. Then another and another, and a fifth. Sores, scars, ear-flap hematomas, fly-bite dermatitis: None of that seemed to matter to the dogs anymore. This one was half blind from an untreated eye infection, that one limped from patellar dislocation, but they seemed happy, and they were uncomplaining. Ragged, tattered, gaunt, freed from a life of cruelty and abuse less than twenty-four hours earlier, they were suddenly and inexplicably socialized, neither afraid any longer nor timid.

Rebecca Cleary, head of the rescue group, knelt beside Cammy. "Pinch me. This has got to be a dream."

"Ben says they all stood up at once, listening to something."

"At least a minute. Listening, alert. We weren't even there."

"What do you mean?"

"Like they weren't aware of us anymore. Almost . . . in a trance."

Cammy held a retriever's head in her cupped hands, rubbing its flews with her thumbs. The dog, so recently fearful and shy, accepted the face massage with pleasure, met her eyes, and did not look away.

"At first," Rebecca said, "it was eerie . . ."

The animal's eyes were as golden as its coat.

". . . then they became aware of us again, and it was wonderful."

The dog's eyes were as bright as gems. Topaz. They seemed to have an inner light. Eyes of great beauty—clear, direct, and deep.

Three

The unpaved turnoff was where he expected to find it, two hundred yards past Milepost 76 on the state highway. He coasted almost to a stop, afraid that his hopes would not be fulfilled, but then he wheeled the Land Rover right, onto the one-lane road.

Henry Rouvroy had not seen his twin brother, James, for fifteen years. He was nervous but inexpressibly happy about the prospect of their reunion.

Their lives had followed different paths. So much time passed so quickly.

At first, when the idea to reconnect with Jim came to Henry, he dismissed it. He worried that he wouldn't be met with hospitality.

They had never experienced the fabled psychic connection of identicals. On the other hand, they had never been at odds with each other, either. There was no bad blood between them, no bitterness.

They had simply been different from each other, interested in different things. Even in childhood, Henry was the social twin, always in a group of friends. Jimmy preferred solitude. Henry thrived on sports, games, action, challenges. Jimmy was content with books.

When their parents divorced, they were twelve. Instead of sharing custody of both boys, their father took Henry to New York to live with him, and their mother settled in a small town in Colorado with Jimmy, which seemed right and natural to everyone.

Since they were twelve, they had seen each other only once, when they were twenty-two, at the reading of their father's will. Their mother died of cancer a year before the old man passed away.

They agreed to stay in touch. Henry wrote five letters to his brother over the following year, and Jim answered two of them. Thereafter, Henry wrote less often, and Jim never again replied.

Although they were brothers, Henry accepted that they were also virtually strangers. As much as he might want to be part of a closely knit family, it was not to be.

But by nature, the human heart yearns most for what it cannot have. Time and circumstances brought Henry here to rural Colorado, with the hope that their relationship might change.

Pines crowded close to the road, and branches swagged within inches of the roof. Even in daytime, headlights were needed.

Years earlier, the University of Colorado had owned this land. Jim's remote house had been occupied by a series of researchers who studied conifer ecology and tested theories of forest management.

The hard-packed earth gave way to shale in places, and nine-tenths of a mile from the paved highway, at the end of the lane, Henry arrived at his brother's property.

The one-story clapboard house had a deep porch with a swing and rocking chairs. Although modest, it looked well-maintained and cozy.

Willows and aspens shaded the residence.

Henry knew that the clearing encompassed six acres of sloping fields, because "Six Acres" was the title of one of his brother's poems. Jim's writing had appeared in many prestigious journals, and four slender volumes of his verse had been published.

No one made money from poetry anymore. Jim and his wife, Nora, worked their six acres as a truck farm during the growing season, selling vegetables from a booth at the county farmer's market.

Attached to the barn were a large coop and

fenced chicken yard. A formidable flock shared the yard in good weather, kept to the well-insulated coop in winter, producing eggs that Jim and Nora also sold.

She was a quilter of such talent that her designs were regarded as art. Her quilts sold in galleries, and Henry supposed she produced the larger part of their income, though they were by no means rich.

Henry knew all of that from reading his brother's poems. Hard work and farm life provided the subjects of the verses. Jim was the latest in a long tradition of American literary rustics.

Following the dirt track between the house and the barn, Henry saw his brother splitting cordwood with an axe. A wheelbarrow full of split wood stood nearby. He parked and got out of the Land Rover.

Jim sunk the axe blade in the stump that he used as a chopping block, and left it wedged there. Stripping off his worn leather work gloves, he said, "My God—Henry?"

His look of incredulity was less than the delight for which Henry had hoped. But then he broke into a smile as he approached.

Reaching out to shake hands, Henry was surprised and pleased when Jim hugged him instead.

Although Henry worked out with weights and on a treadmill, Jim was better muscled, solid. His face was more weathered than Henry's, too, and still tanned from summer.

Nora came out of the house, onto the porch, to see what was happening. "Good Lord, Jim," she said, "you've cloned yourself."

She looked good, with corn-silk hair and eyes a darker blue than the sky, her smile lovely, her voice musical.

Five years younger than Jim, she had married him only twelve years ago, according to the author's bio on the poetry books. Henry had never met her or seen a photograph of her.

She called him Claude, but he quickly corrected her. He never used his first name, but instead answered to his middle.

When she kissed his cheek, her breath smelled cinnamony. She said she'd been nibbling a sweet-roll when she heard the Land Rover.

Inside, on the kitchen table, beside the sweetroll plate were what Henry assumed to be five utility knives, useful for farm tasks.

As Nora poured coffee, she said nothing about the knives. Neither did Jim as he moved them—and two slotted sharpening stones—from the table to a nearby counter.

Nora insisted that Henry stay with them, though she warned him that a sofa bed was all they had by way of accommodations, in the claustrophobic room that Jim called an office.

"Haven't had a houseguest in nine years," Jim said, and it seemed to Henry that a knowing look passed between husband and wife.

The three of them fell into easy conversation around the kitchen table, over homemade cinnamon rolls and coffee.

Nora proved charming, and her laugh was infectious. Her hands were strong and rough from work, yet feminine and beautifully shaped.

She had nothing in common with the sharky women who cruised in Henry's circle in the city. He was happy for his brother.

Even as he marveled at how warmly they welcomed him, at how they made him feel at home and among **family,** as he had never felt with Jim before, Henry was not entirely at ease.

His vague disquiet arose in part from his perception that Jim and Nora were in a private conversation, one conducted without words, with furtive looks, nuanced gestures, and subtle body language.

Jim expressed surprise that someone had drawn Henry's attention to his poetry. "Why would they think we were related?"

They didn't share the name Rouvroy. Following their parents' divorce, Jim had legally taken his mother's maiden name, Carlyle.

"Well," Henry said drily, "maybe it was your photo on the book."

Jim laughed at his thickheadedness, and although he seemed to be embarrassed by his brother's praise, they talked about his poems. Henry's favorite, "The Barn," described the humble interior of that structure with such rich images and feeling that it sounded no less beautiful than a cathedral.

"The greatest beauty always **is** in everyday things," Jim said. "Would you like to see the barn?"

"Yes, I would." Henry admired his brother's poetry more than he had yet been able to say. Jim's verses had an ineffable quality so haunting it was not easy to discuss. "I'd like to see the barn."

Clearly in love with this piece of the world that he and Nora had made their own, Jim grinned, nodded, and rose from the table.

Nora said, "I'll put linens on the sofa bed and start thinking about what's for dinner."

Following Jim from the kitchen, Henry glanced at the knives on the counter. On second consideration, they looked less like ordinary task knives than like thrust-and-cut weapons. The four- and five-inch blades had nonreflective finishes. Two seemed to feature assisted-opening mechanisms for quick blade release.

Then again, Henry knew nothing about farming. These knives might be standard stock at any farm-supply store.

Outside, the afternoon air remained mild. From the split cords of pine came the scent of raw wood.

Overhead, two magnificent birds with four-foot wingspans glided in intersecting gyres. The ventral feathers of the first were white with black wing tips. The second was boldly barred in white and brown.

"Northern harriers," Jim said. "The white one with the black tips is the male. Harriers are raptors. When they're hunting, they fly low over the fields and kill with a sudden pounce."

He worked the axe loose from the tree-stump chopping block.

"Better put this away in the barn," he said, "before I forget and leave it overnight."

"Harriers," Henry said. "They're so beautiful, you don't think of them as killing anything."

· "They eat mostly mice," Jim said. "But also smaller birds."

Henry grimaced. "Cannibalism?"

"They don't eat other harriers. Their feeding on smaller birds is no more cannibalism than us feeding on other mammals—pigs, cows."

"Living in the city, I guess we idealize nature," Henry said.

"Well, when you accept the way of things, there's a stark kind of beauty in the dance of predators and prey."

Heading to the barn, Jim carried the axe in both hands, as if to raise and swing it should he see something that needed to be chopped.

The harriers had fled the sky.

When Henry glanced back toward the house, he saw Nora watching them from a window. With her pale hair and white blouse, she looked like a ghost behind the glass. She turned away.

"Life and death," Jim said as they drew near the barn.

"Excuse me?"

"Predators and prey. The necessity of death, if life is to have meaning and proportion. Death as a part of life. I'm working on a series of poems with those themes."

Jim opened the man-size entrance beside the pair of larger barn doors. Henry followed his brother into the wedge of sunshine that the door admitted to this windowless and otherwise dark space.

Inside, in the instant before the lights came on, Henry was gripped by the expectation that before him would be some sight for which Jim's poem had not prepared him, that the poem was a lie, that the truck farming and the quilting and the simple-folks image were all lies, that the reality of this place and these people was more terrible than anything he could imagine.

When Jim threw a switch, a string of bare light bulbs brightened the length of that cavernous space, revealing the barn to be nothing more than a barn. A tractor and a backhoe were garaged on the left. Two horses occupied stalls on the right. The air was fragrant with the scents of hay and feed grain.

Although Henry's alarming premonition had proved false, and although he knew that fearing his brother was as absurd as fearing the tractor or the horses, or the smell of hay, his sense of a nameless impending horror did not abate.

Behind him, the barn door swung shut of its own weight.

Jim turned to him with the axe, and Henry shrank back, and Jim stepped past him to hang the axe on a rack of tools.

Heart racing, breath suddenly ragged, Henry drew the SIG P245 from the snugly fit shoulder rig under his jacket and shot his twin point-blank, twice in the chest and once in the face.

Henry had come here with the hope that his relationship with his brother would change, and his hope had been fulfilled. Claude Henry Rouvroy was in the process of becoming James Carlyle.

The pistol was fitted with a sound suppressor, and the shots were no louder than a horse cutting wind. Indeed, neither of the horses had been spooked by the gunfire.

Standing over the corpse, Henry strove to quiet his breathing. His tremors forced him to holster the pistol to avoid accidentally squeezing off another round.

He had worried that his brother would grow suspicious of him, and he had feared that he would not be able to pull the trigger when the time came. In the process of assiduously repressing those fears so that he could carry out his plan, he projected his motivations onto Jim, imagining a conspiracy between him and Nora, finding in everyday objects—the knives, the axe—proof of sinister intentions. He had misread menace in innocent actions: Nora watching them from the window, Jim talking about the harriers, about predators and prey.

After a couple of minutes, when his breathing returned to normal and the tremors abated, Henry was able to laugh at himself. Although his laughter was soft, something about it disturbed the horses. They whinnied nervously and pawed the stall floors with their hooves.

Four

Grady Adams lived in a two-story house with silvered cedar siding and a black slate roof, the last of ten residences on a county road. The two-lane blacktop had no official name, only a number, but locals called it Cracker's Drive, after Cracker Conley, who built—and for forty years occupied—the house in which Grady now lived.

No one remembered what Cracker's first name had been or why he was called Cracker. Evidently he was an eccentric and certainly a recluse, because to the locals, Cracker was more of a legend than he was a real neighbor with whom they had interacted.

In their minds, Conley's addiction to solitude forever affected the character of the house itself. They rarely called it the Conley place or Cracker's place, never the Adams house or even the house at the end of the lane. It was known as the hermit's house, and in respect of the name, they tended to keep their distance.

Most of the time, their reticence suited Grady just fine. He was not a misanthrope. But in recent years, he had enough experience—too much—of people, which was why he returned to these sparsely populated mountains. For at least a while, perhaps a long while, he preferred the solitude that Cracker Conley apparently had cherished.

In the kitchen, after returning from the hike on which the intriguing animals had been encountered, Grady prepared Merlin's four o'clock meal. Preparation took longer than consumption.

"You were well named, the way you make food vanish."

The dog licked his chops and ambled to the door to be let out.

Half of the three-acre property lay behind the house. After his dinner, the wolfhound liked to prowl the grounds, sniffing the grass to learn what creatures of field and forest had recently visited. The yard was Merlin's newspaper.

On the back porch, with an icy bottle of beer, Grady sat in one of two teak rockers with wine-red cushions.

A low table with a black-marble top stood beside the chair. Stacked on the table were three reference books from his library.

As intent as a detective at a crime scene, nose to the grass, Merlin vacuumed every clue to the identities of all trespassers.

A large paper birch overhung the north side of the house, and three others graced the yard, their white bark tinted gold in places by the late-afternoon sun. At times, Merlin seemed to be following the intricate patterns the trees cast upon the lawn, as if their shadows were cryptography that he intended to read and decode.

No fence was needed to contain him. He never rebelled against the rule to stay within his master's sight.

Grady's property ended where mown lawn gave way to tall grass. The forest loomed, the land rose under the forest, the foothills broke in green waves against the mountains, and the mountains soared.

From time to time, Merlin marked his territory. For the more substantive half of his toilet, he waded into the tall grass, where there would be no need to pick up after him. Even then he remained within sight, for the grass didn't rise above his brisket.

When he returned to the yard, he raced in great circles and figure eights, chasing nothing, running for the delight of running. His long legs were made for galloping, his heart for joy.

The dog's beauty was not just that of a well-bred breed, but also the more profound beauty that confirms its source and inspires hope. Two things that most comforted Grady were making Craftsman-style furniture—which was his trade—and watching Merlin.

When the wolfhound returned to the porch, drank from his water bowl, and lay in happy exhaustion beside the rocking chair, Grady picked up the first of the books on the table. Like the other two, this one was a reference guide to the wildlife in these mountains.

He had traded bustle for rustic, power for peace, and glamor for the honesty of this artless landscape. Artless it was, because nature stood above mere art, with none of art's pretensions.

Having made this trade, he wanted to know the names of the things he loved about this land. Taking the trouble to know the names of things was a way of paying them respect.

His library contained dozens of volumes about the flora, the fauna, the geology, and the natural history of these mountains. This trio offered more photographs than the others.

None of the three books contained a picture of any animal remotely like the pair in the meadow.

As the sun descended toward the peaks, Merlin rose and moved to the head of the porch steps. He stood as if serving as a sentinel, gazing across the backyard toward the tall grass, the woods beyond.

The wolfhound made a sound that was half purr

and half growl, not as if warning of danger, but as if something puzzled him.

"What is it? Smell something, big guy?"

Merlin did not look at Grady but remained intent upon the deepening shadows among the distant trees.

Five

Walls of shimmering gold and a treasure of gold cascading along the blacktop: The private lane that led to High Meadows Farm was flanked by quaking aspens in their autumn dress, which lent value to the late-afternoon sunshine and paid out rich patterns of light and shadow across the windshield of Cammy's Explorer.

She drove past the grand house, to the equestrian facilities, and parked at the end of a line of horse trailers. Carrying her medical bag, she walked to the exercise yard, which was flanked by two stables painted emerald-green with white trim.

A promising yearling had come down with urticaria—nettle rash, as the older grooms called it. This allergic reaction would eventually clear up naturally, but for the comfort of the horse,

Cammy could relieve the urticaria with an antihis-
tamine injection.

At the end of the yard, a third building housed
the tack room and the office of the trainer, Nash
Franklin. Living quarters for the grooms were on
the second floor.

Lights glowed in Nash's office. The door stood
open, but Cammy could find no one. The enormous tack room also proved to be deserted.

In the first stable, Cammy discovered the stall
doors open on both sides of the central aisle. The
horses were gone.

Stepping outside once more, she heard voices
and followed them to the fenced meadow on the
north side of the building.

The Thoroughbreds were in the pasture: the
yearlings, the colts and fillies, the broodmares, the
studhorses, the current racers, at least forty of
them in all. She'd never seen them gathered in one
place before, and she couldn't imagine for what
purpose they had been brought together.

Many of the horses were accompanied by their
pets. High-strung, sensitive creatures, Thoroughbreds tended to be happier and calmer when they
had a companion animal that hung with them and
even shared their stalls. Goats were successful in
this role, and to a lesser extent, dogs. But the
meadow also contained a few cats, even a duck.

The fact of this assembly, the herd and its menagerie, was not the most curious thing about the scene. As Cammy passed through the gate and into the pasture, she noted that every one of the animals faced west, toward the mountains. They were extraordinarily still.

Heads raised, eyes fixed, they seemed less to be staring at something than to be . . . listening.

Suddenly she realized that she was witnessing a scene similar to what Ben Aikens had described when, in her absence, the rescued golden retrievers had gotten to their feet to listen to something that none of the people present had been able to hear.

The eastward-slanting light brightened the equine faces. Black shadows flowed backward from their heads, like continuations of their manes, flowed off their rumps and tails, reaching eastward across the grass even as the horses yearned toward the west.

Also in the pasture were half a dozen grooms. And the owners of High Meadows Farm, Helen and Tom Vironi.

Clearly perplexed, the people moved among the herd, gently touching the Thoroughbreds, speaking softly. But the animals appeared to be oblivious of them.

The goats, the dogs, the cats, the single duck

were likewise entranced, seeming to hearken to something only animals could hear.

Tall enough to look into a horse's eyes even when it stood proud with its head raised, Nash Franklin spotted Cammy. She and the trainer made their way toward each other.

"They've been like this for almost fifteen minutes," Nash said. "It started with a few in the exercise yard, a few in the pasture."

According to her vet tech Ben Aiken, the golden retrievers had stood in their trance for only a minute or so.

Nash said, "Those in the stables began to kick the walls around them so violently, we worried they'd injure themselves."

"They were afraid of something?"

"That isn't how it seemed. More just . . . determined to be let out. We didn't know what was happening. We still don't."

"You released them?"

"Felt we had to. They came right to the pasture to be with the others. And they won't be led away. What's happening here, Cammy?"

She approached the nearest horse, Gallahad. A deep mahogany, almost black, the magnificent three-year-old weighed perhaps twelve hundred pounds.

Like the other horses, in his perfect stillness,

Gallahad appeared to be tense, stiff. But when Cammy stroked his loin, his flank, and forward to his shoulder, she found that he was at ease.

She pressed her hand against his jugular groove and traced it along his muscular neck. The horse neither moved nor even so much as rolled an eye to consider her.

Cammy stood five feet four, and Gallahad towered, immense. Great Thoroughbreds were usually tractable, and some might be docile with the right trainer, but few were entirely submissive. Yet in this peculiar moment, Gallahad seemed lamblike. Nothing in the intensity of his concentration on the western mountains suggested fierceness or even willfulness.

His nostrils didn't flare, neither did his ears twitch. His forelock fluttered against his poll as a faint breeze disturbed it, and his mane stirred along his crest, but otherwise Gallahad remained motionless. Even when she stroked his cheek, his nearer eye did not favor her.

Following his gaze, she saw nothing unusual in the foreground, only the next wave of foothills and the mountains in the background, and ultimately the sun swollen by the lens of atmosphere as Earth resolutely turned away from the light.

At her side, Nash Franklin said, "Well?"

Before she could reply, the horses stirred from

their trance. They shook their heads, snorted, looked around. A few lowered their muzzles to graze upon the sweet grass, while others cantered in looping patterns as if taking pure pleasure from movement, from the cool air, from the orange light that seemed to **burst** through the pasture. The Thoroughbreds' pets became animated as well, the goats and the dogs, the cats, the duck.

All the animals were behaving only as they ordinarily would, no longer spellbound. Yet here in the aftermath of the event, when all was normal, all seemed magical: the whispering grass, the soft incantatory thud of cantering hooves, the canticle of nickering horses and panting dogs, the season's last lingering fireflies suddenly bearing their wishing lamps through the pre-dusk air, the sable shadows and the gilding of all things by the descending sun, the sky electric-purple in the east and becoming a cauldron of fire in the west.

The grooms and the exercise boys, the trainer and his assistant, Helen and Tom Vironi, and Cammy Rivers all turned to one another with the same unasked and unanswerable questions: **Why did the animals seem enchanted? What did they hear if they heard anything at all? What happened here? What is still happening? What is this I feel, this wonder without apparent cause, this expectancy of I-know-not-what, this sense**

that something momentous passed through the day without my seeing it?

Cammy's vision blurred. She did not know why tears filled her eyes. She blotted them on her shirt-sleeve and blinked, blinked for clarity.

Six

The harrier glided out of the east, into the autumnal light of the declining sun, less than ten feet above the harvested fields, its elongated shadow rippling over the furrowed earth behind it. The bird dropped abruptly and snared something from the ground while remaining in flight. An oarsman in a sea of air, it sculled into the westering sun, passing over Henry Rouvroy as he crossed from the barn toward the clapboard house.

Henry looked up and glimpsed a rodent squirming in the harrier's clenched talons. He thrilled to the sight, which confirmed for him that he was no more and no less than this winged predator, a free agent in a world with no presiding presence.

During his years in public service, he had come to realize that he was a beast whose cruelest in-

stincts were barely governed by the few tools of re-
pression with which his upbringing and his culture
provided him. Not long ago, he had decided to
unchain himself and to be what he truly was. A
monster. Not yet a monster fully realized, but certainly now a monster in the making.

In the house, he found Nora at the kitchen sink,
deftly skinning potatoes with a swivel-blade peeler.

Eventually Henry would want a woman, although not to cook his meals. Nora was sufficiently attractive to excite him, and there was a
perverse appeal to going by force where his brother
had gone by invitation.

She didn't realize he had entered the room until
he asked, "Does the house have a cellar?"

"Oh. Henry. Yes, it's a good big cellar. Potatoes
keep well down there for the better part of the
winter."

She would keep well there, too, but he decided
against her. When the time came to get a woman,
he would be better off with a younger and more
easily intimidated specimen, one who had not
grown strong from farm work.

"Where's Jim?" she asked.

"In the barn. He sent me to get you. He thinks
something's wrong with one of the horses."

"Wrong? What's wrong?"

Henry shrugged. "I don't know horses."

"Which is it—my Beauty or Samson?"

"The one in the second stall."

"Samson. Jim loves that horse."

"I don't think it's serious," Henry said. "But it's something."

After rinsing her hands under the faucet and quickly drying them on a dishtowel, Nora hurried out of the kitchen.

Henry followed her through the house and onto the front porch.

Descending the steps, she said, "So you've never ridden?"

"Only things that have wheels," he said.

"There's nothing like saddling up and riding to the high meadows on a crisp day. The world's never more right than it is then."

Crossing the yard toward the barn, he said, "You make it sound appealing. Maybe I should learn."

"You couldn't find a better riding instructor than Jim."

"Successful farmer, poet, horseman. Jim is a hard act to follow, even for an identical twin."

He spoke only to have something to say, to keep her distracted. Nothing in his words revealed his intentions, but something in his tone or some unintended inflection given one word or another must have struck her as wrong.

Half a dozen steps short of the barn, Nora halted, turned, and frowned at him. Whatever she heard in his voice must have been even more evident in his face, because her eyes widened with recognition of his nature.

Our five senses are in service to our sixth, and the sixth is the intuitive sense of danger to body or soul.

He knew that she knew, and she confirmed her knowledge by taking a step backward, away from him, and then another step.

When Henry withdrew the pistol from under his jacket, Nora turned to run. He shot her in the back, again as she lay facedown.

After putting away the gun, he turned her on her back. He seized her by the wrists and dragged her into the barn and placed her beside her husband.

The first shot must have killed her instantly. Her heart had pumped little blood from her wounds.

Her eyes were open. For a long moment, Henry stared into them, into the nothing that had once appeared to be something, into the truth of her, which was that she had always been nothing.

Until this day, he had never killed anyone. He was pleased to know that he could do it, pleased also that he felt neither guilt nor anxiety.

Like Hamlet, he had no moral existence, no sense of any sacred order. Unlike Hamlet, his condition did not cause him to despair.

Henry's major at Harvard had been political science. He minored in literature.

Prince Hamlet had something to teach those in either discipline. In literature classes, he was assumed to be a tragic figure, sworn to enforce the laws of a sacred order in which he could no longer believe. In certain political-science circles, he was used to illustrate that violence and anarchy can be preferable to indecision.

Henry lived free of despair and indecision. He was a man of his time and, he liked to think, perhaps a man for the ages.

Later, he would use the couple's backhoe to excavate their final resting place. In the Land Rover lay a fifty-pound bag of lime, which he would pour atop them in their grave, to facilitate decomposition and to mask the odor of it, reducing the chances that some carrion eater would try to dig its way to them.

Leaving the cadavers in the barn, Henry went to the Rover, put up the tailgate, and removed two small suitcases. Each of them held a million dollars in hundreds and twenties. He carried them into the house.

Seven

On his way from Chicago to a conference in Denver, Dr. Lamar Woolsey took a side trip to Las Vegas.

The white sun blistered the pale sky. By late afternoon, a heat sink comprised of the towering hotels, the streets, the vast parking lots, and the surrounding desert had stored enough radiant energy to keep the city warm throughout the night.

In the taxi, from the airport to the hotel, Lamar watched rising thermals distort the more distant buildings, making them shimmer like structures in a mirage. In the foreground, windows and glass walls, bright with solar reflections, appeared to buckle, an illusion caused by the changing perspective of the taxi in relation to the buildings.

Illusion and reality. The former enchanted most people these days; the latter had been out of fashion for years. This city of casinos stood as proof that humanity preferred fantasy over truth.

In his hotel room, Lamar changed into white tennis shoes, white slacks, a blue Hawaiian shirt, and a white sport coat.

In a money belt under the shirt, he carried ten thousand in hundred-dollar bills. He folded two thousand more into his pockets.

Wherever he went in the world, he never gambled at a casino in his hotel. That made it too easy for a pit boss to learn his name.

On Las Vegas Boulevard South, he walked north through crowds of tourists. Most wore sunglasses, some with lenses so dark that they seemed not to be shielding their eyes, but instead to be concealing that they had no eyes, only smooth skin where eyes should have been.

He chose a casino and a blackjack table. He bought six hundred dollars' worth of chips.

Sixty years old, with a round brown grandfatherly face that reminded people of a beloved comedian and sitcom star, with wiry white hair, twenty pounds overweight, Lamar Woolsey seldom inspired suspicion. The pit crew glanced at him and showed no interest.

The black dealer was outgoing—"Have a seat, brother"—too young to have grown bored with table talk. Of the three other players, two were loquacious, one sullen.

Lamar identified himself as Benny Mandelbrot, and he chatted up everyone, patiently waiting to learn why he was there.

Decades earlier, when the effectiveness of card counting became widely known, most casinos went to six-deck shoes. Keeping a running mental inventory of a 312-card shoe to calculate the odds in your favor hand by hand was geometrically more difficult than doing the same with a single deck, foiling both amateurs and most hustlers.

When rich veins appeared in a six-deck game, however, they could run longer and be more rewarding than in single-deck play. In three hours, his six-hundred stake had grown to eleven thousand.

The pit crew had become interested in him but not suspicious. They hoped to keep him at the table until he gave back his winnings.

He allayed suspicion with occasional bad plays. When the dealer showed a king and the deck was full of face cards, Lamar split a pair of sevens "on a hunch," and lost. His highly calculated erratic play made him appear to be an ordinary mark on a lucky streak.

Lamar still didn't know why he was there until, at a quarter to six, the cocktail waitress—her name tag identified her as Teresa—asked if he wanted another diet soda.

She was an attractive brunette with a spray of

freckles and a forced smile. When he glanced at her to confirm he wanted another soft drink, unshed tears stood in her eyes, barely repressed.

The current dealer, a redhead named Arlene, finished shuffling the six decks. Lamar had been tipping her well, so they had rapport.

As Arlene loaded the shoe, Lamar looked after Teresa, then asked the dealer, "What's her story?"

"Terri? Husband was a Marine. Died in the war last year. One kid. Marty, eight years old, he's a sweetie. She loves him to death. He has Down syndrome. She's tough, but tough isn't always enough."

Lamar played three hands and won two before the cocktail waitress returned with his soft drink.

Of his stake on the table, he gave seven hundred and change to Arlene. He scooped up the remaining eleven thousand in chips and poured them onto Teresa's drink tray.

Startled, the waitress said, "Hey, no, I can't take this."

"I don't want anything for it," Lamar assured her, "and there's nothing I need it for."

Leaving her astonished and stammering, he followed the bank of blackjack tables toward the street entrance to the casino.

So meticulously barbered, manicured, and well-dressed that he might have been a mannequin come to life, the pit boss caught up with Lamar and stepped between two game tables. "Mr. M., wait," he said, referring to the Mandelbrot name that Lamar had used. "Mr. M., are you sure you want to do that?"

"Yes. Quite sure. Is there a problem?"

"You were only drinking diet soda. I don't see a problem." Still half suspicious of some scheme, he added, "But it's unusual."

"What if I were to tell you that I've got an incurable cancer, four months to live, no need for money and no one to leave it to?"

In the fantasy world of the casino, death was the truth most aggressively repressed. No clock could be found in any casino, as if games of chance were played outside of time. Gamblers now and then petitioned God for help, but they never talked to Death.

The pit boss was disconcerted, as if the C word might break the spell that had been cast upon everyone within these walls, as if the mere mention of metastasis would transform the swank and glitter into mud and ashes. He straightened the knot in his tie, which was not crooked. "That's tough. Take care of yourself. Good luck, Mr. M."

Lamar Woolsey did not have cancer. He had not claimed to have it. But the what-if question served as a sufficient reminder of reality to scare off the pit boss.

Outside, in the sharply angled gold-and-orange

sunlight, the world seemed about to burst into flames. Acres of neon signs welcomed the oncoming evening.

Many people in the crowds of tourists no longer wore sunglasses, but their eyes couldn't be read behind cataracts of brilliant colors.

Eight

With darkness at the windows and with the great mass of Merlin slumped at his feet, Grady Adams ate dinner at the kitchen table. The dog hoped for a piece or two of chicken but did not beg, feigning disinterest to preserve his dignity.

The CD player on a nearby counter provided music. Grady didn't have a TV, and he didn't want one. Although he usually preferred silence even to the most elegant noise, at times Merlin's presence and books did not adequately fill his leisure hours.

At the moment, books were giving him little of what he sought from them, while Beethoven's Opus 27, Number 2—the "Moonlight" Sonata— was both balm and inspiration.

Having exhausted his collection of illustrated volumes, he pored through essays about the

Colorado mountains while he ate, through memoirs of lives passed in these precincts of the natural world. He skimmed pages in search of references to unknown animals, for strange tales about white-furred creatures that were playful but shy.

He suspected the books would not help him, but he searched them anyway. The encounter in the meadow had affected him powerfully for reasons he could understand but for others that he only half grasped. Something more about the creatures than their uniqueness and their mysterious nature affected him, some quality he sensed that they possessed but that remained too elusive to name.

Merlin leaped to his feet so suddenly that he knocked his head against the underside of the table. The wolfhound was at no risk of concussion. The table would collapse long before the dog did.

When Merlin padded out of the kitchen, into the hallway that led to the living room, Grady put down his fork, let his book fall shut, and sat listening for a bark. After half a minute, having heard neither a bark nor the thudding paws of the returning son of Ireland, he opened the book again.

As Grady picked up his fork, Merlin thumped along the hall to the kitchen doorway, where he stood in a posture of alarm. Easily read, his expression said, **We've got a situation, Dad. What do I**

have to do—learn Morse code and beat out a message with my tail?

"All right, okay," Grady said, rising from the dinette chair.

The dog hurried toward the front of the house once more. Grady found him in the open vestibule, off the living room, his back to the front door, facing the stairs to the second floor, ears pricked.

The rooms above were as silent as they should have been, as they always were in a house where a man lived alone with a dog that seldom left his side.

Nevertheless, Merlin abruptly galloped up the stairs two at a time. He disappeared into the second-floor hallway before his master had climbed three steps behind him.

In the upper hall, Grady switched on the ceiling light. Past a half-open door, he found the dog standing in shadows in the master bedroom. The wolfhound was at a window that faced onto the roof of the front porch, alert to something beyond the glass.

Grady left the lamps unlit. With its secondhand light, the moon painted the peeling white bark of the spreading birch that overhung the house, and silvered the autumn leaves that would be sovereign-gold in sunshine.

As Grady moved toward Merlin, before he could

lean close to the window, a tom-tom and pitter-patter quickened across the porch roof. Several racing feet, by the sound of them.

Although Merlin was tall enough to see out of the lower panes, he put his forepaws on the windowsill and rose to a better view.

By the time Grady insisted on a place beside the window-hogging wolfhound and put his forehead to the cool glass, the noise stopped. Whatever once prowled the porch roof had now gone vertical.

In the windless night, the lower branches of the lacy birch first tossed but then merely trembled as the principal agitation shifted to higher realms. As something ascended, the tree opened its autumn purse and paid out a wealth of leaves.

Grady disengaged the window lock, but before he could raise the lower sash, the climbers sprang from tree to house roof: one thud, immediately another. Judging by their footfalls, they seemed to be exploring this way and that, up the slate slope toward the ridgeline.

Paws still on the windowsill, Merlin tipped his head back to stare at the ceiling.

"Maybe raccoons," Grady said.

Snorting dismissively, the wolfhound dropped from the window, turned toward the bedroom, and cocked his head to listen.

The master-bedroom fireplace stood directly above the fireplace in the living room. A metallic rattle and creak echoed down the shared flue, drawing Merlin to the hearth.

Something on the roof was testing the copper spark-arresting hood atop the chimney. Having installed it himself, Grady knew that it couldn't be easily removed.

Because no fire currently burned, the damper was engaged between the smoke chamber and the firebox. If something got into the flue, it could not penetrate the steel-plate damper and enter the bedroom.

Abandoning the chimney hood, the roof-travelers scurried down the west slope.

As the noises faded toward the back of the house, Merlin hurried out of the bedroom. Grady reached the top of the stairs just as the wolfhound arrived at the bottom.

Descending, he wondered if he had locked the back door after they had come in from the dog's late-afternoon exercise. Then he wondered why he was apprehensive.

He could not deny that something less than fear but more than mere disquiet gripped him as he sought Merlin through the first floor and found him in the kitchen. The dog stood at the door. He wanted to go outside.

Grady hesitated.

Nine

The potatoes were stored in a walk-in room within the windowless cellar, behind a stout oak door with iron hardware, as if they were a treasure worth guarding.

Deep shelves lined the smaller room. On the shelves were many well-ventilated baskets that each contained three layers of spuds.

The highest shelves held only a few baskets. Standing on a step stool, Henry Rouvroy put the two suitcases full of currency on a top shelf, flat on their sides and against the wall.

After climbing off the stool, he could not see the precious luggage overhead. He returned to the kitchen. In a day or two, he would find another and better hiding place for the money.

Because he didn't care for potatoes, he would

throw away that starch stash and rip out the shelves. Properly refitted, the potato cellar would be an excellent place to keep a woman when eventually he got one.

In Jim and Nora's bedroom, he selected underwear, socks, jeans, a flannel shirt, and work boots from Jim's limited wardrobe. Although Henry was less work-toned than his twin brother, everything fit him.

The shirt was from Walmart, not from L.L. Bean. The jeans were cut for working and for horseback-riding, not for Sunday in the park. The boots had no style whatsoever. The disguise was perfect, but for a moment he felt displaced, cast down from his rightful position.

Leaving his shoulder rig and pistol on the bed with a spare magazine of ammunition, he wrapped his expensive clothes and shoes in the shirt that he had been wearing, and tied everything together with the sleeves. He would bury those garments in the grave with his brother and sister-in-law.

Posing in front of a free-standing mirror, Henry addressed his reflection: "Look at you, Jim—back from the dead."

To his ear, at least, he sounded like his brother.

If those who knew Henry in his former life could see him now, they would not recognize him.

The clothes alone would ensure that they looked through rather than at him. He could pass for a hick from fly-over country, with whom they had nothing in common except that they, too, were born of man and woman.

In the kitchen, at the sink, he gathered up the potatoes that Nora had been peeling, and he tossed them in the trash can.

After examining the contents of the pantry and refrigerator, Henry found excellent sausages, acceptable cheeses, fresh eggs, a jar of red peppers, and an unfortunate but edible loaf of white bread made of flour so bleached that it glowed as if radioactive.

He opened three different Cabernet Sauvignons, none known to him. Only the third proved drinkable. If this was the best wine that Jim and Nora could afford or, worse, if this was their idea of a good wine—well, sadly, then they were better off dead.

Henry planned to spend two weeks laying in a three-year supply of canned and packaged food. He hoped that somewhere in a hundred-mile radius would be a specialty grocer and spirits vendor offering a sophisticated selection of consumables of the quality to which he had long been accustomed.

Withdrawing from the world for three years

would be an endurable hardship if he was provisioned with canned breast of pheasant, beluga caviar, hearts of palm, vintage balsamic vinegar, and scores of other delectable items that made the difference between living and merely existing.

After dinner, he washed the dishes. This was an annoyance that he would have to tolerate until he found a woman to keep in the potato cellar.

In his elegant townhouse at the farther end of the country, he had employed a housekeeper, but she'd received a salary and benefits. And she had not been the kind of woman who excited lust.

A windowless potato cellar made it possible not only to have the services of a housekeeper without the expense, but also to enjoy sex without the tedious process of seduction and without the tiresome pillow talk women expected afterward. Thus far he could see no other advantage that, in normal times, this crude residence had over his city digs; but normal times or not, a potato cellar might eventually prove to be a more desirable amenity than a home theater and a sauna combined.

Normal times. In spite of having risen before dawn, having driven for hours, having killed for the first time and the second time in his life, and even in spite of having prepared his own dinner,

Henry Rouvroy was not sleepy, not even weary. Being aware of the chaos that would sweep the nation in the months ahead, he was motivated to begin at once to prepare this house to meet his needs in these abnormal times.

Ten

After a brief hesitation, Grady opened the kitchen door and followed Merlin onto the porch. Scatters of dry birch leaves crunched underfoot.

No further sounds came from the roof, and the moonglow revealed no visitors on the porch or on the immediate lawn.

The taller dry grass beyond the mown yard appeared to curl like a line of phosphorescent surf breaking on a dark shore.

Screened by trees and swallowed by distance, the lights of the nearest neighbors could not be seen.

The workshop in which he crafted furniture, an add-on to the garage, stood forty feet south of the house. Those windows were as luminous as the panes of a lantern.

Grady had concluded his day's work before going on the hike with Merlin. He remained certain that he had left the workshop dark.

Something drew the wolfhound toward that building.

Few crimes occurred in this remote land, and those were mostly crimes of passion, seldom theft or vandalism. Consequently, Grady occasionally forgot to lock the workshop door.

He might have forgotten this time, but he hadn't left the door **open,** as it now stood. With the faintest click of claws, Merlin preceded his master across the threshold.

Because fluorescent light created little or no shadow, making it difficult to judge depth and to assess surface textures of materials being worked, pendant fixtures with shallow hoods brightened the room. The fixed machinery was lit from every angle to avoid harsh shadows, so that moving parts clearly could be seen to be moving.

At the moment, the machinery stood silent: circular-saw bench, surface planer, band saw, drill press, hollow-chisel mortiser. . . .

Four large reclining chairs, from a Gustav Stickley design, were in production for a client in Los Angeles. With broad canted arms, square-baluster sides, through-tenon construction, and exposed pegs, the handsome chairs would be comfortable, too, once a leather-covered pillow and spring-supported seat were installed.

The air smelled of freshly sawn oak.

At the back of the large room, a short but double-wide hallway separated the lavatory from the simple kiln in which air-dried lumber was further seasoned to carefully reduce its moisture content.

The lavatory door stood open, and the only reflection in the above-sink mirror was Grady's.

Neither he nor Merlin was startled when a hiss issued from behind the door of the walk-in kiln. To slow the drying process and avoid warping and buckling the lumber, from time to time live steam was injected into the kiln by a tightly calibrated humidifier.

The hook latch on the door hung loose. Either someone lurked in the kiln—or glanced in earlier and then failed to secure the latch.

The latter proved to be the case. The incandescent lamps, under which the wood dried, revealed no one in the kiln.

At the end of the short hallway, Grady opened a heavy door with soft rubber weather-stripping around all four edges. Beyond lay the finishing room, which he kept as free of dust as possible.

He stained and finished his furniture by hand. A dining table, mahogany with ebony inlays, in the style of Greene and Greene, was in the final month of curing after receiving a meticulous French polish with garnet shellac dissolved in industrial alcohol.

To Grady, the aromas of shellac, beeswax, turpentine, and pure copal varnish were no less pleasing than the fragrance of wild roses or the pine-scented crystalline air of a high-altitude forest.

In his best dreams, he drifted through vast houses without residents, through room after deserted room of ever more beautiful furniture, rooms in which no human being would ever betray another or raise a hand in violence, or speak a lie, or out of envy scheme to destroy his neighbor. These were the only dreams of his that featured scent, and waking from them, he was always happy, savoring the lingering memory of the fragrances of the finishing room.

Like the front door, the back stood open, unlocked from inside. Neither he nor the wolfhound detected anyone in the night beyond.

Grady locked the door, and as they returned to the front of the workshop, he opened a few cabinets and drawers, conducting a cursory inventory. No tools or supplies were missing.

After switching off the lights and closing the front door, as he turned his key, he said, "Which is it, big guy—just curious and well-meaning elves or nasty gremlins?"

The dog's answering chuff seemed noncommittal.

The escort moon guided them across ground that would have been black without the pale celestial light.

When Grady thought he heard the thrum of wings, he looked up but saw only stars.

As they approached the back porch, Merlin quickened from an amble to a trot. He leaped up the steps, bounded across the porch, and disappeared through the kitchen door, which Grady had not closed when they left the house.

While they were out, an intruder had taken advantage of the unguarded entrance. Although Grady had been interrupted halfway through his dinner, his plate on the kitchen table was now empty.

He had baked three extra chicken breasts, one for his lunch the next day and two for the dog. They had been cooling in a pan atop the stove. The covering aluminum foil had been torn aside and thrown on the floor. The pan and the chicken were missing.

Eleven

Half an hour after dinner, too excited to sleep, eager to make the house his own, Henry Rouvroy found himself in the bedroom, where Nora Carlyle's garments occupied half the drawers in the dresser and in the highboy, as well as half the closet space. Her clothes weren't likely to fit whatever girl he chose for the potato cellar, and he had other uses for the drawers and the closet.

Henry possessed numerous firearms and a supply of ammunition that he intended to distribute throughout the house and the barn. The highboy drawers were wide enough to take a shotgun or a rifle.

Stuffing Nora's clothes into plastic garbage bags took longer than he expected. No matter what dire days might lie ahead for the nation, regardless of the necessity for him to prepare this retreat in a timely fashion, Henry repeatedly found himself distracted by the silky feel of his sister-in-law's underwear.

When at last he filled four bulging trash bags with her wardrobe, he carried them two at a time to the front porch. Initially intending to take the bags to the barn in the morning, he remained so energetic that he decided to finish the task before bed.

At the corner of the house, near the tree-stump chopping block, stood a deep wheelbarrow that Jim had meant to fill with the split cordwood that now lay scattered on the grass. Henry pushed the barrow to the porch steps, where he loaded it with the bags of clothing.

Under the swollen moon, he didn't need a flashlight to follow the driveway to the barn. The traffic associated with the September harvest had worn the dirt lane, leaving a half-inch of soft dust that wind had not yet scoured away. His feet and the wheel of the barrow made little noise.

Henry had expected this countryside and the surrounding woods to be noisier than they were, not as drenched in sound as the city, of course, but full of buzz and hum, tick and click, rustle, murmur, sibilation. Instead, the night was quiet, almost eerily so, as if all that slithered and crawled and walked and flew had suffered a sudden extinction, leaving him as the only living thing that wasn't rooted to the earth.

At the barn, he parked the wheelbarrow near the man-size door, stepped inside, felt for the switch, turned on the lights. He carried two bags of clothes inside before he realized that the bodies of Jim and Nora were not where he had left them.

Dropping the sacks, he stepped to the spot where he had shot his brother and to which he had dragged Nora's corpse. Some blood on the carpet of straw was still moist, sticky.

Bewildered, Henry crossed to the tractor, circled it, and made his way around the backhoe, as well, seeking the deceased. He was certain they had been dead, both of them, not merely wounded and unconscious.

Bewilderment thickened into confusion when he looked up and saw the horses, Samson and Beauty, watching him over the half-doors of their stalls. Both were chewing mouthfuls of hay and appeared not to have been in the least disturbed by whatever had happened here after he had returned to the house to dress in his brother's clothes and to have dinner.

Henry checked the first horse stall, then the second, expecting to find the dead lying beside the steeds they had once ridden, though he could not imagine how they would have gotten there. Each horse stood alone in its enclosure, no fallen rider with either of them.

Confusion sharpened into perplexity as Henry turned in a circle, surveying the barn. Worry drew his stare up the rungs of the ladder to the dark loft. But that made no sense: If the dead couldn't crawl, they certainly couldn't climb.

Half a minute passed from the discovery that the bodies were missing to the belated realization that he must not be alone on the farm, that someone must have found the murdered pair and moved them.

Henry had left the pistol and the shoulder holster on the bed. Suddenly he was a sheep, shorn and shaking, tender flesh exposed, suspecting every shadow of harboring a wolf.

He hurried to the tool rack and took down the axe. The implement was heavier than he expected, unwieldy. In Jim's hands, it had looked deadly; in Henry's grip, it had little of the quality of a weapon and felt more like an anchor. Nevertheless, the axe was the best defense available until he could get to a firearm once more.

The situation seemed to call for stealth and caution. But Henry was trembling uncontrollably, breathing rapidly and shallowly, unable to calm himself. The telltale heart he heard was not that of either Jim or Nora, not a dead pump drumming out an accusation of his guilt, but his living heart knocking against his breastbone, announcing not his homicides but instead his rapidly escalating fear. At the moment, he was no more capable of stealth and caution than he was capable of juggling the axe with no risk to his fingers.

Desperate rather than brave, reckless rather than bold, axe held in both hands as he'd seen his brother carry it, Henry rushed through the open door, into the night. He plunged along the lane toward his Land Rover, which was parked near the house.

Whoever had taken the bodies could not be an agent of legitimate authority. No cops would move and hide the cadavers, and then torment their prime suspect but never question him. His nameless adversary mocked Henry, and when no more fun could be wrung from mockery, murder would follow.

He stumbled, dropped the axe, tripped over it, and as he flailed to keep his balance and avoid a fall, something passed over his head with a **whoosh**. He thought it must be a blade, perhaps the terrible scythe that had hung in the barn next to the axe.

When he cried out and turned, anticipating decapitation, no one loomed behind him. He was alone in the lane, in the moonlight, in his thrall of terror.

Rather than retrieve the axe, he hurried to the Land Rover. As he raised the tailgate, he expected to find the vehicle empty, but it was packed wall to wall, nothing missing except the suitcases full of cash that he earlier had transferred to the highest shelf in the potato cellar.

He pawed through the cargo, found the large rigid-wall suitcase that he wanted, and pulled it out. He closed the tailgate and pressed the lock icon on the electronic key. Nervously surveying the night, he carried the bag to the house.

Jim and Nora were childless. They lived alone.

Their farm help was seasonal. With the completion of the final harvest, the two hired hands would be gone until spring. Even in season, no laborers lived on the property.

Henry had inferred that much from Jim's poetry, in which the hired hands were sometimes featured. He had confirmed his inferences soon after his arrival, as he chatted with Jim and Nora over cinnamon rolls and coffee.

Immediately inside the front door, he put the suitcase flat on the living-room floor and opened it. Inside, in molded-foam niches, were a pair of short-barreled, pump-action, pistol-grip, 20-gauge shotguns and boxes of low-recoil ammo.

He fumbled with the shells, dropped more than one, but managed to insert a round in the breech of one of the shotguns and four more in the magazine. He stuffed spare shells in the pockets of his jeans.

First, the house. Make sure no intruder lurked anywhere within these walls. Room by room, lock the windows and doors. Pull shut the drapes, lower the pleated shades.

His tremors had diminished but had not subsided altogether. Dry mouth. Moist palms. Eyes hot and grainy.

Although he had practiced with the shotgun both on shooting ranges and in lonely landscapes on the long drive west, he had no experience sweeping a house to find an intruder. Fortunately, the place was small and was arranged in such a fashion that his quarry could not circle quietly behind him as he searched.

The living room harbored no one. Neither did the kitchen nor the dining area.

The door to the cellar, which earlier he had closed, stood open. Wooden stairs with rubber treads led down into darkness.

Beside the door, the wall was marred by a bloody handprint, as if a wounded man had leaned here for a moment before descending into the dark. The blood glistened, wet.

Holding the shotgun with one hand, Henry

pressed the back of his left hand against the wall, next to the print. The length of his pale fingers and the size of his palm seemed to match the hand of whoever had ventured into the cellar.

Twelve

Another blackjack table. Another casino. This time, Dr. Lamar Woolsey was calling himself Mitch Feigenbaum.

This seemed to be an unlikely name for a sixty-year-old African-American. But his resemblance to the beloved star of a long-ago TV sitcom gave him such instant credibility that no one ever seemed to suspect he was someone other than whom he pretended to be.

He was winning bigger than previously, because he enjoyed the double advantage of being a card counter and a man with an intuitive ability to recognize patterns in apparently chaotic systems.

His intuition had been refined and enhanced by a life's work in physics and mathematics, in each of which he held a doctorate. His specialty was chaos theory.

For most of its history, science had been reductionist, seeking to learn how things worked by analyzing their constituent parts. But as successful as the sciences had been, discoveries in the last half of the twentieth century revealed that the sum of human knowledge amounted to a few grains of sand, while what waited to be discovered was an infinite—and very strange—beach.

In every complex system—from solar-system dynamics to Earth's climate, to crystal formation, to cardiological processes—just under the facade of order, which science had discovered and long thought it fully understood, lurked an eerie and disturbing chaos. But also, deep inside every chaos, an eerier kind of hidden order waited to be found.

Even a simple system, like a card game dealt from a six-deck blackjack shoe, was fundamentally chaotic, likely to produce complex and unpredictable results. As a card counter, Lamar Woolsey hoped to **impose** a profitable order on the random flow of cards.

After thirty minutes of play, the composition of the six-deck shoe tipped slightly in Lamar's favor: somewhat rich in aces and face cards, a bit low on fives and sixes, but still ruled by randomness. He couldn't yet justify aggressive betting.

Then something strange happened. A series of Hail Mary draws gave Lamar a glimpse of the eerie nature of reality, of hidden and mysterious order.

The dealer showed a queen above his hole card. Lamar had a ten and a six, to which he drew a five, beating the dealer by a point.

In the next hand, he drew a three and a seven while the dealer showed a six. He doubled down, but drew only a deuce. The dealer revealed a sixteen count—and drew a six, busting.

Now the dealer had an ace up, and Lamar had a four and a three. He drew another four. Then a deuce. Another deuce. Then a six. His final twenty-one beat the dealer, who had a nine under his ace.

None of those three wins involved card counting, and even the most paranoid pit boss would see them as nothing but luck.

Not a believer in luck, Lamar read them instead as one of those curious patterns that expressed a hidden order under the randomness—under the chaos—of any game of chance. This phase of the pattern, which benefited him, was a wave that offered effortless surfing. Until it lost its benign character, he ought to ride it.

He won nine more hands in a row, lost two, then won another eight with such unlikely combinations of cards that counting tens and aces could have had no effect on his fortunes.

Sometimes the power of hidden order can have, with its patterns, such an obvious presence in a system that its precise mechanisms seem within the theorist's grasp—until chaos reappears. Even when Lamar played irrationally, splitting a pair of fours when the dealer showed a face card, he won. When the dealer showed an ace, Lamar doubled down on eight—and won.

After losing three hands in a row, he suspected that the patterns under the apparent chaos of the cards no longer favored him, and he asked to have his winnings converted into high-value chips to make them easier to carry. His thousand-dollar buy-in had grown to nineteen thousand.

At the cashier's window, he converted two chips into folding money. After the two casinos, this left him ahead four hundred for the night. He intended to give away the other seventeen thousand in chips before leaving the building.

Thirteen

Exploring the house bottom to top with Grady, Merlin was as stealthy as an excited pony. They found no intruder.

Whatever had finished Grady's dinner for him, whatever had taken the three baked chicken breasts and the pan on the stove, left no sign that it had ventured farther than the kitchen.

Before returning to the ground floor, Grady turned off the lights room by room. In the darkness, he drew aside any draperies that were closed, raised any shades that were lowered.

On the ground floor again, he made sure that the views from all the windows were likewise unobstructed.

In the kitchen, he washed his dinner dishes. He brewed a pot of coffee, poured it into a thermos bottle, and stood the thermos on the dinette table. He set a mug on the table, too.

Merlin watched as if witnessing a ritual with solemn meaning.

Only two chairs served the table. They were at opposite ends of the window that looked out onto the back porch.

Grady moved one of the chairs to face the window from across the table. He switched off the lights and sat in the chair, in the dark, in the lingering aroma of strong coffee, his mug empty.

Merlin stood very still, as if pondering the situation. He was a contemplative dog, always ruminating on some aspect of his world.

Out of sight above the house, the mirror moon reflected the sun of a day not yet dawned, shining the pale light of tomorrow on the yard and on the paper birches.

The porch lay in shadow.

Merlin padded to the kitchen door, a French door with panes all the way to the bottom, installed specifically to allow the wolfhound to see outside. Alert, he stood there, barely visible in the gloom.

Grady's window had three rows of panes, three panes per row. In another house, miles from here, this was the identical configuration of the window through which Grady's mother had foreseen her future.

*

A year before Grady was born, his father gave his mother a puppy—half German shepherd, half everything else. She named him Sneakers because he had a dark coat and paws as white as tennis shoes.

Growing up with Sneakers was a fine adventure, although the dog reserved the greater part of his devotion for Grady's mother. He loved his human brother, but he **adored** Ellen Adams.

Grady's dad, Paul, worked at the lumber mill. A few weeks before his son's eighth birthday, he was killed on the job.

The huge sizing saw, which cut logs into manageable lengths, had every safety feature. The saw was not the problem.

People were the problem. A group opposed to logging operations had driven dozens of eight-inch spikes into each of numerous randomly selected, mature, mill-ready pines. The spiking didn't kill the trees but rendered them useless for lumber.

Harvesting crews identified most of the ruined specimens. Only one slipped past their inspection.

The giant circular saw ripped the spikes from the wood, tangled them into bristling knots, and spat them out. When the blade met the resistance of the steel spikes, a sensor killed the power to the saw. But already the mangled spikes were in flight at maximum velocity, as was a piece of broken blade like a wide and toothy smile.

Grady never heard exactly what the shrapnel did to his father. Considering the vivid images his imagination conjured, perhaps he should have been told. But perhaps not.

Millworkers, police, friends, and the family priest advised Ellen not to view the body. But Paul had been, she said, "the other half of my heart." She declined to heed their advice.

She accompanied her lost husband from the mill to the coroner's office. Later, she went with him from coroner to mortician.

His mother's courage in a time of terrible loss, and her faith, were profound. Young Grady had drawn his strength from her example.

He loved his dad. The loss was so grievous, he felt as though he had been cut open and robbed of a vital essence. Every morning for a long time, when he woke, he was aware of being incomplete.

Because his mother endured, Grady endured. For him, endurance led to acquiescence, then to acceptance, and at last to peace.

Long before he found peace, only a month following his father's death, after waking past midnight, he went downstairs to get a snack. He wasn't hungry, but he couldn't just lie in bed and think.

A lamp already lit the downstairs hallway. His

mom sat at the table in the kitchen, which was brightened only by the spill from the hall lamp. Her back to him, she gazed at the night beyond the window.

Beside her chair sat Sneakers, his head in her lap. With her right hand, she tenderly, ceaselessly stroked the dog's head.

His mom didn't know Grady stood in the doorway. The dog surely knew, but he would not turn from the woman's consoling hand.

Grady could think of nothing to say. As quietly as if he were the ghost of a boy, he retreated from the kitchen, returned to bed.

A few nights later, waking at one in the morning, he silently went downstairs and found her as before, with the dog.

He stood for a while in the doorway, unannounced. It felt right that he should be with her yet at this distance, watching over her as she stared through the window at the night.

During the next month, he joined her a few more times, as silent and unnoticed as a guardian spirit. When he returned to his bed, he always wondered when his mother slept. Perhaps she didn't.

One night he went downstairs and found the hall lamp off. His mother wasn't in the kitchen, nor was Sneakers.

Grady assumed that she had changed her routine. He, too, was sleeping better than in the weeks immediately after his dad's death.

A year passed before he again discovered her and Sneakers at the kitchen table, in the dark. She had never entirely stopped coming here in the emptiest hours. Perhaps she came more nights than not.

This time he said, "Mom," and went to her side. He touched her shoulder. She reached up and took his hand in hers. After a moment, he said, "Do you think . . . he'll come to visit?"

She had the softest voice: "What? A ghost? No, sweetheart. This is my past and future window. When I want my past, I see your father working out there in the vegetable garden."

They grew tomatoes, carrots, cucumbers, radishes, and more, for their own use.

Grady sat at the table with her.

"When I want my future," she continued, "I see you tall and handsome and grown, with a family of your own. And I see myself with your dad again, in a new world without struggle."

"Don't be sad," Grady said.

"Oh, honey, I'm not sad. Have I ever seemed sad to you?"

"No. Just . . . here like this."

"When I say I see myself with your dad again, I'm not saying that I wish it. I mean I truly see it."

Grady peered through the window and saw only the night.

"Believing isn't wishing, Grady. What you know with your heart is the only thing you really ever know."

By then she had taken a job in the office of the lumber mill. She spent five days a week where Paul died. They needed the money.

For a long time, Grady was concerned about her working at the mill. He thought she suffered the constant reminder of the twisted spikes and the broken saw blade.

He came to understand, however, that she liked the job. Being at the mill, among the people who had worked with Paul, was a way of keeping the memory of her husband sharp and clear.

One Saturday when he was fourteen, Grady came home from a part-time job to discover that Sneakers had died. His mom had dug the grave.

She had prepared the body for burial. She wrapped the beloved dog in a bedsheet, then in the finest thing she owned, an exquisite Irish-lace tablecloth used only on Thanksgiving and Christmas Day.

Grady found her sitting on the back-porch steps, cradling the shrouded body, weeping, waiting for him. Two people were required to put Sneakers in the grave with respect and gentleness.

As the summer sun waned, they lowered the dog to his rest. Grady wanted to shovel the earth into the grave, but his mom insisted she would do it. "He was so sweet," she said. "He was so sweet to me."

Determined to be strong for him, she never allowed Grady to see her crying for his father. She couldn't hide her tears for the dog.

His father had given her the dog. On lonely nights, the dog had grieved with her. Now she'd lost Sneakers, but in a way, she had also lost her husband again.

Later, Grady sat with his mom in the dark kitchen. The dog's grave lay in a direct line with the window, at the end of the yard.

Grady was six years older than he'd been when his dad died. His mother could talk more frankly about love and loss, about grief and faith, about the sharpness of her pain, than she had talked back in the day.

Although she had withheld from him the depth of her anguish and her fear about their future—for a while, they had been in danger of losing the house—she never deceived him. She had always told him as much as she thought he was old enough to handle.

The night of the day that Sneakers died, Grady realized that all of his mother's sterling qualities arose from the same basic virtue. She loved Truth, and she did not lie.

Until she drew her last breath—far too young—

she never told him a falsehood. Because of her, Grady valued nothing higher than veracity.

In this age, lies were the universal lubricant of the culture. A love of Truth and a commitment to it were seldom rewarded and were often punished.

So you came home to the mountains, and you built tables and chairs and consoles in one Craftsman style or another. The simple materials and the clean lines of such furniture revealed where a woodworker dared to take a shortcut or to employ a substandard technique. Honest crafts-manship and a commitment to quality were evident in a finished piece, and no one could spin the truth of your work into a lie.

*

As Grady sat at the table, watching the night, as Merlin sat sentry at the French door, the south end of the moonlit yard suddenly became slightly brighter than it had been. The source of the light lay out of sight.

Grady rose, stepped around the table, and put his face to the window. He expected to see lights in the workshop, which earlier he locked tight. Instead, the glow came from the garage, to which the workshop was attached.

Nevertheless, he knew this intruder must be the same that had toured the workshop and later had taken the baked chicken breasts.

Fourteen

Upon finding the bloody handprint on the wall near the head of the cellar stairs, Henry Rouvroy considered firing the shotgun down into the darkness. Restraint was not a quality of character natural to him, yet he managed to resist the urge to squeeze the trigger.

When he flicked the switch and light bloomed, he found no one waiting at the bottom of the stairs. He let out his pent-up breath.

Listening to the room below, he became convinced that someone down there likewise listened to him.

He almost whispered a name. But he kept his silence for fear of receiving an answer in a familiar voice.

Anyone in the cellar could leave by the outer door, which opened onto exterior stairs that led up to the lawn. Henry couldn't imprison the intruder, but he could prevent him from returning to the ground floor by this route.

After switching off the cellar light, he closed the door and slid the bolt into the latch plate. He doubted it would hold against a determined assault. He fetched a chair from the nearby dinette, tipped it on its back legs, and wedged the headrail under the doorknob.

He continued his sweep of the house, making sure no one was concealed anywhere, checking that windows were securely latched. He felt exposed at every pane of glass while he closed the draperies.

In the bedroom, on the bed, he had left the pistol with which he had killed Jim and Nora. During his absence, someone had taken it. The shoulder holster and the spare magazine were also gone.

A small smear of blood brightened the beige chenille bedspread.

Two spaces remained to be searched: the closet and the bathroom. Both doors were in the same wall, and they were closed.

Taking a wide stance to brace himself against the recoil, Henry leveled the pistol-grip shotgun at the closet, fired, fired again. In this closed space, the sound slammed off the walls with a blowback that he could almost feel. He fired two rounds at the bathroom.

The buckshot punched holes through both of the cheap hollow-core doors, with enough velocity remaining to tear up whoever might be waiting beyond. The absence of a scream suggested that he'd wasted ammunition.

He pumped the last round into the breech, dug spare shells out of his pockets, and reloaded the magazine.

His hands trembled, stomach acid scalded the back of his throat, and his bowels felt loose. But he neither vomited nor soiled his pants.

In such a pressurized situation, with everything at risk, not losing control of bodily functions seemed to be a triumph. Henry gained confidence from the fact that his underwear remained dry.

Killing unsuspecting people was far easier than defending your life against an armed enemy.

That was a truth they didn't teach you at Harvard. At least not in any of the classes that Henry had taken.

The anticipation of violence before a murder was pleasurable, but the expectation of being shot in the head wasn't in the least exhilarating, no matter what psychology professors said about death having a subconscious appeal similar to that of sex. A good-looking woman chained in a potato

cellar had infinitely more appeal than stalking—
and being stalked by—someone who perhaps
wanted to blow your brains out.

He opened the riddled door to the closet and
found no one alive or dead. In the bathroom,
buckshot had shattered the mirror.

Having secured the residence, he felt safer but far
from safe. The house was not a fortress. Anyway,
sooner or later, he would have to go outside.

Fifteen

Standing in the dark, face to the kitchen window, looking south beyond the house, Grady saw lights in the garage windows. And the big roll-up door was raised.

Getting into the garage would not have been difficult for an intruder. Neither of the two windows had a working latch. In a rural county with a crime rate almost as low as that in the Vatican, he'd never seen a need for garage security.

For a minute, he watched for a silhouette of someone against the big rectangle of light. But then he returned to his chair and poured his first mug of coffee from the thermos.

Sitting at the French door, Merlin issued a thin, inquisitive sound.

"I don't know," Grady said, "but I think maybe the idea is to determine if we're watching. If we're watching, we'd be expected to go out to the garage to see what's up."

The dog said nothing.

"My feeling is," Grady said, "it's better if it looks like we've gone to bed. If no one thinks we're watching, then there might be something to see."

Having been seasoned with cinnamon, the black coffee gave off a mellow aroma. The brew tasted as good as it smelled.

Watchfulness and patient waiting were tasks for which Grady possessed the temperament and the skills, and with which he had years of deep experience.

His friend Marcus Pipp had called him Iguana. Like that lizard, he could sit motionless for so long that his stillness became a kind of camouflage. You could see him, yet you forgot he was there.

Marcus had been dead for ten years. Grady still thought of him more days than not.

A United States senator killed Mrs. Pipp's boy. Grady should have seen it coming and should have acted to prevent Marcus's death; therefore, he was in part at fault.

Some would not agree with that assessment. Present when Marcus died, Grady knew the truth. He would neither endorse the official lie nor make excuses for himself.

His mother said the lies you told yourself were

the worst lies of all. If you could not face every truth about yourself, you would not know who you really were. You could not redeem yourself if you failed to recognize the need for redemption.

Grady recognized the need for redemption, all right, and he realized that to finish the task, he would have to live a long life.

Having gotten to his feet again, Merlin padded through the gloom to his water bowl, which was wide and deep. In the stillness of the kitchen, he sounded like a Clydesdale drinking from a trough.

Out in the yard, only the moon now relieved the darkness. The garage lights had gone off.

Seeking affection, the wolfhound came to Grady. Merlin's head was above the table, and Grady gently worked the dog's ears between his thumb and forefinger.

When your task was patient watchfulness, the anchored body frustrated the mind into cutting loose, setting sail. Your thoughts tended to tack through an archipelago of disconnected subjects. The journey could seem to have no destination— yet could bring you to a port worth exploring.

He found himself in a vivid memory of the afternoon woods, at the instant when Merlin passed through the last trees into the golden meadow. Beyond the woods, the sunshine seemed witchy, as lurid as a coppery twilight, glimmering as if a cloud of sequined atmosphere had plumed through an open door from a realm more magical than this one.

He had hesitated to follow the wolfhound, but when he stepped from the forest, he had found the meadow descending in sunshine as ordinary as ever it was. He had dismissed the perception of coppery scintillation as a short-lived phenomenon resulting from his angle of view and from the contrast between dusky woodland and open field. And then the appearance of the white animals caused him to forget the unique quality of the light.

Now, as he sat at the kitchen table, the nape of his neck prickled, and the memory replayed like a film loop. Again, again. And again. Each time, the experience returned to Grady with greater force. He didn't merely recall the shimmering incandescence but saw it as he had never relived a previous memory: in three dimensions, with the true color and the poignant detail of the event itself, hypersensitive to every nuance.

He seemed to be transported to the deer trail, to the pregnant moment. Charcoal and gray, untethered shadow, Merlin strode toward the meadow as Grady hesitated behind him. Overhead: the canopy of evergreen boughs, more feathery than needled, green-dark and still and fragrant. Ahead: pine trunks and limbs almost black against the backdrop of twinkling and glistering coppery light, the compelling and coruscating light, the significant light, the **light**.

The memory relented, the past moment in the woods released him to the present moment in the kitchen, and he found himself standing at the table, having knocked over the chair as he'd gotten to his feet. He had experienced not merely a memory but something else for which he had no name, a re-immersion in a past event, all five senses fully engaged.

And it was as though, earlier in the day, during the actual occurrence, he was blinded to the intense character of the light, and was able to perceive the momentous quality of it only when he experienced it through recollection, from the safety of this later hour.

His scalp crawled, cold sweat slicked the nape of his neck, and he heard his heart knocking.

Grady's eyes were sufficiently dark-adapted that he could see Merlin a few feet away, alert and regarding him with interest.

Beyond the window, beyond the shadowed porch, the burning moon seemed to have dusted the yard and the trees with its phosphorescent ashes. The night lay as still as if it were airless.

Then something moved in the moonlight: quick, lithe, on all fours, white. Two of them.

Sixteen

The most expensive of the hotel-casino's five restaurants had a large holding bar that featured a black-marble floor with small diamond-shaped inlays of gold onyx. The walls were clad in the same marble but without the diamonds. A highly dimensional black-marble ceiling glowed with panels of backlit translucent gold onyx at the bottom of each coffer. Instead of a mirror behind the black-marble bar, huge panels of backlit onyx were inlaid with the silhouettes of Art Deco wolves perpetually leaping.

If Dracula had moonlighted as an interior designer, he might have created a room like this.

Sitting at the bar, Lamar Woolsey ordered his only alcoholic beverage of the evening: a bottle of Elephant Beer, a Danish import.

Some people at the cocktail tables were waiting

to be told by the maître d' that their dinner tables were ready, but those at the bar had not come for dinner. They were mostly men, but whether men or women, they fled the casino for a respite from self-destruction.

Their moods ranged between forced gaiety and somber reflection, but the impression they all made on Lamar was of desperation.

They had come to the games of chance with hope. Emily Dickinson, the poet, had written that "Hope is the thing with feathers / That perches in the soul . . ." But if your hope was hope for the wrong thing, it could be a sharp-beaked hawk that ravaged the soul and the heart.

In his easy way, Lamar chatted up six fugitives from cards and dice, as they came and went. Eventually, in each conversation, he briefly waxed philosophical, and then said, "Don't think, just answer. What's the first word comes into your mind when I say **hope**?"

As he nursed his beer, he didn't know what answer he would find appealing, but it wasn't among the first five: **luck, money, money, change, none.**

The sixth of these brief companions, Eugene O'Malley, appeared to be in his late twenties. He had such an innocent face and such a humble manner that beard stubble and bloodshot eyes didn't make him appear dissolute, only harried.

Both arms on the bar, hands around a bottle of

Dos Equis, he replied "Home," in response to Lamar's question.

"Where's home, Mr. O'Malley?"

"Call me Gene. Home's just down the road in Henderson."

"What's at home that gives you hope?"

"Lianne. She's my wife."

"She's a good wife, is she?"

"Lianne's the best."

"So why're you here, O'Malley?"

"Supposed to be at work. Night-shift construction foreman."

Lamar said, "I don't see anyone constructing anything around here except hangovers."

"In this economy, who needs a night shift? Lost my job a week ago, can't bring myself to tell Lianne."

"But my dear O'Malley, if she's a good woman . . ."

"She was fired in July. We've got a baby coming in six weeks."

"So you figured your luck had to turn."

"Figured wrong, Ed."

Lamar had introduced himself as Edward Lorenz. Now he asked, "You lose a lot?"

"Anything is a lot right now. I dropped fourteen hundred, half my severance pay. Don't know what happened, sort of lost my mind."

After finishing his bottle of Elephant Beer,

Lamar said, "You aren't fighting Irish, are you, O'Malley? Don't take a poke at an old man just because he asks a rude question."

"You're not that old, and I can't see you being rude."

"No lie—are you a degenerate gambler or just a damn fool?"

Gene laughed softly. "You have a way about you, Ed. I'm a damn fool who doesn't ever want to see the inside of a casino again."

"I guess I'll believe you. Never known an O'Malley to lie."

"Have you known a lot of O'Malleys?"

"You're the first one. O'Malley, do you know who Sir Isaac Newton was?"

"A scientist or somebody."

"Both somebody and a scientist. For centuries, Newtonian physics gave science the tools it needed to build the modern world. Newton's theories and methods still work, but we now know that many of them are incomplete or even wrong."

"How can they work if they're wrong?"

"It has to do with reductionist observation and the power of approximation in the reliability of short-term effect."

"Well, of course," O'Malley said, and rolled his eyes.

"Einstein destroyed Newton's illusion of absolute space and time. Quantum theory put an end to the notion of a controllable measurement process."

"How many beers have you had, Ed?"

"This all relates to something good that's soon going to happen to you, O'Malley. You know Galileo?"

"Not personally."

"Galileo was a great scientist, too, and one of his theories, related to the oscillation of a pendulum— that its period remains independent of its amplitude—is still taught in most high-school physics classes more than three hundred years later. But it's wrong."

"I'll bet you know what's wrong with it," O'Malley said, as if he was humoring an eccentric.

"Everyone doing physics for the last thirty years knows it's wrong, but it's taught anyway. Galileo used linear equations. But turbulence is present in the system, so it requires a nonlinear approach. Chaos, O'Malley. Underlying even the simple system of a pendulum is chaos, potential for complex and unexpected behavior. Now, I'm going to give you something."

"What I need are the magic words to make Lianne forgive me."

"Life can sometimes seem hopelessly complex, unpredictable, chaotic. Then a strange order makes itself known. You tell Lianne what you've done and what I've done, so she'll know there's order in the chaos. But first, cash these and take the money home to her."

From a pocket of his white sport coat, Lamar extracted seventeen chips worth seventeen thousand dollars and put them on the bar.

Seventeen

The snowy pair glided across the moon-chilled yard: clearly seen but not in detail, catlike, wolflike, yet little resembling either cats or wolves, both familiar and strange, dreamlike.

When the animals arced toward the house, disappearing around the north end of the porch, Grady hurried from the kitchen, navigating by the LED numbers in the oven clock and by the hum of the refrigerator.

Blind in the windowless hallway, he felt along the left wall until he found a door.

In his study, two pale rectangles silvered the darkness directly opposite the entrance. His familiarity with the furniture arrangement allowed him to make his way quickly toward those undraped windows.

Halfway across the room, he gasped as a figure

loomed against one of the framed panels of moon-light. But at once he realized that it was Merlin, on this side of the glass, paws on the sill. Grady went to the other window.

The night remained for a moment as night had been for millennia: full of myth, mystery, and threat, but in fact less dangerous than the day, if only because more men were sleeping now than would be sleeping after dawn. The venerable stars. The ancient moon. The old Earth, its timeworn beauty under wraps until sunrise . . .

Then suddenly the night was new, as the white enigmas appeared. Having been out of sight, tight against the house, directly under the windows, they raced away from the building, past the trunk of the birch, north across the lawn. They halted at the limit of visibility, faint featureless presences, huddling together as if conferring.

Panting agitatedly, beating his forepaws against the windowsill, the wolfhound wanted to be in the night and in pursuit.

"Settle," Grady said, and again, "settle." A third issuance of the command was required when always before one had calmed the dog.

Out of the darkness, the visitors returned, not directly but obliquely, angling east toward the front of the house.

Dropping to the floor, beyond the rays of the moonlamp, Merlin became a disembodied pres-

ence, a canine poltergeist, knocking across the
floorboards, rapping the furniture and the door-
jamb with an ectoplasmic tail, abandoning the
study for a different haunt.

With the windows at his back, Grady was a
blind man all the way across the room, reaching
with both hands for the doorway. In the hall, he
slid one palm along a wall until he reached the living room.

Already Merlin had materialized at a front window to the right of the door, paws on the sill.

Making his way toward the window to the left of
the door, Grady bumped an end table. He heard a
lamp wobbling, found it, steadied it.

Earlier, when he opened all the draperies and
shades, he hadn't imagined chasing around the
house in pursuit of circling visitors. He merely
wanted to have immediate access to any window
that gave a view of an area where a noise might
arise or entry might be attempted.

By the time he reached the window, he began to
suspect that these mysterious animals were as curious about him as he was about them, that they
were intent on satisfying that curiosity.

Beyond the porch, east of the house, lay the
front yard, part of it overlaid with a faint tracery of
moonshadows cast by the intricate branches of the
huge birch tree.

The visitors were not on the yard or on that portion of the county lane—Cracker's Drive—visible from this vantage point.

Nothing else traveled the night, either. No deer were present, though they frequently came to graze upon the lawn. Often coyotes whidded through the lunar glade, all legs and haunches and sharp shoulders, but on this occasion, they were hunting elsewhere.

As though aware of their audience and timing their entrance for maximum drama, the creatures sprang as one over the railing at the north side of the porch, seemed to cross the deck as fast as two pulses of light, and vanished over the railing at the south end.

The speed with which they moved and the darkness of the porch prevented Grady from learning anything more significant about their appearance than he had perceived from a distance in the meadow. He confirmed their size and their nimbleness, and thought he had seen lushly plumed tails, but their faces remained unrevealed.

They ran on all fours, though it seemed that they reared up as they approached the south end of the porch, that they took the last few steps on their hind feet before vaulting over the railing. Their movement wasn't what he expected of any four-legged mammal in these mountains, though he couldn't precisely identify the difference.

The instant the creatures leaped out of sight,

Merlin abandoned his post and hurried unerringly through the dark living room to the hallway. Most likely, the wolfhound intended to track the animals from one of the library windows at the south side of the house.

Grady was so sure these visitors were intrigued by him and intent upon him that he saw no reason to scramble after them through the gloom, at the risk of falling and breaking a bone. They weren't going to retreat into the mountains and leave him forever wondering about their nature. They had initiated a process of discovery, and they were not likely to relent from it.

This was an extraordinary expectation. Wild animals were by their nature wary. Even confident predators like mountain lions generally slunk away into the brush at the sight of a human being.

In this wooded vastness, only bears were fearless. An eight-hundred-pound brown bear was as ready to charge a man as to ignore him.

Grady felt his way cautiously through the living room, from sofa to armchair to armchair, and as he reached the hallway, he heard a thin cry of doggy excitement.

Eighteen

The moth danced with the false flame of the ceiling light, and its shadow swelled and shrank across the pages of the books through which Cammy Rivers searched for answers.

The horses and other animals at High Meadows Farm had seemed no worse for the time they spent in a trance, if indeed it was a trance. But such behavior surely must be symptomatic of a physical disorder.

In her apartment kitchen, above the veterinary clinic, the table was stacked with reference volumes that had thus far failed her. The Internet had failed her, as well, so she put aside one book and opened another to its index.

Absence seizures, in epileptics, weren't accompanied by abnormal movements. The subject appeared conscious but wasn't, and the seizure could be mistaken for daydreaming or inattentiveness.

The longest absence seizure, however, lasted less than a minute. The Thoroughbreds and their pets at High Meadows reportedly had been in a trance for more than fifteen minutes.

Besides, none of the animals at the farm had been previously diagnosed as epileptic. And it offended reason to suppose that they would all simultaneously manifest a condition that affected on average one in three hundred individuals.

In addition to congenital cases, other incidences of epilepsy could be attributed to birth trauma and blows to the head, as well as to previous cases of meningitis, encephalitis, and bacterial infections of the brain. Symptoms of those preconditional diseases, however, would have been impossible to overlook. None of the animals at High Meadows— let alone all of them—suffered any such illnesses.

After ruling out epilepsy, Cammy moved on to systemic fungal diseases. She had a dim recollection that certain exotic funguses—not more common varieties like coccidioides—could have brain effects that included absence seizures and hallucinations.

Funguses tended to be regional. But she didn't limit her inquiry to Rocky Mountain or even Western varieties.

Rare indeed were the funguses that could cause

such symptoms. Rarer still were those that conceivably could take hold in four different species—horses, goats, cats, and dogs.

She wasn't going to consider the duck. She had never treated a duck. She didn't know how ducks thought or if they thought much at all. The duck was at best a distraction. To hell with the duck.

The problem with pinning the event on a fungus was that none of the animals had exhibited any of the more common symptoms of fungal diseases: diarrhea, fever, chronic cough, difficulty breathing, weight loss, lethargy. . . .

Before leaving High Meadows Farm, Cammy had taken blood samples from seven horses, three goats, and three dogs. In the morning, she would FedEx them to the lab in Colorado Springs.

Considering that none of the animals was suffering and that none had shown any disturbing symptoms other than the communal trance, she would fulfill her responsibilities merely by waiting for the report from the laboratory. But from funguses, she moved on to several thick volumes concerning rare and exotic protozoan diseases.

She had quite literally given her life to healing animals and relieving their suffering. She lived for nothing else. Her patients were her family, her children, her passion, her mission, her only path to peace.

No animal had ever betrayed her. No animal had

ever robbed her of her dignity. No animal had ever oppressed and debased her. No animal had ever tortured her.

The shadow of silent wings swelled and shrank across the stacks of books, across the white pages of the open volume, across her badly scarred hands.

Nineteen

Off the south side of the downstairs hall lay the dining room, which Grady had lined with shelves to store the book collection that spilled over from his study. He didn't need a dining room. He always ate at the two-chair table in the kitchen, and on the rare occasions when he had company for an evening, he invited only one guest.

Following the wolfhound's cry of excitement, Grady crossed the threshold of the library.

In silhouette, Merlin stood with his paws on the windowsill, as he had in previous rooms.

Grady took three steps before he froze at the sight of what lay beyond the window, unable to make sense of it.

In relation to the house, the moon was farther to the east than to the west, farther north than south.

No porch roof overhung this side of the residence, but moonlight was no more able to reach these southern panes than those in the living room.

Suspended as if weightless in the darkness beyond the glass, slightly higher than the dog's burly head, were four luminous golden spheres, each approximately three inches in diameter, as bright as candlelight but constant in their radiance, without any throb or flicker. Two were side by side on a horizontal plane, and two floated at an angle.

Bubbles, he thought, not only because they seemed to levitate but also because their color was less constant than their brightness. They revealed a subtle iridescence. Shades of gold played through them, and quivers of copper, and streams of silver, much the way that a more complete spectrum of colors manifested across the surface of a soap bubble.

As easy as it was to think of the floating objects as bubbles, he intuited that they were not that ephemeral. They possessed more substance than a first impression suggested.

Although full of light, the spheres seemed to emit none. The panes took no shine from them, and neither did the wolfhound on this side of the glass. The tarnished-silver cedar frame of the window remained uniformly dark. These globes weren't truly radiant, weren't luminous in the sense that they shared their light and color, but somehow contained them.

Grady moved toward the window, and as he drew close to Merlin, the iridescence of the objects increased. In two, sapphire washed through the gold, and then many shades of blue at once, and the gold repeatedly bloomed through the other hues, like the base-weave color in a rippling garment of lustrous silk. The third and fourth spheres changed entirely from gold to blues and greens.

The wolfhound continuously expressed excitement and eagerness in a voice pinched so thin that he sounded like a much smaller dog.

As beautiful as the spheres were, their most affecting quality was strangeness. A perpetual aurora borealis in gem-bright colors, captured in weightless globes the size of tennis balls, hovering to no apparent purpose . . . They seemed to be so far beyond anything in Grady's experience, so mysterious, so resistant to explanation, so dazzling, that the longer he contemplated them, the more disoriented he became.

He began to feel light-headed and curiously weightless, as though he might suddenly break the bonds of gravity and rise off the floor, float in the darkness on this side of the glass as the four spheres floated in the outer dark.

Then one of the pair blinked, and the other

blinked, blinked, and this suggestion of function gave Grady a fresh perspective that resolved the mystery. Eyes. A darkness at the center of each, the irises open wide. Impossibly huge, luminous, color-changing eyes.

The creatures were crowded onto the windowsill. One held its head upright, and the other cocked its head: two eyes aligned on a horizontal plane, two at an angle.

For a minute, the iridescent orbs had so captivated Grady, so riveted his attention, that he was all but mesmerized by them. Now he was able to register the totality of the window, everything that it framed. Dimly, he saw their pale forms, the faintest suggestion of faces, perhaps a forepaw clinging to the casing.

The pair dropped away from the glass.

Constrained to stalk from behind windows but nonetheless full of enthusiasm for the hunt, with a rough growl to express confidence in his prowess, Merlin abandoned his post.

Grady pressed past the dog to the panes that were still partly feathered with the fog of canine breath.

Bearing their lantern eyes, the animals fled into the night.

Merlin galloped out of the library and thundered toward the kitchen.

Grady stood as if concussed, shocked into immobility, not by a physical blow but by a mental one. Having at last seen the pair from the meadow more clearly, he should have understood them better, but he was more mystified than ever.

Merlin rarely barked. He barked now.

Twenty

Henry Rouvroy picked up shotgun-shattered fragments of his face from the bathroom floor and dropped the pieces of broken mirror into a heavy-duty plastic trash bag.

He paused repeatedly to study reflections of his stare in the silvery shards before throwing them away. He saw nothing in his eyes, certainly nothing like guilt. No such thing as guilt existed, except in the weak minds of those who believed in the false gods of various authorities. He saw the same nothing he had seen in the eyes of Nora Carlyle's corpse, the universal nothing of the human gaze.

The eyes were not the windows of the soul, and what could be seen beyond them was only a thousand hungers, needs, desires, and one thing more—fear. Henry knew his hungers and did not need to discover them in his eyes. His needs and desires were insatiable, and he would feed them, feed them as no glutton ever born had ever fed. The first woman in the potato cellar would not be the last, and if he lived long enough, the fields of his brother's farm would be a six-acre cemetery without headstones.

Henry challenged himself to acknowledge the fear in his eyes, and he saw it clearly. He was not afraid of any variety of authority. He feared only others like himself, monsters in the making or already made. He knew that legions of them stalked the world. He knew of what they were capable, because he knew of what he was capable: anything.

He saw nothing exalted about the human animal, nothing elevated or dignified, or exceptional. Only two roles existed for any human being: prey or predator. Rule or be ruled. Act or be acted upon.

Somewhere nearby, a predator intended to prevent Henry from establishing a survivalist retreat on this property. The unknown adversary could have but one motivation: to seize the property for himself and live there to ride out the coming storm.

If that was the case—and it **had** to be the case—then he must be someone **who knew the storm was coming,** someone who traveled the same Washington circles in which Henry had once moved. He must have discovered that Henry had stolen a fortune from the operation, and he must have put Henry under observation to discover what further intentions he might have.

Those circles were infested with people who possessed limitless resources for investigating and tracking a subject of interest. Henry had taken great care to conceal his theft and to cover his trail when he came west, but evidently he had not been careful enough.

He didn't for a moment believe that his brother, Jim, might be stalking him. Jim was dead. Shot three times. The third time in the face. Even if Jim survived—which he had not—he would be blind and brain-damaged.

After picking up the last of the broken mirror, Henry carried the bag to the kitchen and put it in the trash can. He took the shotgun with him.

At the cellar door, the chair remained wedged securely under the knob.

Putting one ear to the space between door and jamb, he held his breath and listened. No sound rose from below.

Perhaps some people would have been superstitious enough to wonder if Jim might have returned from the dead for revenge. Henry didn't believe in life after death of either the spiritual or the zombie-movie kind.

The missing bodies, the bloody handprint, and the smear on the bedspread were just theater. Somebody out there had an adolescent sense of humor. He wanted to torment Henry.

Whoever the sonofabitch might be, he was evidently a sadist. No surprise. Most people in Henry's Washington circles were sadists. In a certain kind of personality, sadism and a craving for power were entwined character traits.

Henry put the shotgun on the dinette table. Still standing, he poured another glass of the wine that he had tolerated with dinner.

A year previously, Henry had become aware of a sadistic streak in himself. He first recognized it when, while watching a woman chef on the Food Network for half an hour, he imagined sixteen violent and grotesque things he wanted to do to her. At the end of the show, he had no memory of a single dish that she had prepared.

He then switched to Home and Garden Television, where he found a program hosted by a cute interior designer. By the end of the show, in Henry's vivid imagination, the woman sagged naked and broken against a limestone column to which she had been lashed with lengths of barbed wire.

For the past year, no woman on television was safe when Henry picked up the remote control.

Certain celebrities inspired in him such extravagantly savage fantasies that he bought the largest flat-screen TV on the market.

Jim and Nora didn't have a TV. No cable service existed in these boondocks, and they refused to spring for satellite service.

If Henry Rouvroy's plans were fulfilled, he would have no time for television, anyway. He doubted very much that he would be able to find celebrity chefs to imprison in the potato cellar, but even rural Colorado had plenty of tender flesh to suit his purposes.

Because he considered himself an intellectual, Henry had spent considerable time thinking about his sadistic impulses. He understood that they were not triggered by the cooking show. Extreme sadism always had been a fundamental quality of his nature. For most of his life, he repressed it in order to avoid imprisonment. He channeled that energy into his career, powered his ambition with it.

A year earlier, however, because of his insider knowledge, he recognized that a time was coming when societal upheaval and chaos would result in widespread failures of local authority, creating circumstances in which a sadist could surrender to his compulsions with little fear of punishment. The nation would soon be a thrill park for men like him.

To be ready for that time of infinite delights, he had much to do. Stock the place with years' worth of consumables. Seed the first hundred yards or so of the dirt lane, this side of the highway, so that weeds and grass would make it vanish. Create a natural-looking deadfall of trees that further blocked entrance, but only after charting a drive-able path through the forest, to get an SUV around the deadfall.

He must sell the horses and chickens, too, or otherwise dispose of them. His assumption of his brother's identity had not been for the purpose of becoming a farmer.

The thought of feeding chickens and collecting their eggs made Henry shudder. And he would not slaughter and pluck them, either. A man of his education, sophistication, and accomplishments should not be reduced to killing the food he ate.

Before he killed the women he intended to keep in the potato cellar, he would most likely bite them, as part of his play, but he had no intention of **eating** them. That was so twentieth-century Hollywood, and Henry had as much contempt for clichés as he had for people who ate fast food, people who wore off-the-rack suits, people who believed in things, and people in general.

For a while, waiting for his enemy's next move, Henry didn't think about anything. Sometimes it was a relief not to think. He could at will become the blank, the vacant flesh, the nothing that was the truth of every human being.

Ralph Waldo Emerson, the literary genius, a hero of Henry's, believed that each of us must be a circle, inventing his own truth moment by moment, consuming his truth as a snake consumes its tail, always rolling forward, living for this moment and the next, only this moment and the next, always seeking the new, becoming the new, metamorphosing, ever changing with our ever-changing truths. In transition, in progression toward the ever-new self, said Emerson, "I the imperfect adore my own Perfect."

Now imperfect Henry was a perfect circle. Nothing inside the circle. Nothing outside. Just a thin line curving to meet itself.

This was a kind of meditation, meditation without even the awareness of meditating, meditation without purpose.

When he stopped being nothing, he sat at the kitchen table, sipping the mediocre wine. He waited for a development that would break the current impasse between him and his unknown enemy.

The moment arrived when he heard footsteps ascending the wooden staircase in the cellar.

He got to his feet and picked up the shotgun. He went to the chair-braced door.

The footsteps were plodding, as if the intruder carried a heavy burden or was weary. Finally he reached the top step.

Henry waited in silence. So did the man on the cellar stairs.

After a while, the doorknob turned back and forth, squeaking against the headrail of the tipped chair. Then it stopped moving.

Twenty-one

After dinner, Lamar Woolsey returned to his Las Vegas hotel room and switched on his laptop. He had six e-mails.

He answered five quickly but took time to consider his response to the sixth, which was from Simon Northcott. Simon was already in Denver, where the conference would begin the following afternoon.

Scheduled to give a speech on Tuesday, he proposed instead that he and Lamar dedicate the time to debate. Simon listed three related propositions, which were all ground they had covered before.

Debating Simon would be as pointless as debating an issue of constitutional law with a Broadway tenor who cared only about winning over the audience by belting out show tunes. If the audience cared about law, the singer didn't stand a chance of winning the debate; but because everyone appreciates a rousing rendition of "Yankee Doodle Dandy," there would be enough applause to convince him that he had indeed won.

Having once been a man of reason, Simon had become more of an evangelist than a scientist. His new version of reason did not allow him to abandon or even to revise a cherished theory as a consequence of new information. Instead, Simon required that new information be interpreted in such a way as to support a theory to which he and so many others had devoted their careers.

At last Lamar Woolsey answered the invitation to debate.

Dear Northcott: For centuries, from the beginnings of science until the year I was born, the universe was believed to have existed forever in the same condition we observed it. Then came the big bang theory and decades of accumulating proof that the universe had a cataclysmic beginning and has been expanding ever since. If I live long enough, another revolution in science may make it unnecessary for us to debate your favorite issue. Then I will simply need to say I told you so. I look forward to hearing your speech.

After changing into pajamas and brushing his teeth, Lamar sat on the edge of the bed and keyed in his home number in Chicago. He listened to the voice-mail message: "You have reached the Woolsey residence. No one is available to take your call right now, but please leave a message, and we **will** get back to you."

He could access existing messages, but he was too weary to deal with them now. He would call for that purpose in the morning.

He didn't leave a message. There was no one to receive it.

He called only to hear his wife, Estelle, who recorded the greeting. She'd been gone almost three years, taken suddenly by an aortal aneurysm, but Lamar had not changed the recording.

When he switched off the bedside lamp, her voice remained clear in his memory. Closing his eyes, he could see her. Lying on the edge of sleep, he hoped to dream of her.

He wasn't concerned about having a nightmare about Estelle. Her presence guaranteed a dream of great comfort and gladness.

Twenty-two

Entering the dark kitchen, Grady whispered reassurances to the agitated wolfhound.

At the French door, peering out, Merlin stopped barking but began whining as though other dogs were at play in the yard and he was eager to romp with them.

Grady leaned over the table, squinting through the window at which he had earlier sat sentinel. His eyes were by now so dark-adapted that he saw the two creatures at once.

One of them sat as a dog might sit in the chair that Grady had occupied in the late afternoon, when Merlin had chased coveys of scents around the yard. The other sat on the marble-topped table on which Grady had earlier stacked three reference books about the fauna of the mountains.

Because the two had their backs to the house,

Grady couldn't see their eyes. Their impossible, inexplicable eyes.

The meadow had been more than a place. The meadow had been a moment. A moment and a motion, a pivot point and a lever, where and when his life had changed, and not just his life, much more than his life, maybe everything.

He thought of his mother at another window much like this, after the death of his father, the window through which she saw her past and her future.

This was a night of windows, upstairs and down, north, east, south, west, past and present and future. He went to the door where Merlin waited, and the door was in fact a window with nine panes.

On the porch, the animals continued to face out toward the yard, toward the night and the mountains and the moon.

They had to be aware of Grady's presence, if only because of Merlin's barking earlier and his eager entreaties now. Yet they didn't look toward him.

Grady switched on the kitchen and porch lights.

Beside him, Merlin stopped whining and began to pant excitedly. The wolfhound appeared to be neither afraid nor aggressive. His wagging tail slapped, slapped, slapped against the wall.

Grady hesitated with his hand on the doorknob.

He thought of the shimmering light as he had

moved through the piney woods toward the meadow.

He wondered who earlier turned on the lights in his workshop, and then in the garage. Who opened the workshop doors, raised the garage roll-up?

Hesitating with his hand on the knob, he rapped knuckles against one of the panes of the door.

The mysterious animals sat motionless on the chair and on the table, declining to reveal their eyes.

He thought of Marcus Pipp, who had given him the name Iguana, who had died violently, killed by the senator. He didn't know why he should think of Marcus now, in this amazing moment, except that he had thought of him often over the past ten years.

Once more he raised his knuckles to the glass, but he didn't rap the pane. He wanted to see their eyes, wanted very much to see them, but he did not rap.

He took a deep breath.

He opened the door of nine windows, and where the door had been was a threshold, and where the threshold had been was a porch floor underfoot.

The animals turned to look at him and at the suddenly shy dog.

Twenty-three

Standing at the braced door, Henry waited for the knob to turn again, but it did not.

The hollow-core doors of the bedroom closet and the bathroom had offered little resistance to a blast of buckshot. Had anyone lurked on the other side, he would have been grievously wounded.

This cellar door, however, was a solid oak slab, hard enough and thick enough to stand up to the 20-gauge. There might even be some ricochets, which Henry chose not to risk.

Whoever stood on the landing at the head of the cellar stairs must be listening, as Henry listened. For a minute or so, neither of them gave the other anything to hear.

The mediocre wine had left a less than mediocre aftertaste. Now Henry's mouth soured further. His lips were dry under the nervous passage of his dry tongue.

Beyond the door, the tormentor at last spoke in a rough whisper. **"Henry?"**

Low and hoarse, the voice could have been that of anyone. It had no recognizable character.

"Henry, Henry, Henry, Henry."

Three of those four repetitions were slurred, as though the tormentor had a malformed—or damaged—mouth.

Henry didn't know anyone with a speech impediment. The man beyond the door could be no one he knew. No one.

Because his adversary might be well-armed, Henry didn't speak or otherwise make a sound that might reveal his presence and position.

Among the weapons packed in his Land Rover was an Urban Sniper, a pistol-grip shotgun that fired only slugs powerful enough to stop a charging bull. If the tormentor had armed himself with the Sniper, the oak wouldn't provide sufficient protection for Henry.

From the farther side of the door came a shuffling as the intruder turned around on the landing. Heavy footsteps descended into the cellar, faded into silence.

Quietly, Henry returned to the dinette table. He put down the shotgun but remained standing.

Although the wine wasn't worthy of him, he drained his glass and poured another serving.

He expected to hear noises below, but silence endured.

If the tormentor had seen Henry carry two heavy suitcases into the house, and if he was someone who knew what might be in those bags, perhaps he already found them.

Henry waited to hear the outer cellar door opening and the rain doors being swung out and back from the exterior stairs. Nothing.

After a while, he sat at the table.

If the tormentor had somehow left quietly with the two million dollars, that would be a blow but not a disaster. Henry had with him five million in cut diamonds, another ten million in bearer bonds. In safe-deposit boxes in domestic and foreign institutions, he kept fortunes in commodities-grade gold coins, also in rare coins of greater value than their precious-metal content.

In the circles in which Henry once moved, embezzlement had such a long history that some viewed it as an honorable tradition. The sums drained from the system in the past, however, were pittances compared to the fortunes gushing from the spigots in recent years.

Those who stole billions were whales, and schools of them plied the waters, majestic superthieves to whom pilferers like Henry were mere pilot fish. He had assumed that the thirty million he filtered out of the flow would not be missed.

Now he wondered if he might be wrong to think that a small fish could swim safely among leviathans. Perhaps the whales devoured small fish as readily as they ate krill or plankton.

The climber and descender of the stairs wanted Henry to search the cellar. The subsequent silence was meant to wear his restraint to a fragile filament.

He was being baited. He would not take the hook.

Neither would he go outside at night to check on the remaining contents of the Land Rover. Dawn would be soon enough.

The thought of dawn led him to consider how his situation might deteriorate if his enemy cut power during the night. He didn't want to be feeling his way through a strange house in absolute blackness.

When the University of Colorado had used this place for forest-management research, it paid to have the power company trench the dirt lane and bury cable. But the line must come out of the ground before entering the house, which was a point of vulnerability.

In the cellar, he'd seen a service panel. If his tormentor was still down there and decided to flip a few breakers, Henry would be effectively blind.

He imagined groping warily through lightless

rooms and hearing, close at his side, a low, rough voice whisper **Henry**.

Anxiety spiking, he searched kitchen cabinets and drawers until he found a flashlight and spare batteries. All right. He would be all right.

Now, at a few minutes past ten o'clock, dawn lay at least eight hours away. If he spent the night alert for sounds of an attempted break-in, he would be exhausted by daybreak. Already weary, he needed sleep to regain the necessary edge to stay alive.

He wanted to leave all the lights on. But he had always needed darkness to sleep. If he switched off the lights in only one room, anyone outside would know where he must be sleeping.

After consideration, he switched off the kitchen fluorescents. In the dark, he saw a bright line at the bottom of the cellar door, which might mean either that his tormentor was down there or wanted him to think as much.

He left the lights on in the hallway but turned them off in the study where Nora had intended to prepare the sofa bed for him.

In the living room, he clicked off one lamp but left another aglow near a window.

He would sleep in the bedroom, but not where anyone would expect to find him. The situation required precautions, deception.

He propped the shotgun against the bedroom

armchair. He put the flashlight and the package of batteries on a footstool.

In the closet with the riddled door, from a high shelf, Henry took down two extra pillows and two spare blankets. With these, he could create the illusion of a sleeper, under the covers.

Approaching the bed, he saw the gloves.

The pillows and blankets fell from his arms.

On the chenille spread lay the pair of leather work gloves that Jim had worn to chop wood. They hadn't been there before. They were saturated with blood. The blood had leached into the chenille.

Twenty-four

Cammy Rivers in her kitchen, in the ceaseless throbbing shadow of the light-drunk moth, eliminated protozoan diseases as possible causes of the behavior of the animals at High Meadows Farm.

She seemed to be left with only the possibility that a toxic substance or a drug had been administered to the Thoroughbreds and their pets. The method of delivery would most likely have been through accidentally or intentionally contaminated food.

The different species—horses, goats, dogs—would not have been fed the same things. Even some of the horses might have been on diets different from the others. Consequently, the contamination surely would have been intentional.

This explanation struck her as melodramatic and implausible. But she had no other avenue to explore.

Although she was old-fashioned in her approach to research, preferring books to Internet sources that more often contained misinformation, the time had come to go downstairs to the computer. The large number of drugs with their lengthy lists of side effects and the even larger number of natural and man-made toxins could be considered and eliminated only with the use of carefully composed search strings.

As she pushed her chair away from the table and got to her feet, the wall phone rang. She plucked the handset from the cradle: "Cammy Rivers."

"Hey, Doc," Grady Adams said, "hope I didn't wake you."

"It's not even ten-thirty yet, Grady."

"Well, I know you get up early. Listen, could you maybe come out here?"

"What—now?"

"That's what I'm hoping."

"Tell me nothing's wrong with Merlin."

She had given Grady the wolfhound as a puppy almost three years earlier.

"No, no, he's fit enough, you could saddle him up and ride him. There's this other thing."

"What thing?"

"This thing—I want you to take a look at it. At them. Bring your bag, whatever you need, 'cause you might want to examine them."

"They have a name?"

"That's just it—I don't think they do. I've never seen anything like them. Right now, they're chasing Merlin around the room, and he loves it."

"I have to ask you, furniture guy—you been breathing too many shellac fumes?"

"Maybe I have. Maybe I've been drinking the stuff."

Twenty-five

After finding the blood-soaked gloves, shotgun at the ready, Henry Rouvroy searched the house, found no one, then searched it again, with the same result.

The chair still braced the cellar door. The front door remained locked, as did the back door between the kitchen and the rear porch.

The explanation became obvious. The enemy possessed a key. No doubt he took it off either Jim's corpse or Nora's.

While Henry had sat at the dinette table, listening for sounds in the basement, drinking dismal wine that might as easily have been pressed from plastic grapes as from real ones, his tormentor used a key to come in quietly through the front door. He left the bloody gloves on the bed, gloves he had worn while moving the bodies, and he left by the way he entered, locking up after himself.

Henry could see how it was done, but he couldn't understand **why**.

Earlier, this kind of prankish behavior seemed to indicate that his tormentor must have an adolescent sense of humor. With so much at stake, however, and with every prank performed at a mortal risk, such behavior was unreasonable if not irrational.

If someone in Washington had become aware of Henry's theft even as he had been industriously embezzling, if that person monitored him to discover the extent of his larceny and to determine his ultimate intentions, and if that person had either followed him to Jim's farm or been waiting here for his arrival, common sense argued that Henry should have been killed, shot in the back of the head, before he even realized anyone had become aware of his thievery and his plans to make the farm his redoubt.

Evidently, his tormentor wanted more from him than his money and the farm. He tried to imagine what that might be, but his imagination failed him.

To ensure that his enemy could not get in with a key, Henry braced the kitchen door with a dinette chair. He used another chair to prevent the front door from being opened.

Henry thought of himself as a monster of limitless cruelty and perfect self-interest, whose absolute amorality ensured that he would reliably do the best thing for himself without hesitation. Now he reluctantly recognized that he could nevertheless make mistakes.

For one thing, he had equipped his Land Rover with a roadside-assistance and anti-theft service. Via satellite, it allowed real-time conversations in the event of breakdowns, accidents, and other emergencies. His primary purpose when having the service installed was to receive reliable advice about the best restaurants and the finest hotels wherever he happened to be at mealtime during his leisurely drive west.

In his Washington circles were people who could secretly hack into the satellite-service computers and follow him by the signal from the transponder that had been installed in the Land Rover as part of the package.

He purchased the Rover using fake ID and paid for it with a wire transfer from a bank in Bermuda, which itself received the funds from the account of a fabric-design firm in France, which was only a shell corporation acting on behalf of a nonexistent textile mill in the Philippines, which was owned by a wealthy Hong Kong man who could never be questioned or subpoenaed to testify in court because he was a figment of Henry's imagination.

Evidently, using a homeless bum as proxy, he should have instead bought a used and spavined SUV for cash and should have driven west in rattletrap style, dressed in the tacky garb of a typical middle-class tourist, subsisting on Twinkies and Big Macs and mystery-meat tacos, sleeping in cheap motels where he was at risk of death either from swarms of mutant bedbugs or from exposure to such tasteless decor that it could inspire a weak cerebral artery to pop.

Never in a millennium would anyone in his Washington circles have thought to look for him—or for anyone of their acquaintance—in such a vehicle or in such déclassé establishments. They had all benefited from the same quality education, and they shared a set of standards by which they lived, and they expected of one another adherence to those standards.

Being one of the anointed elite meant **belonging,** meant freedom from self-doubt, meant always knowing what you thought and what you should think, meant **comfort.** But now Henry realized that it also meant being so intellectually cozy that you could not easily think out of the box. He thought he had risen above the past by freeing his inner beast from all restraint, yet he had planned his flight from D.C. in these dangerous times much as he might have planned a motor trip to the Hamptons in the old days when the world had not yet begun to slide into an abyss.

The tormentor clearly retained the ability to think outside the box. This sonofabitch wanted something more than the money and the farm, and he sought what he wanted with a strategy and tactics that left Henry confused and off balance.

Henry needed to be more mentally nimble. He must strive to expect the unexpected. To think the unthinkable.

After taking a trash bag from a box of them in a kitchen drawer, Henry returned to the bedroom. He put the blood-soaked leather gloves in the bag and placed the bag on the armchair.

As he removed the bloody chenille spread from the bed and set it aside to be laundered, he reminded himself that survival required mental nimbleness. Expect the unexpected. Think the unthinkable. He tried to think of something unthinkable so that he could consider it.

But as a monster in the making, he found nothing unthinkable, no motive or action shocking or even alien. Limits and transgressions had no meaning for him.

Then into his mind's eye came the image of his twin brother taking a bullet in the face. He saw the event as it had been. Then he saw his brother on the barn floor, face broken as it had been.

None of that was unthinkable.

But then he saw something that had not occurred: the hemorrhaged eyes clearing, the occluding blood draining away, the eyes alive once more and capable of sight.

No. That was not merely unthinkable; it was impossible. There could be no return from death because there was no place after death from which to return.

The poet Emerson, grandfather of the modern intellectual, said to trust your will, trust in the power of will, and all things would be possible. He said, "What a man does, that he has." He said men didn't need hope and fear, meaning the hope of anything beyond themselves, meaning the fear of eternal consequences.

Henry Rouvroy had nothing to fear from his murdered brother, only from an unknown tormentor who, when the truth was at last known, would be a man like him, not his dead identical come back to life, but a man **like** him, shaped by the same influences, with a mind clear of all superstition.

He used spare pillows and blankets to shape a body on the bed. He drew the bedclothes over the faux sleeper.

In the kitchen, he removed the chair from under the doorknob and returned it to the dinette table.

Likewise, he returned the chair with which he had braced the front door. For the time being, he left the chair bracing the cellar door.

Let the tormentor use his house key again. This time, Henry would be prepared for him.

Twenty-six

These rural roads were deserted at an hour when no logging trucks were en route to the mill and when no loads of lumber were outbound.

The Explorer's headlights worked across various combinations of geometrical white ranch fencing and caused tree shadows to swing open like dark doors across moon-frosted meadows.

The forested mountains were blacker than the sky, and the moon rode high across a sea of stars.

At the end of the county road, Cammy followed Grady's driveway past the house and parked behind.

On those occasions when she came to dinner, they always ate at the table in the kitchen, so she usually knocked at the back door instead of the front.

She and Grady were nothing more than friends.

No man—or woman—in her life was more than
that, but she counted Grady Adams as an especially good friend.

He possessed the grace of knowing what to ask
about and what to leave unasked. He understood
that caring didn't require that every curiosity be
satisfied.

Perhaps they got along so well because she,
too, knew the limits of therapy talk in a society
that counted nothing higher than the therapeutic.
She didn't expect to heal a friend or to be healed
by him.

Sharing didn't have to involve complete revela-
tion. In fact, the more you shared of the past, the
less people saw you for who you were in the now,
the more they saw you as who you had been and
who you had struggled so long not to be.

Neither words nor time healed anyone. Only living healed, if it healed at all, living as you were
meant to live, as best you could with your learned
habits and confused intentions, living through
time and finally beyond time, where neither thera-
pists nor surgeons were any longer needed to
smooth away the pain or cut it out.

Cammy carried her medical bag to the house. As
she climbed the back-porch steps, Grady opened
the kitchen door.

As always, she liked the look of him: big, a little
rough, an impression of determination in the set

of his jaw and in the line of his mouth, but then the kindness in his eyes, the kindness that was as apparent as the blue of his irises.

Some might argue that kindness could not be seen in a kind man's eyes any more than evil could be seen in the eyes of an evil man. But she could see them both when they were present: evil because she had much experience of it, kindness because she'd had no experience of it for such a long time that the absence of it had made her acutely sensitive to its eventual presence.

She had read about a man named Homer who, as a six-year-old child, suffered a mysterious neurological disorder that left him unable to smell anything for the next thirty years. One day, when he was thirty-six, as he picked a rose to savor the sight of it and the texture of its petals, his sense of smell returned to him full power, so overwhelming him that he fell to the ground in shock. In the years thereafter, while he enjoyed every bewitching scent of a world rich in them, he was so sensitive to the fragrance of a rose that he could smell a bush of blooms two blocks away and knew before he opened the door of a flower shop if it had a generous supply of roses or was temporarily out of stock.

Kindness in a man's eyes was as apparent to Cammy as the promise of roses was manifest to Homer at a distance and beyond closed doors.

This time, as Grady greeted her, she saw something additional and less familiar in him: a childlike exuberance and wonder.

He said, "I should've prepared you better."

"Prepared me?"

"On the phone. For this."

As he ushered her into the kitchen, she said, "I brought my medical bag."

"I don't mean prepared that way. I mean, you know, **prepared.**" He closed the door. "But there's no way you could be. Prepared, I mean. For this."

"Are you babbling?"

"Sounds like babbling, doesn't it? A lot's happened. I don't know what to make of it. Of them. Maybe you will. They're in the living room."

Cammy followed him across the kitchen. At the threshold of the hallway, he halted. She almost collided with him.

He turned to her. "I'm half afraid to take you in there."

"Afraid—why?"

"Maybe you won't be surprised. You'll have a name for them. Then it's not something, after all. It sure seems like it is. Something, I mean. But what do I know? I'm babbling, aren't I?"

"Which sure isn't like you."

"They ate my chicken. Some was Merlin's chicken. I'm assuming it was them. I don't have actual proof."

"I'm not here to make an arrest."

"But who else would've eaten it? Maybe whoever switched on the lights in the workshop."

Clueless but game, Cammy said, "Maybe the light switches smell like chicken. That would be proof of something."

After turning away from her, he at once faced her again. "I don't care they ate it. What surprises me is they would come right in. In the house, I mean. Wild animals aren't that bold."

He started toward the living room, but three steps along the hallway, he stopped and turned to her. She collided with him.

Steadying Cammy with one hand, Grady said, "Wild, bold—but not dangerous. Just the opposite. Almost tame. Like somebody's pets."

He let go of her and headed along the hallway again.

Expecting him to halt suddenly, Cammy hesitated to follow.

At the living-room archway, he glanced back. "What're you doing? Come on, come on."

In the front room, Merlin sat at attention. He glanced at Cammy, and his tail twitched, but he didn't hurry to her as he usually did. He was captivated by the two creatures in front of him, on the sofa.

They were the size of six-year-old children. They sat as kids might sit, not on their haunches as a dog or a cat, but on their posteriors, legs straight in front of them.

In its forepaws, each held a dog toy, which it was examining with interest. A plush yellow duck, a plush purple bunny.

They were almost like plush toys themselves: dense, lustrous, snow-white fur. Furless and coal-black noses, lips, and paws.

Grady said, "Well? Is this really something? Is this something or isn't it?"

Cammy glanced at him. Nodded. Found her voice. "Yeah. It's something, all right."

She put down her medical bag. Her knees had gone weak. She sat on a footstool directly opposite the animals.

Their skulls were not long like those of dogs, but round, and their faces were flat compared to the faces of dogs. Their nose leather and lips seemed feline. They looked more like otters than like cats, but they were not otters.

Because their heads were larger in proportion to their bodies than was usually the case in animals, the enormous eyes didn't seem grotesque, and they weren't protuberant. When they blinked, their lids were as black as their noses and lips.

Other aspects of the creatures were different from anything Cammy expected in furred mammals. Above all else, however, their eyes compelled her attention.

Some nocturnal animals, like African bush babies, had large eyes in proportion to the size of their heads. None she could think of was a fraction as enormous as these.

"Large eyes aren't essential to night vision," she said, as much to herself as to Grady, thinking aloud. "Diurnal-nocturnal animals, like dogs and cats—they're able to see well in the dark because they have large pupils and a lot of photoreceptors in their retinas."

Many animal eyes lacked a sclera—the white—as prominent as it was in the human eye. In most dogs, the sclera became visible largely when the animal looked sideways. The pair on the couch seemed to have no sclera whatsoever.

"The iris," she said, "the pigmented portion, appears to wrap the eyeball far enough that the sclera never rotates into view."

This alone suggested the possibility of numerous structural differences from the eyes of other animals. The cornea's convex arc was a more impressive engineering feat here than in the human eye. The anterior and the posterior chambers of the aqueous humor must be shaped differently and must integrate in a unique fashion with the iris at the iridocorneal angle.

As a veterinarian, she was compelled to study them more closely, but she was simultaneously restrained by amazement, by astonishment, her mind and heart equally affected. Her stomach muscles fluttered, and her hands trembled as if palsied.

The animals shook-smelled-chewed the plush toys. The one with the duck offered it to the other, and they traded duck for bunny.

Merlin wagged his tail, as if pleased that they seemed to like his stuff.

A kind of wonder had overcome Cammy, akin to what she felt among the horses at High Meadows Farm. But the word **wonder** didn't do this feeling justice. This was more profound. The right word eluded her.

However many differences might exist between these eyes and those of other animals, only their color impressed as much as did their size. They were golden but not uniform in hue. Several shades played through them: from gold dust to flax, to amber. . . .

"The irises don't appear to be striated," she said.

From the arm of the chair on which he now perched, Grady said, "Appear to be what?"

"Striated. The light and dark crossbands of muscle fiber—the striae—that radiate from the center of the iris and give texture to it. Sometimes the way light plays in light-colored eyes, they seem to be cut like jewels, to sparkle."

"Sure. Okay. Striated."

"But these aren't. There's a wholly different texture. I'd sure like to look at their eyes with my ophthalmoscope."

"I think they might let you."

She raised her hands to show him how she trembled.

He said, "You're not afraid of them, are you?"

"No. No, they seem docile. It's just . . . just what they might mean. My God."

"What? What're you thinking?"

"I'm not thinking anything."

"You're thinking something."

"No. I don't **know**. But they sure as hell mean **something**."

"I told you they were something. But I thought you'd have some idea what."

"I don't. I don't know what."

"I thought you'd at least have a theory."

"I do medicine. I don't do theory."

He said, "I'm gonna turn off the lights. Wait till you see their eyes in the dark."

The creature with the purple bunny found the squeaker in it.

"Wait," Cammy said as Grady moved toward the light switch.

"Wait for what?"

Squeak, squeak.

In case the squeaking meant a play session was imminent, Merlin got to his feet.

"Their forepaws," Cammy said. "I didn't notice

till now. I was so taken with their eyes, I didn't notice their forepaws."

"What about them?"

Squeak, squeak, squeak.

Cammy's knees still felt loose, her legs shaky, but
nervous energy brought her to her feet. "They
aren't paws. They're hands."

"Yeah," Grady said. "Like monkeys."

Her hands were suddenly damp. She blotted
them on her jeans as she said, "No. No, no, no.
Not like monkeys."

Twenty-seven

As a man of impeccable personal hygiene, Henry Rouvroy longed to take a bath. His activities since arriving at the farm had caused him to break into a sweat more than once.

He would be forced to costume himself as a rustic for the next few years, to pass as Jim. But he refused to be reduced to one of the Great Unwashed, either intellectually or physically.

With his tormentor on the prowl, however, he dared not be naked and vulnerable. The noise of the bathroom shower would leave him deaf to an enemy's approach.

The most he could do was wash his hands. As he quickly filled the sink with hot water, he rolled up his shirtsleeves.

From the soap arose a cheap scent, a poor imitation of the fragrance of roses. The lather was not as rich as that of the fine soaps to which he was accustomed. In fact, it felt like slime.

When Henry stocked the cellar for the possibility of society's collapse, he would have to lay in a good supply of the right soaps. No doubt their shampoo, hair conditioner, toothpaste, and various toiletries were also purchased because of price and were inadequate.

The condition of his fingernails distressed him. Unspeakable grime was embedded under every one.

How could he have eaten dinner with such filth under his nails? Perhaps, like a malign fog that begins as wisps of mist, the rural way of thinking crept into a newcomer's mind without his awareness. One day you neglected to clean under your fingernails, and a week later you found yourself chewing tobacco and buying bib overalls **because you liked them**.

He must guard against an unconscious slide from sophistication into uncouth practices and boorish ideas.

In the soap dish lay a small rectangular brush with medium-stiff bristles, clearly meant for scrubbing the stubborn grime of farm work out of knuckle creases and from under fingernails. Henry applied it vigorously to the disgusting scum under his nails.

As he labored, he realized with dismay that he

would no longer be able to avail himself of the services of a manicurist twice every month. Ensuring the health and attractiveness of his nails, of his cuticles, would henceforth be his responsibility and his alone.

His hair. With a shiver of horror, he suddenly understood that he would have to cut his own hair.

In the surrounding county, in this kingdom of rubes and hicks, barbers could no doubt be found, but he suspected that they learned to cut hair by shearing sheep and would do him up in full redneck style. Anyway, when anarchy swept the nation, venturing out to a barber would be as foolhardy as walking barefoot through a snakepit.

The water was foul, lukewarm. He had cleaned four fingernails to his satisfaction. He drained the sink and filled it again.

He scrubbed, scrubbed. He drained the sink once more and filled it a third time.

When his hands were clean, he felt that he had washed away not only the filth but also every stubborn vestige of superstition. He believed that he would suffer no further from paranoid fantasies of the resurrected dead. Good-bye, Jim.

With the shotgun in hand, Henry toured the house one more time.

In the kitchen, he stared at the glow leaking under the braced cellar door. He was disturbed by the

light pooling below, down there where only darkness ought to be—pooling, rising, insinuating.

He stood there for so long, gripping the shotgun
so fiercely, that eventually he became aware that
his hands ached.

He returned to the bedroom and stood staring at
the faux sleeper under the bedclothes, the make-
believe Henry composed of pillows and rolled
blankets. The simulacrum was convincing.

As his flashlight brightened in his hand, he
doused the overhead light with the switch by the
door. He left the door open. The hallway light was
too dim to relieve the deep gloom in the bedroom.

He retrieved his shotgun and took it into the
empty half of the closet, from which he earlier removed Nora's clothing. He sat on the floor with
his back against the wall, leaving the riddled door
open. He clicked off the flashlight.

Outside, the tormentor would see the glow of
the living-room lamp, the other rooms dark. He
would most likely sense a trap and wait for Henry
to step out of the house before making his move.
If the sonofabitch dared to use his key to come inside, Henry would be ready for him.

The simulacrum under the bedclothes looked
like someone sleeping.

If the tormentor stepped into the room,
switched on the lights, and opened fire on the fake

Henry, the real Henry would return fire from the closet, killing him.

Sitting in the dark, Henry recalled the shape on the bed, under the covers. He could see it clearly in memory.

A real man lying on the bed would present exactly the same form as the pillow-and-rolled-blanket dummy. Exactly.

He knew the sleeper was nothing but pillows and blankets because earlier he arranged them under the covers. He knew. Just pillows and blankets.

Henry listened for a distant door to open. He listened for the stealthy footsteps of an intruder. He listened intently for the sound of the bedsprings adjusting to a shifting weight.

Nothing. Nothing. Nothing. Yet.

Twenty-eight

For Cammy Rivers, the sudden recognition of the nature of the creatures' hands was a wardrobe-to-Narnia, tornado-and-Toto moment, when the well-known land of a lifetime suddenly proved to be—to have always been—one door away, one wind away, from another reality.

The creature with the plush yellow duck found the pressure point that made the toy speak: **Quack, quack.**

At once, its companion answered with the purple bunny: **Squeak, squeak, squeak.**

Panting in anticipation of play, Merlin stood poised to move whichever way the action might go, looking from one to the other of his new friends.

Quack. Squeak, squeak. Quack, quack. Squeak.

Throughout most of her childhood, Cammy had wished desperately for a magic moment, for a wave of change to wash away the way things were, for all that seemed impossible to become possible in a wink. Having given up long ago, having been old and without dreams even before her brutal childhood ended, she now found herself on the brink of an event potentially so momentous that it seemed to have the power to put her past in a new perspective, to diminish the memory of her suffering, and to open a door through which she could step and be transformed.

Squeak. Quack. Squeak. Quack, quack, quack.

The word **wonder** was inadequate to describe the feeling—both emotion and sensation—that flowered in her more fully by the minute, and the right word no longer eluded her. But she feared that speaking it even to herself would jinx her, would ensure that what seemed to be momentous would turn out to be mundane.

Squeak, squeak. Quack. Squeak, squeak. Quack.

Sitting on the footstool again, Cammy remained riveted by the animals' hands as they squeezed the toys. "No, not like monkeys. There's over a hundred species of monkeys, some with hands instead of paws, but not all. Those with hands don't always have thumbs."

Grady rose from the arm of the chair behind Cammy and knelt beside the footstool on which she sat. "These guys have thumbs."

"Oh, yeah. Yeah, they sure do. And some monkeys have thumbs that help them hold things. But only capuchins and one or maybe two other species can pick up things between their thumb and forefinger."

Squeak. Quack. Squeak, squeak. Quack, quack.

One of the animals made soft chortling noises that seemed to express delight, and the two appeared to grin at each other.

Making a timpani of the floor, Merlin galloped out of the room.

"Of monkeys, only capuchins and—I think maybe—guenons can move the thumb around to touch a couple of the other fingers."

Grady counted, "One, two, three, four," as he moved his right thumb to each finger on his hand.

"I don't know of any monkeys that have fully opposable and extendable thumbs, capable of such dexterity," Cammy said. "A lot of monkeys can't hold things with their thumb, they just press the object between their fingers and palm."

"Anyway," Grady said, "these guys aren't monkeys. They don't look anything like monkeys."

"Definitely not monkeys," she agreed. "Some

lemurs have pretty flexible hands, but these hands aren't like the hands of any lemur."

"What has hands like theirs?"

"We do."

"Besides us."

"Nothing."

"There must be something."

"Yeah. There's them."

Having made a selection from his toy box in the kitchen, the wolfhound thundered into the living room with a plush raccoon in his mouth.

The animals on the sofa reacted to that ring-tailed treasure with interest.

Hoping to tease them into a chase, Merlin bit the raccoon, and it produced a squeak identical to that made by the purple bunny.

As if disappointed that the raccoon lacked a unique voice, the creatures returned to the examination of their toys.

"Look at the way they handle those things," Cammy said.

"What way?"

"The way they stroke the fabric."

"So?"

"Look at that one, Grady. Look how it likes the feel of the duck's rubber bill."

"Yeah, and Merlin loves to chew on it. So what?"

"The other one. See? The way it keeps rubbing its thumb across the bunny's nose? I bet there's something else they share with us besides the shape and function of their hands. A richness of nerve endings in the fingertips. Did you know, compared to other species, the human sense of touch is highly refined, it's unique on Earth?"

"I didn't know," he admitted.

"Now you know. Unique on Earth. Or it was."

As if tiring of the toy, one of the creatures tossed the purple bunny across the living room, where it bounced off the fireplace mantel and fell to the hearth.

Merlin dropped his raccoon and scrambled after the rabbit.

The second creature threw the duck to a far corner of the room.

The wolfhound seized the rabbit, dropped it, and plunged after the duck.

One of the animals began to pry up a sofa cushion, apparently to see what might be under it.

The other had taken an interest in Cammy. It slid to the edge of the sofa and leaned forward, staring intently.

At the centers of its beautiful golden eyes, the pupils were not black but a dark copper color.

Merlin returned with the duck. He squeaked the toy twice, but neither of the creatures wanted to play.

"Calling them 'it' doesn't feel right," Cammy said. "We ought to name them."

"I don't name every animal in the woods."

"They aren't in the woods. They're here now."

"Probably not for long."

"Are you paying attention?" she asked.

"I thought I was."

"They've moved in."

"Wild animals don't just move in."

"**Wild** isn't the right word for them. You yourself said they were almost tame, like somebody's pets."

"I did. I said that. You think they're someone's pets?"

She shook her head. "No. Not pets. But they're something."

"We aren't making any progress. We're back to the something theory."

After discovering that neither of his new friends was in the mood for a chase, Merlin came to Cammy with the duck, squeaking it teasingly.

She rubbed his head and said, "Not right now, you big sweetie."

Astonishment and amazement affected the heart and the mind only momentarily and couldn't be sustained. The wonder that gripped Cammy was continuous, however, in part because the longer she observed the creatures, the more they intrigued her.

Their nostrils quivered frequently, suggesting that their nasal cavities were richly supplied with blood vessels and nerves, like the noses of dogs, and that their olfactory sense was highly developed. Their teeth were those of omnivores, quite human in shape, sharpness, and arrangement. In spite of the masking fur, their facial muscles allowed a wide range of expressions. Their toes were longer than those of humans, and the great toe appeared to be a kind of thumb, not fully opposable but functional enough to make them good climbers.

With every new observation, Cammy was further energized. Ideas, questions, and suppositions that gave rise to additional questions spun through her mind. The flint of one idea sparked against the flint of another and another and another.

Indicating the animal that perched on the edge of the sofa and stared intently at her, Cammy said, "She's so totally mysterious, I'm going to call her Puzzle."

Because the genitalia were well-concealed in fur and folds, Grady asked, "How do you know it's a female?"

"I'm guessing. But she's slightly smaller than the other one. And her tail isn't quite as plumey."

"Male peacocks are always showier than female, huh?"

"It holds for a number of species, though not all. Male golden retrievers tend to have plumier tails than females."

Puzzle slid off the sofa, onto all fours, cocked her head, and continued to study Cammy.

Immediately, the other animal turned to the cushion on which Puzzle had been sitting and tipped it on end to look underneath.

Grady said, "So you think the one searching for loose change is a male?"

"I'm pretty sure. But the names work either way. I'm going to call him Riddle."

"Puzzle and Riddle. I guess that's better than Ebb and Flo."

"You should be forbidden by law from naming animals."

"I still think Howard would've been a good name for Merlin."

"You were going to call him Sassy, for God's sake."

"That was only to scare you into letting me call him Howard."

Pointing at the female, Cammy said, "Puzzle. That's you. But every puzzle has a solution."

Seeming to confirm the judgment that these animals were not wild, that they were familiar with people, Puzzle scampered to the footstool, climbed into Cammy's lap, and curled up for a cuddle, as if she were not a fifty-pound package but instead a lap dog.

Laughing, Cammy stroked Puzzle's coat—and exclaimed at the density and singular softness of the fur. "Grady, feel this."

He put a hand on Puzzle. "So soft, like mink."

"Softer than mink," Cammy said. "Softer than sable. Softer than anything."

Under Cammy's ministering hands, Puzzle purred with pleasure.

"Look at you," Grady said. "You're glowing."

"I'm not glowing," Cammy objected.

"I've never seen you glowing like this."

"I'm not a lamp."

"Your face is like the face of a saint in a painting."

"I'm no saint."

"Well, you're glowing, anyway."

Twenty-nine

The incident occurred in the afternoon, and Tom Bigger thought about nothing else all day and into the night before deciding what he must do.

He was vomiting into a trash barrel when it happened.

Without a shriek or shrill, a flock of seagulls swooped out of nowhere, wings beating the air low over his head. The mere act of ducking, turning, and looking up into the sun was enough to trigger vertigo.

A trash barrel stood a step away. If it hadn't been there, in his confusion he might have thrown up on his shoes. He had done that before.

The barrel served a small rest area off the coastal highway. Two concrete benches offered vantage points from which to enjoy the sun-spangled sea and a curve of coastline.

Occasionally, on days when he looked as presentable as he got, Tom climbed up from the beach to panhandle the motorists who stopped to commune with nature. If he tried to beg when he was too rough-looking, the marks didn't get out of their cars.

The name Bigger fit him better in his youth. At forty-eight, more than fifty pounds lighter than in his glory days, he was gaunt, although at six foot five, he still towered over most people. Large-boned, with wrists as thick as axe handles, with sledgehammer hands, he could knock down any-one, but the condition of his face ensured that no one ever challenged him.

Three times over the years, when the self-hatred became too poisonous to contain, he pounded his massive fists into his own face until the pain burned as fiercely as he deserved. Each time, someone found him, and he was hospitalized.

He accepted basic care but refused reconstructive surgery other than some dental work. He wanted to look like what he was: broken, the non-functional wreckage of a man. He wanted people to see the real him and to witness their pity, their disgust.

Humiliation kept his acrimony focused on himself. He feared only that one day his bitterness would turn to hostility against others and that he would act upon his enmity. He dreaded what violence he might perpetrate, what a horror he might become.

When he panhandled, he held a sign that identified him as a veteran, the survivor of a bomb blast in one Middle East conflict or another, but he was a veteran only of the war within himself.

On this day, shaved, hair freshly washed in the sea, wearing rumpled khakis and a parrot-pattern Hawaiian shirt, Tom appeared sufficiently presentable to take in thirty dollars and change in three hours.

He was alone in the rest area when the seagulls dived at him, the vertigo overcame him, and he vomited into the barrel.

Stomach purged, he took a pint of tequila from a pants pocket to wash the foul taste from his mouth. As he put the bottle to his lips, the incident occurred.

When Tom Bigger at last could move, he walked north from the rest area, until the sheer bluff became a steep sandstone slope. He descended in a shambling rush to the shore. On the beach, he realized that he had neither taken a swallow of the tequila nor held on to the bottle.

For some months, he had been sheltering in a ten-foot-deep cave at the base of the bluff, directly below the scenic viewpoint. With his bedroll and his few belongings, he kept a supply of tequila and a tin filled with joints of sinsemilla.

In recent years, he drank more than he smoked. Now, he wanted both, until he achieved oblivion.

For the first time in memory, however, he denied himself what he craved. Instead, he waded fully clothed into the sea and sat where the low surf broke gently against his chest.

On this stretch of state-owned coastline, in respect of certain endangered species, the beach was permanently closed to swimmers, surfers, campers, and fishermen. Bankrupt California didn't have the funds to enforce much more than the tax laws, however, and Tom didn't worry about being hassled by any kind of shore patrol.

The outer limits of the town lay almost a mile to the south, once a community filled with promise but now just another place where people waited for the end of one thing and the beginning of something worse. He walked into town most days, but no one from there ever came this far north on foot.

Over the years, he'd lived in many places: tents, culverts, junkyard cars, a half-collapsed barn, abandoned buildings. His hope had been that the cave in the sandstone bluff might be his last home.

Six months ago, he twice had a dream about living just above the high-tide line in a cave with smooth sinuous walls, where inflowing wind sometimes spoke in many voices. In the dream, the sea rose in a monster swell and came to him as he lay watching the water claim the stars.

After the second dream, he came to the coast and walked miles of lonely beaches and sandless shingle, until he found his current quarters with its smooth and sinuous walls. He had believed in the promise of the tsunami, and he had known what to do: Wait for the great wave, the drowning rush.

The incident in the rest area changed everything. He no longer knew what he should do.

He sat in the surf while the day waned. If the sea would not keep its promise to him, then perhaps it would wash into him an understanding of what he had seen, what it meant, and what he must do now instead of waiting for the wave.

Twice people in the rest area high above shouted down to him. He didn't acknowledge them. Later, two young men descended from the bluff, either to see if they could help him or, more likely, to see if they could have some cruel fun with him. As they approached, one of them said, "Hey, dude, where's your surfboard?"

When he turned to look up at them, they halted at the sight of his face. Their attitude and expressions changed, and they backed off a few steps.

As the two conferred in whispers, Tom raised his

hands out of the surging water and showed them his huge fists.

The young men retreated to the bluff and did not return.

After a while, Tom moved farther back on the beach, so the surf broke at his feet.

Neither twilight nor nightfall brought under-standing.

The moon silvered the froth of the breaking surf.

Far out on the black sea, ship lights moved north, moved south, grew brighter, then dwindled.

As if stepping out of time from a prehuman world, a great blue heron of singular size appeared to the south of him, a prehistoric presence almost five feet tall, wading through the shallow purling water of the collapsed surf, feeding as it pro-gressed.

Heron often trumpeted during a hunt. This one stalked silently. The bird stopped near Tom's feet and regarded him with its tiny moon-monocled eyes. Instead of spreading its immense wings and taking flight or issuing its threatening cry of ag-gression, it paused only briefly and then dismis-sively moved past him, continuing north along the shore, spearing small fish with its sharp bill.

The moon, the ships, the hunting heron seemed to have the same message for Tom Bigger: **Rise, go, keep moving.**

Suddenly chilled, he stripped out of his wet garments and left them on the beach. He dressed in one of his two changes of clothes: thick socks, walking shoes, jeans, and a denim shirt.

He packed six pints of tequila in his backpack and left the rest of his supply buried in the sand at the back of the cave, although he suspected that he would never return.

Because his bedroll was worn and greasy, he left it in the cave, but he packed his tin of sinsemilla joints and the pistol.

With no destination yet in mind, he took his direction from the traffic on the sea. At the moment, two clusters of ship lights were visible. Both vessels were sailing south, so Tom Bigger walked south toward the town.

He didn't believe the town would be his ultimate destination. On arrival, perhaps he would receive a sign by which he would know where to go from there.

Sometimes he made decisions based on dreams that seemed to be predictive, as when he followed a dream to a cave by the sea, hoping for an obliterating tidal wave. The dreams in which he believed and from which he took direction were always death dreams, foreboding but at the same time alluring.

He never previously expected to see signs and portents in the waking world. Perhaps he would see none now. But the incident in the deserted rest area had upended him. He would not be surprised if at least he sensed being guided by mundane things—like blue herons and distant ships—that suddenly seemed to have greater significance and require interpretation.

The damp, compacted sand underfoot. The vast night-shrouded sea to his right. The sky hard and cold but stippled with stars. To his left, the land, the highways and the cities, the people and their pain, the infinite possibilities, the unspeakable horrors, the world long lost to him, everything that might have been for him but never was, perhaps now his future.

Thirty

Cammy on the footstool, holding Puzzle on her lap, started with the furry ears, the shape of which reminded her of calla lilies, and proceeded down the neck to the shoulders, working her fingers all the way into the undercoat, massaging the creature's sleek muscles. She was surprised by what she found—or, rather, by what she didn't find.

"I'm not feeling a tick anywhere. Not one. And she doesn't seem to have any fleas, either."

Grimacing, Grady said, "I didn't think about ticks and fleas when I let them in the house."

"No ticks, no fleas—she can't have been roaming around fields and woods more than a day or so, probably a lot less than that."

"When Merlin and I saw them in the meadow

this afternoon, they were romping as if they'd just been set free. Maybe they were."

"No papillomas or cysts," Cammy reported.

She raised her hand to her face and found that no offensive odor had been transferred from the white fur to her skin. Leaning forward, she put her nose to Puzzle's ventral coat.

"She smells fresh, as if she was just groomed."

Feeling ignored, Merlin dropped the toy duck and thrust his big head into the moment, resting his chin on Puzzle's chest, rolling his eyes at Cammy.

Before Cammy could pet the dog, Puzzle took Merlin's muzzle in both hands and began to massage his face with her small fingers, which was his favorite form of attention.

"Look," Cammy whispered, as if a loud word would break the spell.

"I see."

"Shouldn't she be at least a little afraid of such a big dog?"

"I don't think she's afraid of anything," Grady said. "I don't think . . . well, I don't think she even knows she should be afraid of some things."

"What an odd idea."

He frowned. "Yeah. Isn't it? But there's something about these two . . . something makes me think maybe they've never known real fear."

Watching Puzzle stroke the wolfhound's face, Cammy said, "If true, that would be the biggest difference about them. Everything alive knows fear."

Leaving the cushions in disarray, Riddle sprang down from the sofa and, as if having noticed it only now, scurried to a Stickley desk that Grady had made during the first few months after his return to the mountains. It was a lovely walnut piece with hammered-copper hardware, ornamented with inlaid pewter.

Riddle sat on his hindquarters and with one finger repeatedly flicked the dangling copper pull on the right-hand door, which rang musically against the escutcheon plate.

In Cammy's lap, Puzzle pushed Merlin aside and raised her head far enough to see what her companion might be doing.

Riddle turned his head to look at her.

For a moment, Puzzle held his stare.

Riddle moved to the left-hand door and flicked the dangling pull as he had flicked the first. Again, he turned his head toward Puzzle.

As before, she met his stare, and after a hesitation, he turned away from the desk.

By some subtle expression or even more subtle gesture that Cammy failed to register, they seemed to have communicated with each other regarding the desk.

Grady appeared to have the same impression. "What was that about?"

Riddle scampered to the purple bunny, snatched it with his teeth, raced out of the living room, into the vestibule, and up the stairs, squeaking the toy as he went.

Game for a chase, Merlin pursued him.

Thirty-one

In the bedroom closet, Henry Rouvroy listened for movement in the house and tried not to think about the body lying on its side in the bed. It was not a real body, only a dummy constructed of pillows and blankets, a deception that he had created himself, that and only that, that and nothing more.

No one could have entered the house, jammed the components of the faux body under the bed, and slipped beneath the covers, taking the place of the fake sleeper. Henry would have heard. He would have encountered the intruder in the act.

Of course, after arranging the bed, he spent as much as half an hour in the bathroom, scrubbing grime from under his fingernails. Standing at the sink, he had his back to the door and could not see the bedroom.

Thereafter, during his final search of the house, he stood for a long time at the cellar door, studying the light that leaked beneath it, listening for any sound from below. In that position, he would have known if someone tried to come in by the back door, but he would not have been aware of an intruder entering by the front.

"Ridiculous," Henry hissed in the dark closet where once Nora's clothes had hung.

His faceless tormentor was bold but not reckless. No adversary this clever would make himself vulnerable by taking the place of the dummy.

Only a lunatic would pull such a stunt, a lunatic or someone who had no fear of death because . . .

"Don't go there," he muttered.

Because he had already thought **faceless tormentor,** his line of thinking progressed as inevitably as an avalanche. His brother, Jim, was faceless because he'd been shot in the face, and Jim had no fear of death because he was already dead.

Logic like that would have gotten Henry hooted out of the Harvard debating society.

To get his mind off this absurd line of speculation, he tried to picture his favorite female TV chef spread-eagled on the bed, tied to the four posts, prominent features of her naked body pinched by wickedly designed clamps, a choke chain around her neck.

He thought of himself as a highly imaginative

person. Therefore, he was dismayed to discover that he couldn't conjure in his mind satisfying scenes of sadistic sex without an image of the desired woman in front of him.

He couldn't very well sit sentinel in the closet with a TV tuned to the Food Network and expect that an intruder wouldn't notice him. Besides, the house had no television.

If his primary entertainment in the years to come was to be a woman in the potato cellar, he had better keep more than one chained down there. To ensure against boredom, he ought to construct a couple of additional cells and keep a variety of women at the ready.

Once he sold all the noxious chickens or otherwise disposed of the gabbling creatures, he might insulate the chicken coop and turn that into a series of cells, as well. And the barn. The horse stalls could be easily retrofitted as cells, and the big building offered plenty of room for additional penitentiary units, as many as he had the energy and time to build.

Henry thought how cozy he would feel on a winter night, going to bed here in the house with the knowledge that in the barn were penned and shackled a herd of beautiful women, with perhaps a barn cat to keep them company, each of them snug in a sleeping bag, in the straw, and dreaming about her turn with the master. On wintry mornings, he would lead his choice through the snow to the house, where she would cook breakfast, something that a cow could never do, and while he ate, she would sit naked at the table and tell him all of the latest gossip among the girls. After breakfast, he would use her, savage her, and kill her or not, depending on his mood.

Although he was a young and virile man at thirty-seven, he was not inexhaustible. In addition to food and drink, he had better lay in a couple of thousand tablets of Viagra. The drug would probably remain potent if he vacuum-packed the pills in groups of ten and kept them in the freezer. That would work unless civilization entirely collapsed and power companies were unable to function. Fortunately, Jim had a propane-powered backup generator with half a dozen tanks of fuel already on hand. If Henry added to the propane supply and if he used the generator only for essential maintenance like keeping the Viagra freezer operating in warm weather, he would be happy here on the farm for a long, long time.

Unless, even now, dead Jim was out there in the generator shed, sabotaging the machinery.

"What the hell is the matter with me?" Henry asked the darkness, and at once wished that he hadn't spoken, for fear he would receive a response in a familiar if slurred voice.

No dead man replied, of course, and Henry had

no answer to the question he asked. His regressive superstition was as inexplicable as it was dismaying.

No dead man had ever come back to life, neither Count Dracula nor Jesus Christ, neither Lazarus nor the insatiable cannibalistic legions in George Romero's movies. The dead stayed dead and the living were only the dead of the future, and the future would have its end, too, in the heat death of the universe and the collapse of time into nothing. Men were meat and nothing more, no soul survived the body, nothing came back from the dead because there was no spirit to return and nowhere to return **from,** and that was the sum of it, men were nothing from nothing on a journey to nothing, nada, zip, zero, nil, naught, cipher.

To avoid thinking about Jim, Henry decided, as an intellectual, to busy his mind with the lessons of the intellectual giants whose work had shaped him. He brooded on James Joyce and **Finnegans Wake,** in which there was such brilliant mockery of Jews and of the Jewish faith, a parody of Psalms in which God was reduced to Lord and Lord was jokingly renamed Loud. "'Loud, hear us!'" Henry quoted from the Joyce novel, "'Loud, graciously hear us!'" and he laughed. He focused on the most poignant remembered wisdom of, one by one, James Joyce, Sigmund Freud, Karl Marx, Marcel Duchamp, Ralph Waldo Emerson, that Madonna who is Ciccone, Bertolt Brecht, Jacques Derrida, Michel Foucault, Peter Singer, Friedrich Nietzsche, and so many others, all so wise, so brilliant, so courageous that his memory of their works easily distracted him from thinking about Jim, not merely distracted him but by virtue of their magnificent one note, their truth drone, their heroic reductionism of all of creation to a single machine hum, they also put him to sleep.

He dreamed of Jim.

Thirty-two

The excitement of the evening, culminating in the chase upstairs and down, inspired in Merlin a need to pee. He informed them of his condition by the intense and insistent look that Grady called his "flood warning."

No doubt Puzzle and Riddle also needed to toilet, but in the kitchen, as Grady was about to open the door for the trio, Cammy said, "Wait, we need to take pictures of them, in case they don't come back."

"I thought you said they were moving in."

"They are. I'm pretty sure of it. But just in case."

Pointing to a digital camera on the kitchen table, Grady said, "I took a slew of pictures before you got here."

"You're sure they're clear?"

"Yeah. I've reviewed them. They're great. But

you haven't seen their eyes in the dark. I want you to slip through the door first, go out on the lawn, watch them come toward you."

When told to sit and stay, the wolfhound obeyed, although he grumbled.

As if they understood what was wanted, but more likely following the dog's example, Puzzle and Riddle sat flanking their new playmate.

Grady let Cammy out and closed the French door, watching as she descended the porch steps. She went into the yard, turned toward the house, and knelt on the grass.

"All right, gang. Last chance till morning."

When Grady opened the door and released Merlin from the sit-stay, the wolfhound and his posse raced out of the house.

Grady stepped onto the porch in time to see the dog bound past Cammy as she let out a wordless cry of astonishment at the spectacle of the other animals' color-changing, lantern eyes.

Puzzle and Riddle gamboled around her for a moment, giving her an opportunity to admire them, and then they sprinted after Merlin, toward the place where yard met meadow.

Remaining on her knees, Cammy said, "Oh, my God. Grady. Oh, my God. **Their eyes!**"

She laughed so merrily, she sounded like a young girl. Grady sat on the porch steps, grinning at her.

When the animals returned from their toilet,

Merlin sat beside his master. But in a playful mood, Puzzle and Riddle rejoined Cammy, swarming around her and over each other. They appeared to understand that they enchanted her, and they were in turn pleased by her admiration.

Their eyes lustered, as though reflecting the memory of the most spectacular aurora borealis ever to grace the northern sky.

Grady had never before seen Cammy laugh with such joy. She had always seemed too cautious to delight unreservedly in anything.

Each man or woman was a mansion in a condition between grandness and disrepair, and even in a grand palace, sometimes a room existed in which no one but the resident would ever be welcome. Cammy's heart contained more than one forbidden room, contained an entire wing of doors locked with bolts of guilt or grief, or both. Grady sensed that she denied even herself the power to open them, to let in the light.

Nevertheless, she was his best friend. He had never known her to lie or to deceive by omission, or even to finesse a matter to her advantage. Parts of her life were off limits not because she wished to deceive but because, right or wrong, she judged the architecture of those rooms to be so inconsistent with the design of the rest of the structure that they added nothing to an understanding of it.

Grady valued her judgment, admired her commitment to animals, respected her standards as a veterinarian, cherished her kindness, which he sensed came from an experience of cruelty, and loved her because in this world of whiners and self-declared martyrs, Cammy Rivers never complained and never portrayed herself as a victim, though Grady suspected that she had more reason than most to claim that status.

Cammy in the night, on the lawn, playing with Puzzle and Riddle, astonished by their eyes, enraptured by the mystery of them, laughing with delight: Grady had never known a finer moment in his life.

Thirty-three

In his hotel room in Las Vegas, Lamar Woolsey dreamed, but not of his lost wife, Estelle.

He dreamed of a casino so vast that he could not see as far as any wall. From the gold-leafed ceiling depended an infinite number of perfectly aligned chandeliers swagged with symmetrical ropes of crystal beads, each great lamp icicled with exactly the same number of crystal pendants in precisely the same arrangement.

Under this exquisitely ordered ceiling, he sat at a blackjack table with three other players: a one-eyed woman, a one-armed man, and a nine-year-old boy with one missing front tooth.

The woman wore a low-cut dress and repeatedly withdrew black hundred-dollar chips from between her ample breasts. Each time that she put them on the table, they transformed into black beetles and scurried across the green felt, much to the dealer's annoyance.

Every time the one-armed man received a card, he looked at it and in disgust threw it angrily at the dealer, who then dealt it to the boy. The boy didn't know the rules of the game and kept asking, "Has anyone seen my sister? Does anyone know where she's gone?"

The six-deck shoe contained ordinary playing cards but also tarot cards and picture cards from a children's game. Regardless of what Lamar drew, he won. A six of diamonds and a rabbit holding an umbrella: winner. The tarot hangman and an eight of hearts: winner.

When Lamar's winnings had grown sizeable, the one-eyed woman said, "There's the Pipp boy."

Glancing at the gap-toothed child who sat farther around the elliptical table, Lamar said, "That's not Marcus. Not him at all."

"Over there," she said, "at the roulette wheel."

The roulette game lay behind them, not in their line of sight. Turning on his stool, Lamar saw Marcus Pipp where she said he was.

Lamar left the table with his winnings in a chip rack, intending to give everything to Marcus. By the time he got to the roulette game, Marcus had gone.

The roulette table was one in an infinite row of them. Surveying the casino, Lamar saw Marcus four tables away and hurried toward him.

Rotors spun, balls danced and clattered, and croupiers called the results, which suddenly were the same: "Double zero . . . double zero . . . double zero . . . double zero. . . ."

The dream didn't descend into a full-blown nightmare, but it became a drama of fleeting promise and enduring frustration. Table after table, Lamar pursued Marcus but couldn't reach him or catch his attention. Later, glimpsing him in the slot-machine maze, Lamar sought to intercept him without success. Later still, he spotted Marcus at a craps table, then at others, but Marcus drifted away.

Dead in reality, alive in the dream, Marcus Pipp was in both cases outward bound and beyond contact.

Thirty-four

During the walk into town, Tom Bigger worked up an appetite.

At a convenience store that offered prepackaged deli creations, he bought a submarine sandwich, a bag of potato chips, and a sixteen-ounce bottle of Coke.

A couple of customers shied away from him. The clerk had served him before, however; she took some of his panhandled money and gave him change without saying a word to him, without glancing at his face.

In a nearby park, under an old iron lamppost that provided more atmosphere than light, Tom sat on a bench that looked out onto the street. He watched the passing traffic as he ate.

Behind the bench rose an enormous phoenix palm. During the lulls in traffic, he could hear rats agitating one another in their nest high in the crown of the tree.

Tom didn't have much overhead, but panhandling alone couldn't pay for his needs. Every other month, he took a bus to the nearest city and, working at night, stole enough to cover his expenses.

Primarily, he burglarized suburban homes where a lack of lights and a few days' of newspapers scattered on the driveway suggested he would not risk coming face-to-face with a homeowner.

If he found a likely target walking alone on a lonely street, he robbed him at gunpoint. Tom's face and the pistol turned even strapping young men into situational pacifists.

The gun wasn't loaded. He didn't trust himself with cartridges.

He never worried that in a frenzy of self-hatred he might kill himself. Suicide required either more courage than he possessed or more despair than afflicted him.

His hatred was directed inward, his rage outward. With bullets in the weapon, he would sooner or later kill somebody.

From experience, he knew that once he indulged in a vice, that indulgence became a habit, then an obsession. Murder would be no less addictive than tequila or weed, or the other drugs that he consumed so recklessly when he could get them.

He was a lot of things, none of them good. He dreaded adding **murderer** to the list of words that described him.

As he ate the sandwich, his mind reeled back more than once to the incident in the bluff-top rest area.

Initially, he had been astonished. Astonishment turned to shock that rendered him bewildered and emotionally numb. On the walk from his cave to the town, numbness relented to a creeping disquiet.

Watching the passing traffic, Tom saw a bumper sticker that proclaimed I STOP SUDDENLY JUST FOR THE HELL OF IT.

Across the street, a multiplex was playing a movie about the end of the world.

In memory, he heard a fragment of what at the time had seemed to be a perpetual argument, conflict without end.

"Why are you doing this, Tommy?"

"Just for the hell of it."

"You're throwing away your life, your future."

"There isn't a future. It's the end of the world."

"It isn't the end of the world."

"Bastards like you are the ones destroying it."

"How can you talk to me like that?"

"How can you be the shit you are?"

The fitful breeze brought a handbill to his feet.

In the wan lamplight he saw that it was for a restaurant called Magic Pizza.

After a moment of consideration, he carried the handbill, the sandwich wrapper, the empty bag of potato chips, and the half-empty bottle of Coke to the nearest trash can and threw everything away.

He needed a joint of sinsemilla. Local authorities were tolerant of the discreet use of pot. He took the tin of hand-rolleds from his backpack, fished a joint from the supply, and put the tin away.

Deeper in the park, he found a more secluded bench.

He had a butane lighter. He struck the flame but didn't light the joint.

If he smoked one, he would smoke a second, perhaps a third. He would wash away the pot taste with tequila. In the morning, he would wake up behind a screen of bushes, with dirt matted in his beard stubble and spiders in his hair.

The creeping disquiet inspired by the incident on the bluff was growing into a motivating apprehension.

He put away the lighter. Instead of returning the joint to the stash in the tin, he shredded it in his fingers and scattered it on the breeze.

This action so surprised him that for a moment he seined the air with his fingers, trying to recapture the debris that he'd cast away an instant earlier.

Already, the disquiet that thickened into apprehension was further thickening into dread.

While he'd been eating a late dinner on the first bench, he was given signs from which he deduced where he must go. He suspected that time was running out for him to do what he must do.

The thought of riding for three hours in a bus chilled him. If this weight of dread became too heavy, he would feel oppressed in a bus. Claustrophobia would overwhelm him.

Intuition told him to begin the journey on foot. He set out for the coastal highway.

Thirty-five

After watching Merlin drink from his large water bowl, Puzzle and Riddle attended Grady's preparations with interest as he chose two bowls from a cabinet and filled each with cold water from the kitchen tap.

As she extracted the memory stick from Grady's camera and tucked it in a side compartment of her medical bag to take home, Cammy said, "Neither of us seems to want to speculate."

"About what?"

"About what do you think?"

"You said earlier—you do medicine, you don't do theory."

"Speculation isn't theory," she said. "It's not even up to the level of hypothesis. It's just blue-skying. It's what-if, if-maybe, could-it-be stuff."

"I don't want to speculate about them."

"That's what I just said. Neither of us wants to speculate."

"All right, then. Good. We're agreed."

"But why do you think that is?"

He said, "I don't do self-analysis."

She watched him put the two bowls of water on the floor.

Immediately, Puzzle and Riddle went to the bowls, lowered their heads to the water, smelled it, and drank.

Cammy said, "I think the reason we don't want to speculate about them is because most of the what-ifs we come up with are likely to be scary, one way or another."

"There's nothing scary about Puzzle and Riddle."

"I didn't say there was. I just said speculating about their origins is going to lead to some scary what-ifs."

"Right now I just want to experience them," Grady said. "If I think too much about what they might be, that's going to color how I interpret their behavior."

Watching the animals drink, Merlin seemed to strike a proud pose, as if they were good students to whom he had successfully imparted the right technique for drinking from a bowl.

"Anyway," Cammy said, "you can't know for sure there's nothing scary about them."

"There's nothing scary about them," he insisted.

"Not now, they're as cute as Muppets now, but maybe later when the lights are off and you're asleep, that's when they reveal their true grotesque form."

"You don't really believe that's a possibility."

"No. It's a what-if, but it's a ridiculous what-if."

"Anyway, they're a lot cuter than Muppets," he said. "Some Muppets creep me out. Nothing about these two creeps me out."

"Muppets creep you out? Freud would find that interesting."

"Not all Muppets creep me out. Just a few."

"Surely not Kermit."

"Of course not Kermit. But Big Bird's a freak."

"He's a freak?"

"A total freak."

As predictably steady, reliable, and self-contained as Grady might be, his conversation could take unpredictable deadpan turns. Cammy liked that. He was smart and amusing, but he was safe.

"Big Bird," she said. "Is that why you don't have a TV?"

"It's one of the reasons."

Riddle and then Puzzle finished drinking. They sat up on their haunches like a couple of giant prairie dogs, folded their hands on their bellies, and regarded Grady with expectation.

"Maybe they're hungry," Cammy suggested.

"They already ate three chicken breasts. And as far as I know, they ate the pan, too."

"You don't know these guys are the chicken thieves. There might be another factor—whoever went in your workshop, the garage, whoever switched on the lights."

"See, this is why I make furniture."

"What's furniture got to do with it?"

"When I make furniture, I don't have to think. My hands do all the thinking for me."

"Even if Puzzle and Riddle **did** eat the chicken," Cammy said, "maybe that's the only thing they've had to eat all day. You don't want to send them to bed hungry."

"Because they might eat me alive in the middle of the night? Problem is, I don't have any more chicken."

"Give them some of Merlin's kibble, see if they like it."

"If I pour bowls of kibble for them, I'll have to give Merlin some, and he's already had all he should have for one day."

"Merlin isn't fat. You'd have to dole out kibble with a shovel to overfeed him. Give him a bowl, let him celebrate his new friends."

"They **do** look like they expect something. Maybe you're right, maybe they're hungry."

He kept forty pounds of Science Diet in the pantry—twenty pounds in a large aluminum can with an airtight lid, and an unopened twenty-pound backup bag. He put a large scoopful in Merlin's food bowl and a smaller serving in each of two cereal bowls.

The wolfhound was trained to sit in front of his bowl and wait for permission to eat. The word **okay** released him to his meal.

Puzzle and Riddle studied Merlin and mimicked him, sitting at their bowls. When the dog ate, the two tasted their kibble, found it acceptable, and chowed down.

Needing to go home and get to work with the memory stick from Grady's camera, still too enchanted to leave, Cammy watched the three eat. "In his way, Merlin's as wonderful and mysterious as they are."

Grady seemed surprised. "I was thinking the same thing."

After his return to the mountains, near the end of his first year, Grady had told Cammy that he'd rediscovered the mystery of the ordinary. He said, if you allowed yourself to be enchanted by the beauty to be seen in even ordinary things, then all things proved to be extraordinary. Shortly thereafter, she gave Merlin to him, a puppy as large as some grown dogs, rough-coated, shaggy-browed, and as magical as the magician for whom he had been named.

Cammy said, "You know High Meadows Farm?"

"That's the Vironi place, they raise Thoroughbreds?"

"Yeah. Something happened at High Meadows this afternoon, right before twilight."

She told him about the strange condition of the horses and the other animals.

"Diagnosis?" he asked.

"I was working on it when you called me out here. Now I don't think there can be a diagnosis because there wasn't an illness."

"But you said, they were in something like a trance."

"I don't know what this means, it's just what I feel. . . ." She took a deep breath, blew it out. "There wasn't anything wrong with them, something was **right** with them."

"I can understand why you wouldn't know what that means."

She told him about the incident with the abused breeder dogs that had been rescued from the puppy mill. "I didn't witness the trance part, but I saw the change in the dogs after it, they were happy, totally and suddenly socialized. Somehow, what happened at our clinic and what happened at High Meadows Farm must be related to Puzzle and Riddle."

"I don't see how, but I think you're right. This many wheels of weirdness have to be on the same train."

The wolfhound and his new companions finished eating. Merlin noisily licked his chops. With their fingers, Puzzle and Riddle meticulously combed the fur around their mouths.

Picking up her medical bag, Cammy said, "I'll make my inquiries before I go to bed. By midmorning sometime, I should have replies, but I doubt there's any chance we'll be enlightened. Then we'll have to decide what to do next."

"Come here for lunch?"

"Yeah. Okay. Unless I have an emergency the techs can't handle and that I can't pass along to Amos Renfrew. He's the best cow doc in the county, and he's good enough with horses, but his heart isn't in small-animal care. I wouldn't recommend him for a dog in serious shape, he might overlook something."

Merlin settled to the floor in a weary heap. Puzzle and Riddle snuggled against opposite sides of him, apparently at last worn out. The wolfhound was like a great woolly coat that had been thrown down, and the golden-eyed pair were the coat's dazzling trim.

When Cammy opened the back door and stepped onto the porch, Grady followed her, but the animals remained behind.

"I'm pretty sure they're already asleep," Grady said. "Sometimes I think it would be a great blessing to walk on all fours and have a smaller brain."

She shook her head. "It's not their smaller brains that let them sleep so easily. It's their innocence."

"Then I'll be awake all night, maybe forever."

His singular smile was the best last sight to any evening, so she said, "Call you in the morning," and moved toward the steps.

He put a hand on her shoulder, requiring her to face him once more. "This isn't a theory or hypothesis or even something as grand as speculation. It's a gut feeling. Nothing's going to be the same."

"Not all change is for the better," she said.

He took her by both shoulders, and his face lowered toward hers, and for a moment she thought he might, with the purest of intentions, do the worst of wrongs that he could do. But the kiss he gave her, the first between them in these four years, was a brother's kiss, his lips chaste against her forehead, and that was an expression of affection with which she could cope.

"Thank you for Merlin," he said. "Whatever Puzzle and Riddle might be, I don't believe they'd have followed me home if I had been on that walk alone. I think it was Merlin who drew them here."

"He's a magnet, sure enough," she said. "He was from the moment he was born. Be careful tonight, Grady. I know they're not a threat, they're as innocent as Merlin, but innocence always has its enemies. Always."

In the car, driving away, she hoped that she had not tensed when he bent down to kiss her brow, that he had not felt her stiffen defensively. She should have had faith that, though he knew nothing of her younger years, his intuition would always be that of a heart healer who knew the seriousness if not the precise nature of those wounds that could not be seen, for that's what he had been as long as she had known him, a good man of exquisite intuition, not just a friend but a grace for which she was profoundly grateful.

If Puzzle and Riddle were more than one kind of curiosity or another, more than a quick stranger-than-fiction item on cable news, more than mere mutation, if they were **something,** as she believed they were, something momentous, they could not have entrusted themselves—or been entrusted—to better hands than Grady's.

She drove out of the foothills, to the lower meadows, where the moonlight pooled in the pale grass.

The strange night appeared to have wrought subtle changes in the familiar land, and the well-known road seemed to be leading her into unknown places.

For twenty years, since she was fifteen and at last free, Cammy had wanted only what she possessed now: a veterinary practice and a life with animals, a life of service to the innocent of the Earth, to those who could not lie because they could not speak, who did not envy or covet or steal, who never betrayed and never took pleasure in the pain and despair of others, who did not enslave and brutalize and humiliate those weaker than they were.

But tonight, in the light of those beautiful unearthly eyes, she glimpsed something that she needed in addition to what she had. She hesitated to want it, for fear that by wanting it, she would ensure it was withheld, but she wanted it desperately nevertheless. Her life was filled with beauty, the flora and the fauna of the mountains, but she longed also to have what for now she only dared to call **mystery**. She wanted mystery in her life, things unknowable yet not imagined, things her mind could touch that her hands could never feel, mystery that could fill her half-empty heart with wonder.

Over gently rolling land, the road rose and fell, while in the geometries of the white ranch fencing, she saw embedded symbols that she had not recognized before, that the builders of the fence had not intended. The symbols now apparent to her were only a consequence of the principles of proper construction, yet they were icons that since time immemorial had been metaphors for hope.

As in the pasture at High Meadows Farm, her vision blurred. She pulled off the highway where the shoulder widened, put the Explorer in park, plucked Kleenex from the console box, and blotted her eyes.

With the magnificent horses and their attendant animals, Cammy had not understood what sentiment had brought her to tears. Whether the same feeling might have been at work then as now, she didn't know, but she knew what moved her this time. Her life before her fifteenth birthday had been unspeakable. Her life these past twenty years was in many ways austere. She found a kind of happiness by demanding much of herself, by expecting nothing of others, and by seeking to balance those years of slavery with years of willing service to what was good in the world, as a way of expunging any stains the past had left on her. Now she stood at the center of a mystery, a significance. Although she had been wretched and without courage in her youth, Cammy knew—**knew** without doubt, as geese knew in their blood when the time had come to fly south ahead of winter—that the presence of these two creatures in her life meant, if she had once been damaged, she was now whole.

Thirty-six

In the bedroom, treading on his large plump pillow bed, Merlin turned three times before settling with a sigh, his head between his forepaws, his tail tucked between his hind legs.

Grady had brought another dog bed from the downstairs study and put it in the same corner with Merlin's. He felt sure that from the wolfhound's example, their visitors understood where they were to sleep.

Puzzle and Riddle, however, declined to turn in for the night. They circled the room, sniffing this and that, peering under the dresser, taking a quick taste of the water in all three of the water dishes, while Grady pulled the draperies shut at the windows.

As he folded back the thin bedspread and draped it neatly over the footboard, as he turned back the covers and the top sheet, and as he plumped his pillows, the pair sat watching him, heads cocked to the right, as if fascinated by his rituals.

"I hope you noticed," he said, "that before I undid it, my bed was made as tight as a drum skin."

Riddle cocked his head to the left.

"Once army, always army."

Puzzle cocked her head to the left, and Riddle cocked his back to the right.

When Grady removed his shoes and put them by his nightstand, Puzzle scurried forward to smell them and to pluck tentatively at the loose laces.

In the walk-in closet, as Grady took off his shirt, jeans, and socks, Riddle followed him—and discovered the mirror on the back of the door. Intrigued by his reflection, Riddle made a thin sound—**"Eee, eee"**—and reached out to this apparent other of his kind. Surprised when the other reached toward him as he reached toward it, Riddle hesitated, considered the situation, then touched his hand to the reflection of his hand.

Over the years, Merlin had seen himself in mirrors many times, and he showed no interest in his reflection.

Riddle's ears twitched, and he scurried out of the closet.

Returning to the bedroom, Grady found his two

guests at the son of Ireland's bed, watching their new friend with interest. Evidently they had been drawn by the wolfhound's snoring, which was indeed impressive.

In the bathroom, after Grady squeezed toothpaste on his brush and turned on the cold water, Puzzle suddenly sprang onto the closed toilet seat and sat prairie-dog fashion, watching him with interest. Half a minute later, Riddle ascended to a position on the side of the bathtub, as intrigued as Puzzle appeared to be by their host's dental-hygiene regimen.

After he finished brushing, they watched him floss. They watched him wash his face and trim a hangnail and wipe splashes of water off the countertop with a towel.

When the time came to toilet, Grady shooed them out of the bathroom and closed the door.

No sooner had he taken the throne than a soft, rapid, irregular rapping arose at the door.

"Go away," Grady said.

The sound came again: **rap-rap-rap, rap-rap, rap, rap-rap-rap-rap-rap.**

"I didn't go out in the yard and stare at you when you were peeing," Grady reminded them.

Rap-rap, rap-rap, rap-rap-rap-rap-rap-rap.

"Good grief."

The rapping stopped.

When he heard one of them sniffing along the crack between the bottom of the door and the threshold, he considered renaming them Nosey and Snoopy.

The silence that followed the sniffing was welcome, but then seemed to have a suspicious quality.

Although the skeleton key had long ago been lost, the old door featured a keyhole. Grady leaned sideways on the toilet, lowered his head, and clearly saw a luminous golden eye on the farther side of the keyway.

"You're a little Peeping Tom. You two ought to be ashamed of yourselves."

The golden eye blinked.

By the time Grady washed his hands and returned to the bedroom, Puzzle and Riddle were on his bed, lifting his pillows to peer under them.

"Off, off," he told them.

They dropped his pillows, sat on his bed, folded their hands on their bellies, and watched him.

Having been awakened after such a short snooze, Merlin yawned extravagantly.

Grady went to the empty dog bed, fluffed it, and said to Puzzle and Riddle, "Here. This is yours."

They stared at him attentively but didn't leave his bed.

In the closet, where he kept a few dog toys,

Grady selected a blue monkey. He returned to the bedroom, knelt beside the empty dog bed, and squeaked the monkey to entice Puzzle and Riddle to come to him.

Merlin grumbled, displeased to be disturbed.

A different toy might possibly lure the pair to their proper place. Instead, Grady decided to show them what was wanted, as he might show a puppy.

He went to his bed and scooped up Puzzle. She not only allowed herself to be lifted and carried, but she also curled into the cradle of his arms, exposing her belly, bending her forelimbs at the elbows and the wrists in an expression of happy compliance.

When Grady put her down in the big fleece-covered dog bed that he intended for her to share with Riddle, he said, "Stay," as if the commands of canine-obedience school were universally understood in the animal kingdom. He gave her the blue monkey to keep her occupied.

At his bed once more, he scooped up Riddle, who proved to be as cooperative as Puzzle. Grady carried him to his appointed lodgings—where only the plush blue monkey waited.

With Riddle still in his arms, he turned and saw Puzzle on his bed again. He deposited Riddle with the blue monkey and returned to his bed for Puzzle.

She virtually leaped into his arms, nearly knocking him down. But no sooner had he turned to take her to Riddle than he heard the monkey squeaking on his bed behind him.

Merlin no longer grumbled. Head raised, ears pricked, he watched with interest.

Instead of taking Puzzle to the empty bed, Grady put her down beside the wolfhound. He lifted one of Merlin's sturdy forelimbs and draped it over the golden-eyed animal.

"Stay," he told Merlin.

In a sterner tone, narrowing his eyes like Clint Eastwood, he issued the same command to Puzzle. He also extended his arm in an accusatory fashion and pointed a finger at her.

She cocked her head to the right.

Grady turned away from her. As he crossed the room to get Riddle and the damn monkey, Merlin and Puzzle sprinted past him and leaped onto his bed.

Riddle put the monkey under Grady's pillows. With expressions of blissful contentment, the dog and the two somethings curled around one another.

The wolfhound and his posse watched Grady turn out the bedside lamp. They watched him turn out the overhead light.

Leaving on the lamp beside the large Stickley-style reclining chair, Grady went into the closet to retrieve a spare pillow and a blanket.

The snuggling animals raised their heads as he came out of the closet, and they tracked him as he went to the reclining chair. They seemed unmoved by the sour look he gave them.

Grady sat in the roomy chair, which he had built and upholstered the previous year. He stretched out his legs on a matching footstool.

The three compadres watched him solemnly.

He draped the blanket across himself and put the pillow behind his head.

They watched him adjust the pillow and the blanket until he got everything as right as he could. The chair made a comfortable bed, and he was too tired to play here-we-go-'round-the-mulberry-bush with these animated plush toys.

He said, "Just so you know . . ."

The three caballeros remained interested in him, although he couldn't honestly claim that they waited with bated breath for what he would say next.

". . . I consider this mutiny," he informed them. "Mutiny indeed. And in the morning, discipline will be administered."

He switched off the lamp beside the chair.

Their colorful eyes seemed to float in the darkness.

"I see you watching me," he said.

They didn't blink.

"I'm counting on you, Merlin. Don't let them devour me in my sleep."

Thirty-seven

At the computer in her office at the veterinary clinic, Cammy Rivers wrote e-mails to Dr. Eleanor Fortney of Tufts University's Cummings School of Veterinary Medicine in North Grafton, Massachusetts, and to Dr. Sidney Shinseki of Texas A&M University's College of Veterinary Medicine in College Station, Texas. She attached JPEGs of photos of Puzzle and Riddle.

Eleanor Fortney was an eminent zoologist, an internist, and a surgeon who had been a guest lecturer for a month at Colorado State University's College of Veterinary Medicine and Biomedical Sciences in Fort Collins, when Cammy had been in her last year of studies at that institution.

As one of the very few CSU students who ever achieved a perfect grade-point average in every semester of her studies, both as an undergraduate and a graduate student, Cammy had been able to receive a guaranteed seat in every one of Eleanor's small-class lectures but had been invited also to participate in three one-on-one conferences that proved to be some of the most intense educational experiences of her life.

By the time Eleanor completed her month in Fort Collins, she had made a persuasive case that, upon graduation, Cammy should come east to Tufts. Eleanor offered a three-year contract to work in a canine-cancer research project of which she was the director, a program with deep funding provided by an alumnus.

Cammy was tempted by the opportunity to advance her career and contribute to research that might save the lives of countless dogs. But ultimately, she declined. She had dreamed for so long of serving animals not in the research lab, but in the course of their day-to-day suffering; she wanted the satisfaction of healing animals whose names she knew and into whose eyes she had looked.

She and Eleanor had remained in touch, however, and were friends who regarded their work not solely as a profession and primarily as a mission. If Puzzle and Riddle were extreme teratogenic individuals, Eleanor's broad, deep zoological background might enable her to see through the mutations to underlying characteristics that identified their species.

As for Sidney Shinseki: After receiving her veterinary degree, Cammy had done a year of postdoctoral work with him to refine her surgical techniques. He was a sweet old gruff bear of a guy who had a keen diagnostic sense and a talent for making intuitive leaps from a few perplexing facts to the truth toward which they pointed.

After sending the e-mails, Cammy trolled a few institutional zoological archives that could be accessed with ease, searching for photographs of nocturnal creatures with unusually large eyes.

The aye-aye, inhabiting the rain forests of Madagascar, appeared to have larger eyes than it really did. In the photos, they were such a bright orange that the stunning color contributed to an illusion of immensity. Anyway, with its big batlike ears and pointed muzzle, it wouldn't qualify for a show about mammalian beauty on Animal Planet.

Bush babies' eyes were markedly larger than those of an aye-aye, especially in proportion to their small heads, but they were ocular nobodies compared to Merlin's new playmates.

The loris, native to south and southeastern Asia, had large eyes in proportion to its head but not in comparison to Puzzle and Riddle. A tree-creeper feeding largely on lizards and insects, the largest loris weighed only four pounds.

After the excitement of the night, she thought she would not be able to sleep, but she soon began hitting too many wrong keys and too often misclicking the mouse, and she logged off. When she dropped into bed at 1:50 A.M., the room seemed to turn slowly like a carousel . . . a carousel, and all the beautiful horses were facing in the same direction, toward the mountains and the twilight sky, and something momentous was passing through the day, something so gigantic that she could feel its presence looming, yet it remained invisible, or if it was not invisible, then it must be visible only by indirection, only from the corner of the eye. . . .

Thirty-eight

Cool and dry, the California night provided perfect weather for walking with a backpack.

To the west of the highway, the dark land sloped to the ocean, which Tom Bigger could see only because the moon trailed a satin train across the water and the breaking surf threw white spray like flung rice to rattle on the shingled shore.

In the east lay hills, visible because they were silhouetted against the star-speckled sky and because, following a rainless summer, they were dressed in pale parched grass. Widely separated hursts of live oaks made Halloween shapes against the pallid meadows.

To every quarter of the compass, the lonely land revealed no signs of habitation.

He knew where he must go and what he must

do. But it was a long walk to the city and a hard thing that needed to be done.

Well past midnight, little traffic cruised the highway. These were the hours when long-haul truckers reigned, and they traveled the interstate farther inland.

Even in the darkness, Tom received signs. The headlights of a southbound car revealed a dead rattlesnake on the pavement, its eyes glittering as if sequined, and he knew that it was there only for him to see.

He passed a DEER CROSSING sign that vandals had riddled with bullet holes. And a short distance farther along the shoulder of the highway, his trudging feet scattered small objects that clinked off one another with a brassy sound. When he switched on his flashlight, perhaps twenty expended shell casings gleamed in the dirt and gravel.

Snakes and bullets. Evil and violence.

A low smooth rock formation rose like a bench made by Nature for a weary hiker. He stopped and unburdened himself of the backpack.

He unzipped the storm flap on the lower compartment and withdrew a stuffsack that contained his unloaded pistol. He returned the empty stuffsack to the lower compartment, and zipped shut the storm flap.

Bearing the backpack once more, carrying the

gun in his left hand, at his side, out of sight of any motorists who might pass, he continued north.

Since leaving the town, he felt that he was not alone. Mile by mile, the impression of an unseen companion intensified.

From time to time, he stopped and turned slowly in a circle to study the night. He never glimpsed movement other than the swaying of grass and the trembling of leaves in the languid breeze that came off the sea. He never saw a ghostly form, or moonglint in an eye.

He walked about half a mile before he heard the engine of a northbound vehicle. Judging by the sound, it must be a light truck or an SUV, but he did not look back.

Motorists disposed to pick up hitchhikers were less charitable to him because of his size and face. He seldom attempted to thumb a ride. Consequently, he walked facing oncoming traffic, which was safer anyway.

Engine noise grew, headlights washed the pavement, and a Chevy Suburban swept past in the farther lane. Brake lights brightened.

A hundred yards ahead, the vehicle made a U-turn and came south, coasting to a stop beside the highway, about fifty feet from Tom. Doors opened.

The headlights half blinded him, but he saw the silhouettes of two men at the front of the

Suburban. A third stood just forward of the driver's door.

Tom didn't try to sprint off the highway and into the dark land because even gentle terrain could be treacherous to a blind runner.

Besides, he didn't run from anything, neither from violence junkies cruising in search of kicks nor from a tsunami. If someone or something killed him, he would only be getting the death that he wanted but that he had no courage to embrace by suicide.

He walked toward them, keeping his head high.

When they got a good look at his face, with the grisly details no doubt exaggerated by the extreme light and shadows, one of them said, "Holy hell, Jackie, look at this," and the one named Jackie said to Tom, "Hey, where you goin', Frankenstein?"

"Leave me alone," he warned, and kept moving toward them as he raised the pistol from his side and transferred it to his right hand.

"Whoa, whoa, whoa!" shouted the guy by the driver's door. "Stop right there, Karloff. I got you covered."

To prove his claim, he fired a round over Tom's head. The report sounded like a rifle.

Through the years, each time that he committed an armed robbery with an unloaded gun, Tom expected his victim to be carrying heat and to do him the favor of shooting him dead.

Here seemed to be the men who would set him free at last. He was surprised, therefore, when he didn't continue toward them.

"Drop the gun," the shooter commanded.

Jackie's pal said, "Blow his brains out, George, do it."

George warned Tom, "I'll do it. Drop the gun or I'll do it."

Instead of casting the pistol aside, Tom tucked it under his belt, against his abdomen.

Less than twenty feet separated him from the two men in front of the Suburban. Wary, they moved toward him, careful to remain out of their armed companion's line of fire.

"I'm not alone," Tom said.

Jackie laughed, and the guy beside him said, "Problem is—that's an **imaginary** friend you been talking to, rummy. What've you got in the back-pack? Take it off and give us a look."

Out of the night to Tom's left, from the long slope that led down to the sea, came a low and sin-ister form, its eyes radiant with the reflected beams of the headlights. A lean coyote with its sharp teeth bared.

The beast didn't even glance at Tom Bigger. With boldness not characteristic of the species, it

moved menacingly toward those who were threatening him.

"Is that a dog?" Jackie asked, and his pal said,
"Shit, no."

As if conjured with invocations and pentagrams,
another coyote slunk out of the darkness, close behind the first. And then a third.

Backing away, Jackie said, "Scare them off,
George."

The shooter fired a round in the air, but the animals weren't frightened.

From the deep dark and the tall grass, a fourth
coyote, a fifth, a sixth, a seventh materialized.

The rifleman, who was the driver, got behind
the wheel of the Suburban, and the slam of his
door triggered the retreat of the other men to the
safety of the vehicle.

Now that he was the only prey remaining, Tom
Bigger expected the pack to turn on him, but their
attention remained fixed on the three occupants of
the SUV.

For a minute or two, the driver waited, surely
expecting the coyotes to roam away into the night.
But the seven maintained their vigil, eerily still.

Through the windshield, Tom could see the two
men in the front seat, the third leaning forward
from behind them. They appeared to be arguing.

The driver released the emergency brake, put the

Suburban in gear, and pulled onto the highway. He drove south, back the way he had come.

Tom watched until the taillights dwindled from view.

He took the unloaded pistol from under his waistband, held it at his side, and walked north.

The coyotes accompanied him through the moonlight, three ahead of him, one on each side, and two behind.

So high that the sound of its engines didn't reach the earth, a jet transited the sky from west to east, and for Tom its lights signified that his journey, too, would continue, must continue.

After a quarter of a mile, the coyotes moved away from him in single file, diagonally across the blacktop.

He stopped to watch them leave.

One by one, the seven leaped across a drainage swale beyond the farther shoulder of the highway, eastbound as silently as the jet, and vanished into a moonlit meadow.

He did not know what to think of them.

After they were gone, he walked north again for about a mile, until he came to a small stone bridge over a currently dry creek. He took off his back-pack and placed it on the waist-high wall of the bridge.

He put away the pistol. From the upper com-

partment of the pack, he took one of the six bottles of tequila, each of which was wrapped in its
own stuffsack.

Two cars appeared in the south, but the thugs
were not returning with reinforcements. A sedan
and a pickup swept past without slowing.

Tom twisted the cap, broke the tax stamp,
opened the pint. He brought it to his nose and inhaled.

The aroma made his mouth water and his stomach flutter with anticipation. The shakes took
him, so he held the tequila with both hands.

After he stood there for a while, perhaps for five
minutes, he screwed the cap back on the bottle.
He took no satisfaction in his self-control. He
knew his willpower would not long endure.

Cursing himself for his sudden temperance, he
threw the bottle off the bridge. He heard it shatter
on the stones in the waterless waterway.

He zipped shut the storm flap, shouldered the
backpack once more, and adjusted the hip belt.

Soon twelve hours would have passed since the
sobering incident in the bluff-top rest area, above
his cave home. He'd been awake for twenty hours,
and he'd walked a long way in the past four. He
should have been asleep on his feet, but he was
awake, alert, and grimly focused.

He knew where he must go. A long, long walk
remained ahead of him.

He knew what he must do. The task would not be easy. He might not have the courage to complete it.

As Tom Bigger walked north into the last few hours of the night, he was overcome again by the feeling that he was not alone, that he was followed step by step, and not merely by coyotes. And he was afraid.

Thirty-nine

For a walk in the suburban Seattle woods, Liddon Wallace wore Brioni loafers protected by rubber overshoes, gray wool slacks by Ermenegildo Zegna, a Mark Cross belt, a Geoffrey Beene shirt, an Armani sweater, a black leather jacket by Andrew Marc, and a Patek Philippe wristwatch.

The hard-packed dirt footpath proved easy to follow in spite of the mottling shadows and the mist. Dawn had come nearly an hour earlier. But fog veiled the face of the sun and allowed only this indirect light.

In the morning murk, the towering Douglas firs and hemlocks appeared to be black, and the ferns were more blue than green. Even the clusters of Pacific dogwoods, with their flurries of scarlet and gold leaves, blazed less than smoldered in the dripping gloom, and their enormous white flowers, which usually resembled clematis, now looked like dead birds in their branches.

After little more than three hundred yards, the footpath led out of the forest. Beyond lay the putting green at the eighteenth hole of the golf course.

An electric cart, used by groundskeepers, stood on the green. Even as Liddon Wallace came out of the trees, Rudy Neems, chief of the landscape-maintenance crew, took the eighteenth-hole flag from the cart and stood it in the cup.

Half surrounding the green and beyond it were three sand traps and then a fairway that sloped down to a water hazard. The first half of the fairway, beyond the water, faded into the mist, and the tee was far beyond sight. A narrow rough lay along each flank of the fairway, and behind both roughs the forest continued.

Rudy Neems stood by the grounds cart, watching Liddon approach. The landscaper was thirty-eight, stocky, with a blond mustache and thick hair that grew naturally in ringlets. Ironically, as a boy, he was often picked to play an angel in Christmas pageants.

"This weather sucks," Liddon said.

Neems was soft-spoken to such a degree that even in the morning stillness, his voice didn't carry far: "Good for the skin."

Indeed, the groundskeeper had a superb complexion.

Liddon said, "So you reviewed the package."

"Yes."

"Do you have any questions?"

"No."

"You see how it can be done?"

"Yes."

"Then you'll do it?"

"The money?"

Liddon handed him a manila envelope containing forty thousand in hundred-dollar bills. "Forty thousand more when it's done."

Neems didn't bother to count the deposit. He dropped it in the cart and returned to Liddon another envelope that contained numerous photographs of his house in California, the floor plan, and detailed information about the security system.

"Plus expenses," Neems reminded him.

"Yes, of course. Forty thousand more plus expenses. When are you flying there?"

"This afternoon."

"As I told you, I'm only in Seattle on business until Wednesday noon. When will you do the job?"

"Tomorrow night."

"Tuesday evening."

"Yes."

"Good. Excellent. I'll be having drinks and dinner with a client from six o'clock till eleven or later."

"Your wife looks nice," Neems said.

"Yes, she does, she's a beautiful woman, but I should never have married. I'm not the marrying kind."

"I want her."

"You want her? No. Not a good idea, Rudy. You were acquitted, but your DNA is still on file from the court-ordered blood sample, it's still in the system, you don't dare leave semen behind."

"I won't."

Four years earlier, in California, Rudy stood trial for the murder of a fourteen-year-old girl. Liddon was his defense attorney.

"It's too risky," Liddon reasoned, "because I got you off in the Hardy case. They find your DNA, they'll know I hired this done."

He had not merely won a not-guilty verdict for Neems, but he had also made two straight-arrow police detectives appear so corrupt that they were ultimately fired from the force.

A network-TV news magazine did a two-hour feature on the case that brought Liddon millions in business. The camera loved him. He was a natural. Now and then he watched a DVD of the program just to remind himself of how good he looked.

"Judy didn't have any."

Judy was Judith Hardy, the fourteen-year-old who was kidnapped and raped.

Liddon said, "Didn't have any what?"

"Any of my DNA."

"She was largely dissolved by acid in a pit on the beach. The best forensic team wasn't going to get anything from that body."

"So I burn Kirsten."

Kirsten was Liddon's wife.

"Fill the bathtub with gasoline," said Neems.

Looking past Rudy Neems, Liddon surveyed the foggy fairway. No one was in sight. The course didn't open for at least another hour. Nevertheless, this was taking too long. To minimize the chance of their being seen together, they needed to meet in places as discreet as this **and keep the meetings brief**.

"Bathtub of gasoline?" Liddon said, boggled by the flamboyance.

"Sink her, burn her," said Neems.

"I've got a lot of expensive art, antiques."

"And a fire-sprinkler system."

"Still. A bathtub of gasoline."

"Studied it," Neems said.

Liddon looked at the manila envelope full of photos and details about the house, which Neems had returned to him.

"You'll lose the bathroom," Neems said.

"Obviously."

"Master bedroom. Some attic."

"What about water damage?"

"Sprinklers only go off in rooms with heat."

"Ah. So there's no widespread water damage. Smoke?"

"I'll close the bathroom and bedroom doors behind me."

Neems was as dependable as he was soft-spoken. He thought things through, cared about details.

"I guess the alarm system will get the fire department there in a hurry," Liddon said.

"Probably under four minutes. They're nearby."

Because the apron of the putting green sloped up slightly to the surrounding fairway, the contours of the land pulled faint currents of morning air into the depressed green, where they circled, circled, drawing in a thicker knee-high scrim of fog that moved around Liddon and Neems, a slow-motion whirlpool, around and around.

"You really want Kirsten that much?" Liddon asked.

Neems nodded. "I gotta have her."

"How long will you . . . take with her?"

"Two hours. Three."

"You're confident about this?"

"Absolutely."

"It's kind of wild," Liddon said.

"So wild, it's not the way hired killings are done."

"Good point. Well . . . okay, then."

Neems's smile was so sweet, he would still be good for Christmas pageants. "Two things. First— you sure about Benny?"

Benny was Benjamin Wallace, Liddon's three-year-old son.

"I'm no better at parenting than marriage," Liddon said.

"There's nannies."

"I'd either end up with some harridan who ruins the mood of the house or some young thing who files a phony civil suit against me for sexual harassment. Is Benny a problem for you?"

"Why would he be a problem? He's three years old."

"I didn't mean a physical problem."

"I'm fine with it," Neems said.

"All right. Then it's set."

"I just wanted to be sure you were okay with it."

"It is what it is," Liddon said. "What's the second thing?"

"Just my curiosity."

"I've got to get going."

"You come to me for this—you had to know I did Judy Hardy."

"Obviously."

"When did you figure it out?"

"Before I took your case," Liddon said.

"You did my case pro bono."

"You didn't have any money."

"Thought you defended me because you believed."

"In your innocence? No. Never."

"So you did it pro bono because . . . ?"

"What do you think, Rudy?"

"In case one day you needed someone like me."

"There you go."

"Were you married when you took my case?"

"Only a few months."

"Did you know then that maybe . . ."

"No, no. I loved her then."

"That's sad."

Liddon shrugged. "Life."

"You do a lot of pro bono work."

"I try to give what time I can."

"So you have others like me?"

"A couple. If I need them."

"Well, I want you to know I'm grateful."

"Thank you, Rudy."

"Not just for back then, but for this opportunity, too."

"I know you're meticulous. Now I better be going." He took two steps across the green, toward the woods, then turned to look once more at the groundskeeper. "I'm a little curious, too."

"About what?"

"Since Judy Hardy, have you . . ."

"Yes."

"Often?" Liddon asked.

"I make myself wait between."

"Is it difficult—waiting?"

"Yes. But then it's sweeter when I do one."

"How long is the wait?"

"Six months. Eight."

"Have you ever come under suspicion again?"

"No. And I never will."

"You're a smart and careful man. That's why I took your case."

"Besides, people like me," said Neems.

"Yes. They do. That's always a plus."

Liddon continued across the green, across the rough, to the footpath through the woods. He was two hundred yards from the most terrifying encounter of his life.

Forty

"Henry."

The dream was a montage of action close-ups: long bare limbs thrashing, blond hair tossing, red-nailed hands clutching with desire and striking out defensively, ripe mouth open in rapture but then shaping a silent scream of sublime terror.

As he woke, Henry Rouvroy thought he heard someone whispering his name.

"Henry."

In sleep, he had slid onto his side. Now he sat up, his back against the closet wall.

The shotgun. He had let go of it. He fumbled in the dark, found the 20-gauge.

More likely than not, he dreamed the voice. He listened but heard nothing.

Beyond the open door, the bedroom was

brighter than when he had taken up his post in the closet, but it wasn't as bright as it would have been with a lamp on.

Dawn had come. Morning sun seeped around the edges of the closed draperies.

Wincing, flexing his left foot to defeat a cramp, Henry rose and moved cautiously to the doorway.

Again he listened. After a silence, he heard the thinnest of whistles—and his heart clenched for a moment, until he realized that the sound was his own flatulence.

Sausage, cheese, and a plebeian bread for dinner had been a mistake, a shock to the system.

Less than a day on the farm, and already his standards and conduct had begun to deteriorate. One could not overestimate the dangerous effects that a rustic way of life could have on a man's personality and intellect, even after he had been prepared in the finest private schools and polished to a high finish at Harvard. Without the daily stimulation of life in a big city, without continuous wit-sharpening interaction with other well-educated and sophisticated people, he might become countrified, coarse, uncouth. The **Times** probably wasn't distributed in this benighted region's one-horse hamlets and jerkwaters, and the illiterate inbred clerk at the newsstand no doubt sold **Vanity Fair** in a plain brown wrapper.

While Henry listened to his oscillating butt

whistle as it diminished to a final peep, he realized that when he stocked the potato cellar and the converted horse stalls with women, he should attempt to find at least one who had gone away to the right schools and returned to this intellectual wasteland for whatever misguided reasons. If he couldn't find one who was witty **and** sexy, he might be wise to imprison a plain woman who was a good conversationalist with refined tastes, strictly for the purpose of honing his intellect and maintaining his clarified and supreme aesthetics.

The unfortunate consequences of his rectal recital prevented Henry from remaining in the closet. In need of fresh air, he decided that if his name had been spoken, the whisperer had been a figure in his dream, and he moved into the bedroom.

When he switched on the ceiling light, he focused at once on the bed. The covers seemed to drape exactly as he had arranged them, and the shape of the fake sleeper was as he designed it.

If someone had taken the place of the dummy, Henry would have been murdered while he slept. His fear had been irrational.

Nevertheless, he rounded the foot of the bed to stand over the blanketed form. Holding the shotgun in both hands, with a finger on the trigger, he used the barrel to hook the bedclothes and flip them back from whatever they concealed.

Having been hostage to his absurd expectations, his breath blew free of him in a gust of relief.

He pulled the draperies back from the windows and let the early light into the room. He would no longer cower in closets. With the new day, he would follow a fresh strategy. Instead of reacting, he would act, and take the fight to his tormentor.

The hallway light was on, as it should have been, and one lamp in the living room, but the kitchen was not dark, as he had left it.

On the dinette table were the leather work gloves. When he found them on the bedspread the previous night, he had put them in a trash bag and set the bag on the bedroom armchair, intending to dispose of them come morning.

Now morning found them here. They appeared to be more saturated with blood than they had been before, much of it crusted and dry, but some still wet, gluey.

Beside the gloves were a pencil and the notepad that earlier had been by the kitchen phone. The yellow paint on the pencil was mottled with dried blood.

A few smears of blood also stained the top sheet of the notepad, but they did not obscure the message. The three handwritten lines were centered to one another.

So suddenly did Henry's dread return and with

such force that at first he could make no more
sense of the words than he would have if they had
been from the lost language of an ancient civilization. Fear rendered him momentarily illiterate.

When he could read, he saw that before him
were three lines of verse. They didn't rhyme because they comprised a brief poem in that seven-
teen-syllable Japanese form called haiku.

Of course, Henry knew about haiku because he
had graduated from Harvard, but also because his
brother, Jim, had written fifty-two of them that
were published in a slender hardcover.

Swooping harrier—
calligraphy on the sky,
talons, then the beak.

Henry remembered the pair of harriers gliding
in intersecting gyres as he had walked to the barn
with his brother.

Calligraphy. Beautiful Japanese writing done
with a brush.

Henry was neither a poet nor much of a reader
of poetry, but he supposed that to describe a
swooping bird, a brush painting graceful strokes
might be an acceptable metaphor.

The last line disturbed him more than the others. The final four words made this a poem about

death, a poem less about the harrier than about the unmentioned mouse that would be pierced by the talons and torn by the beak.

If Henry was the harrier, then his twin brother must be the mouse, and this poem was about Jim's murder in the barn.

On the other hand, if Jim was the harrier, then **his** brother was the mouse, and the poem must be about the impending murder of Henry.

He remembered Jim's words spoken just before they entered the barn: **"Predators and prey. The necessity of death, if life is to have meaning and proportion. Death as a part of life. I'm working on a series of poems with those themes."**

Infuriated more by the mockery than the threat, by being played for a fool, Henry Rouvroy wanted to rip the top page off the notepad, tear it in pieces and flush it down the toilet, but the thought of touching it repulsed him.

. . . talons, then the beak.

Those cold words seemed to promise a cruel death by stabbing, slashing.

. . . talons, then the beak.

Jim had not been stabbed. He had been shot. The poem was not likely to be about Jim's death.

Henry remembered the five knives that had been on the table when he first came into the kitchen with Jim and Nora.

Five knives with four- and five-inch blades, nonreflective finishes. Assisted-opening mechanisms for quick blade release.

Before the three of them had coffee and sweet-rolls, Jim moved the knives to the counter by the refrigerator.

Henry turned away from the haiku and went to the counter.

Three knives lay there. Two were missing.

Forty-one

The fragrance of fir, the wry significance of hemlock, and the irony of dogwood comforted Liddon Wallace as he followed the footpath through the forest after arranging for the murders of his wife and child.

The law was a magnificent thing. His legal career had brought him wealth, a measure of fame, powerful friends in high office, a young and stunningly beautiful wife, the means to resolve problems that would daunt or destroy other men, and the freedom to make even radical changes in his life to increase his happiness and to ensure that he was always as fulfilled as he had every right to be.

His parents and most of his teachers over the years, from preschool through law school, had stressed that nothing was more important than self-esteem, that self-esteem was **the** ticket to a satisfying life journey. In Liddon's case, they were wasting their time preaching to a true believer who from a tender age was well aware of his many superior qualities, not the least of which was decisiveness.

When he saw what needed to be done, he did it. Or hired someone like Rudy Neems to do it. Liddon never dithered, and once he acted, he never had remorse.

Sometimes, if he possessed the right information, he neither had to do the job himself nor pay to have it done. A lot of people lived with secrets that could destroy them, and if you knew their secrets, you could manipulate them to do things for you that reduced them to the condition of puppets. Because Liddon had friends in high office with unlimited public funds to investigate any member of the public, he never had difficulty getting the dirt on those he targeted, assuming that they had secrets worth learning.

As much as he loved the law and money and himself, he loved nothing more than pulling people's strings. He was born to be the master of his universe. Power was better than sex. Power was better than wealth. Power was better than anything.

All of these thoughts and a great many more of a diverse nature were bursting through Liddon Wallace's ever-busy mind as he walked through the woods toward the service road along which he had parked his rental car. Preoccupied with details of universe management and with thoughts related to the oncoming changes in his life, he was all but oblivious of the beauty of the forest.

He was not enthralled by nature as so many people seemed to be these days. He liked grass that was mown, trees artfully shaped by a talented arborist, flowers in orderly rows in well-designed beds, water contained within pools and fountains. He didn't appreciate the riotous quality of the natural world, everything thrown together in a wild sprawling mess, the fertility, the variety, the chaos.

Perhaps because he was unimpressed by nature, Nature decided to give him a slap upside the head. One second he was hurrying through the fog in a fog of his own, and the next second, **wham!**

The thing happened so abruptly, he reeled from it with a cry of terror, but there was nowhere to reel **to,** because the thing happened all around him, so that he either had to surrender to it or resist and endure. Liddon Wallace had never surrendered to anything in his life, never; and he refused to start capitulating now. If any strings were going to be pulled, **he** would do the pulling, he would not be pulled, he would never yield, **never.**

The energy of the event, the absolute power of the thing, took his breath away. Literally, he could not breathe. The air became as thick as water, compressed by an irresistible force of inconceivable might. And it seemed to him that the sunlight was being condensed, as well, concentrated not into greater brightness but into a rich golden densification, into a **substance** that he could feel and smell, into a shimmering coagulum that swelled, bent, buckled, and brought forth impossibilities.

He sensed also that something had gone wrong with time. **Wrong** wasn't the correct word; something about time had changed—the flow, the rules, the purpose of it. The past, the present, and the future were as one, twisted together like spaghetti on a fork, then twisted tighter, tighter, until countless millennia were wound into a single instant. He became aware of every moment of his past and of all the possibilities of his future, saw himself as a fetus, an infant, a growing child, an adolescent, an adult, a feeble octogenarian, all simultaneously.

As deeply strange and terrifying as the event was, although it overwhelmed all the senses and oppressed the mind nearly to the point of mental implosion, Liddon knew instantly what was happening, the cause and the intention. He knew also that the hideous stress upon him, the crushing power, the choking awe that arose from the sheer immensity of the thing, would be at once relieved if only he didn't resist, but he resisted.

Subjectively, the event seemed to go on for hours. But as he opened his mouth in a soundless scream of denial and self-assertion, as he fisted his hands so tightly that his fingernails cut his palms and his knuckle bones felt as if they might split through his skin, Liddon knew that in fact only a few seconds were passing, a sixth of a minute at most.

As abruptly as the thing began, it ended. Just as he had tried to reel back at the start of it, Liddon reeled forward when it was over, and this time no power impeded him. Neither the lifting fog nor the perpetual shadows offered adequate conceal-ment, neither the trees nor the ferns, and the one path was the one way, not back to Rudy Neems but forward. Liddon lurched and staggered along the last hundred yards of the footpath, to the oiled-dirt road that was used mostly by forest-ser-vice personnel and primarily in times of fire.

In the rental car, he locked the doors, threw the manila envelope on the passenger seat, and sat gasping, shuddering.

He flipped down the sun visor to consult the mirror on the back. He expected his face to be scorched or in some other way branded by the en-counter, but he bore no mark of his experience. When he peered into the reflection of his eyes, he immediately looked away.

Only when his heart slowed a bit and his fear abated did he realize that he had lost one loafer and the rubber overshoe with it. No expensive

Italian footwear could be expensive enough to motivate him to return to the woods.

His gray wool slacks by Ermenegildo Zegna were shapeless, as if processed by an incompetent dry cleaner. Half of the top stitching in his Mark Cross belt was unraveled, and the tongue of the buckle was bent.

The Geoffrey Beene shirt, soaked with sour sweat, had shrunk in curious ways, binding at the underarms and pulling tight across the yoke.

From the badly snagged Armani sweater dangled scores of yarn loops, and the black jacket by Andrew Marc stank as if the leather had begun to rot.

When he consulted his Patek Philippe, the hour and the minute hands seemed to present the correct time, and the second hand swept smoothly around the face. But the watch indicated that the day of the week was Thursday when in fact it was Monday, and that the month was December instead of September.

Eventually Liddon started the rental car and switched on the heater, for he felt cold to the bone.

He was not yet ready to drive.

He didn't look toward the forest. Nothing there interested him. Nothing ever would. He wouldn't be returning to those woods. Never again would he go into any forest, anywhere.

Neither did he turn his eyes to anything else beyond the windows, nor even to the windows themselves.

The thing happened, Liddon would never forget that it happened, but in the end it didn't matter. He would never mention the event to anyone. What would it profit him to do so?

He opened the envelope that Rudy Neems had returned to him, and he took out the photographs. Pictures of the house and grounds were of no interest to him. He found photos of Kirsten and Benny. Wife and son. Woman and boy. Other and other. Unknown and unknowable.

He returned the photos to the envelope.

Later, when his tremors subsided, he made a U-turn on the narrow road and headed out of the forest.

Forty-two

At 6:35 A.M. mountain time, Dr. Eleanor Fortney phoned from Massachusetts, waking Cammy Rivers, who sat up in bed to take the call.

Eleanor had a gift for small talk, but she didn't make use of it this time. "Knowing you, how responsible you are, this can't be a prank. Those aren't altered images."

"No. They're real, Eleanor. They—"

Interrupting, the zoologist said, "You've secured them?"

"Secured them?"

"The animals. In a cage. A dog crate. A padlocked crate. With those hands, they'll be clever about simple latches."

"No, they're not in a crate. They're with Grady at his place."

"Please call him now. Tell him to lock them in a

closet or a room without windows. Windows have latches."

"I don't think he'd do that."

"Why? Why on earth wouldn't he?"

"They're very appealing. They seem attracted to people the way dogs are, they're affectionate."

"That can't be a fully informed opinion. Not in the little time you've had. That's just a first impression."

"All right, sure," Cammy acknowledged, "a first impression. But it feels right. Eleanor, you'd understand if you were here and could see them firsthand."

"Maybe I would, but you can't let these creatures get away."

"They don't want to get away. They want a home. They're cozy with Grady."

"You're ascribing human motivations to them. You can't know what they want. Cammy, I **know** you must understand what they are."

Unable easily to put into words the ineffable quality of Puzzle and Riddle, which suggested that they were something different from any of the easy explanations that came to mind, Cammy merely said, "We've been avoiding theories."

"They're engineered," Eleanor declared. "Multiple-species DNA."

"It crossed my mind." Cammy tossed back the

covers and sat on the edge of the bed. "But creatures this complex? Nobody's that far along yet."

"These days, it's not just engineering new bacte-
ria to make them into little factories producing
insulin and interferon. It's not just modifying
Thiobacillus ferrooxidans so it'll be a better ura-
nium-mining bacterium. We're way beyond that."

"Sure, I know. Some Chinese scientist imported
a gene into pigs that makes them glow green in the
dark. All kinds of crazy things are happening out
there. But if Puzzle and Riddle were engineered,
the science that made them would be magnitudes
beyond the glowing-green-pig stunt."

"Let me bring you up to date," Eleanor said.
"Let's stay on pigs for a minute. Did you know
pigs are being radically engineered to have organs
suitable for transplantation into people?"

"I've heard something about it."

"Pig organs that will be structurally, chemically,
genetically so human that the recipient's body
won't reject them. It's coming fast."

Getting to her feet, Cammy said, "But still—"

Eleanor interrupted once more: "Pigs again. At
universities here and in other countries, there's a
race on to be the first to engineer a pig with a human brain."

The cordless phone allowed Cammy to move to
the nearest window. "For God's sake, why?"

"Arrogance. Because it negates the idea of a soul. There's no practical application. The creature will be tortured by loneliness, by the incongruous nature of its body-brain relationship. It'll have no refuge but insanity. It's Frankenstein to the tenth power."

Hard flat morning light. The sky a pale, pale blue.

Cammy said, "You're talking about monsters. These animals aren't like that. They're . . . quite wonderful."

"They might be as peachy keen as Mickey Mouse, but if they were engineered, there's no way of knowing what havoc they might wreak on the environment. Like . . . if they give birth to large litters and they make good use of those incredible hands, they could displace one or more indigenous species."

The window glass felt cold. The air temperature had fallen at least fifteen degrees after midnight.

"If they were born in a lab," Cammy said, "how did they get here? There's no university in this county, no companies in the bioengineering business."

"They probably wouldn't have gotten out of the lab on their own. Maybe some animal activists did it. That bunch is causing havoc these days. Vandalizing scientists' homes, raiding laboratories in the night. Some of them—they're fanatical enough and ignorant enough to turn an experimental species loose in the wild. They could've brought them from anywhere."

"An experimental species," Cammy said dubiously. "This is just gut instinct, Eleanor, but that isn't what they are."

"Then what are they, Dr. Rivers? They're not in the encyclopedia of known species. Their eyes alone qualify them as an astonishing singularity."

"I don't know. I don't know what they are."

"Previously undiscovered species of insects, various aquatic forms, even mice are turned up from time to time. But we haven't overlooked any large mammals, not in an area as fully explored as the Colorado Rockies, not anywhere. The moment I hang up, call this Grady and tell him to secure those animals. Insist on it. Then wait by your phone."

"Wait for what?"

"You'll be getting a call. I had to report this."

Misgiving honed an edge on Cammy's voice: "Report? To whom?"

"To a man I know at the National Science Foundation. He gave me the name of someone at the Environmental Protection Agency, and it's snowballed from there."

"But I contacted you as a friend. I expected discretion."

"Cammy, even as much as I like you, I can't possibly conspire with you regarding something like this. I have professional and legal obligations to report it."

"Yeah. Okay. I guess I understand. I just didn't realize . . ."

Eleanor said, "Sidney Shinseki called me from Texas this morning, as soon as he read your e-mail. We reported this together. Anyone in our positions would have done the same."

"I see. Of course."

"Now call Grady and make sure those animals are secured. Then wait by your phone. I think the name of the man calling you will be Paul Jardine. He works out of Denver, I believe."

"What're they going to do?" Cammy asked.

"The authorities? They'll take custody of the animals."

"And then what?"

"Then you're out of it. You didn't steal the animals. You're cooperating, doing the right thing."

"No, I mean then what happens to Puzzle and Riddle?"

"Research animals have embedded microchips under the skin of their necks. Or at least ear tattoos. They'll be easy to trace."

"Then . . . they'll be sent back where they came from, to the lab."

Evidently hearing a note of dismay in Cammy's

voice, Eleanor said, "You know that's where they belong. They don't belong in the wild."

"I wish you could see them."

"Get straight about this, Cammy. If you turn the animals loose, you could be criminally prosecuted."

"Okay. I get it."

"**Do** you get it?"

"I totally get it."

"Good."

"I don't know what I was thinking. I'm embarrassed. I was caught up in the . . . the magic of it. I should have realized."

"Make Grady secure the animals. Then wait by your phone."

"All right."

"I'm sorry, Cammy. If I snapped at you, I mean."

"I was a little obtuse. I needed a snap."

"We'll talk later," Eleanor said, and hung up.

Cammy pushed the END button on her cordless phone.

She did not at once call Grady.

She touched the cold windowpane again. The day would quickly grow warmer, though not as warm as Sunday. A change in the weather was coming.

Deciding against taking the time to shower,

Cammy quickly dressed in a sweater, jeans, and boots.

Using her cell phone, she called Cory Hern, her senior vet tech, and put him in charge of the office for the day. Any cases he and Ben Aikens couldn't deal with should be referred to the usual competitors whom she backed up when they were on vacation.

The house phone rang as she returned to the bedroom. The caller was Paul Jardine.

"Some of us are en route, and I'll be airborne in half an hour." He had the demeanor and the melodic voice of a game-show host. "As I understand it, the two individuals are with Mr. Grady Adams."

"That's right." Jardine recited an address, and Cammy said, "Yes. The last house on the county road. If you need directions—"

"We're fine, don't worry about us, we're all coming in with satellite navigation. Doctor, we'll be doing an extensive debriefing, an interview."

"I've cleared my schedule for today."

"That's great. Thank you so much. But I'll need you to clear it for tomorrow, as well. Just in case."

"In case of what?"

"You never know. Doctor, not to spook you, but this matter may fall under the National Security Secrets Act, which provides for a spectrum of penalties that range all the way to life imprisonment. Do you understand?"

"Yes, I guess, but—"

"You must not speak to anyone further about the two individuals in your photographs. I need the names now of everyone you've told about them, in addition to Eleanor Fortney and Sidney Shinseki."

She found herself pacing back and forth at the foot of the bed as she assured him, "There's no one else."

"Ah. Good. That's excellent. Simplifies the situation. Later, I will need you to repeat that statement under oath."

In spite of Jardine's cheerful manner and appealing voice, every sentence he spoke intensified Cammy's sense of foreboding.

She said, "Mr. Jardine, am I going to need an attorney?"

"Good question. I don't think so. But we'll make a determination about that when we're on scene. I am hoping that you can go now to Mr. Adams's residence and wait there with him until we arrive."

"Yes, all right."

"If you would be so good as to bring with you the memory stick from Mr. Adams's camera and any copies you might have made of the photos he took, that would be terribly helpful."

"Of course. No problem."

"Finally, please pack clothes and toiletries for a two-night stay at the site."

"Site?"

"The Grady Adams residence."

"Why would that be necessary?"

"We never know. Things happen. Questions arise. I know it's an inconvenience, but it's just better if the principals are all in the same place for the preliminary investigation."

"We can all gather in the drawing room for a reenactment," she said, "but there's no butler, suspicious or otherwise."

"That's funny," Jardine said with delight but without a laugh. "That really is clever. I'm looking forward to meeting you, Doctor. Please be at the site sooner than later."

"I will. Oh, Mr. Jardine. Are you with the National Science Foundation or the Environmental Protection Agency?"

"Neither, Doctor. This investigation is being run by the Department of Homeland Security."

Forty-three

When Grady woke in the Stickley-style reclining chair shortly before 7:30 A.M., he switched on the nearby lamp and discovered that the three chums and co-conspirators were not on the bed where he had last seen them. They were nowhere in the bedroom, and when he called Merlin, the dog didn't appear from either the adjoining bathroom or the closet.

The door to the hall stood ajar. He was certain that he had closed it before retiring.

Yawning, scratching his head, he got out of the chair and padded barefoot into the hallway. The doors to the other upstairs rooms were closed.

Downstairs, in the living room, morning light flooded in through the windows and drew his attention to the items arrayed on the carpet in front of the walnut desk with the hammered-copper hardware and the decorative pewter inlays. The contents of every drawer and shelf in the desk lay in neatly aligned rows: a stapler, a staple remover, a ruler, pencils, pens, a box of rubber bands, a box of paper clips, a small container of Sortkwik fingertip moistener, a packet of plain white envelopes. . . .

The tableau suggested that someone might be conducting a meticulous inventory of his business supplies. Maybe Merlin planned to drive over to the Costco in the next county and needed to compose a shopping list.

In the hallway, the end door to the kitchen was closed, as was the door to his study on the right. To the left, the library door stood open, and lights were on in that room.

On the floor were approximately twenty books in three stacks. Grady had not left them there.

Curious, he knelt to examine the volumes. They were a mix of nonfiction and fiction in various genres. At first he could see no connection between them—and then he realized that all of the dust jackets of all the chosen books had exceptionally colorful spines: red, yellow, hot pink, orange. . . .

Because his books were arranged alphabetically, Grady knew that the selection had been taken from both low and high shelves and from half a dozen points around the room. Cold reason suggested he could dismiss from consideration the possibility that Merlin had learned to climb.

The suspicion arose that he had been prudent to go barefoot and not to announce himself in any fashion since coming downstairs. In the hallway, he listened attentively and heard furtive noises behind the end door.

Stepping into the kitchen, he found the wolfhound sitting at the open pantry. At first there was no sign of Puzzle and Riddle, but then from the pantry appeared a white furry arm ending in a coal-black hand that offered a Ritz cracker slathered with peanut butter.

For a dog his size, Merlin routinely accepted any treat with a gentleness that was surprising, taking it with soft lips and quick tongue, never with a rudeness of teeth, finessing it from fingers instead of snatching. He accepted the Ritz cracker with his usual good manners.

As the dog munched the cracker and lavishly licked his chops, he turned his head to Grady. His expression suggested that henceforth his dad could sleep late every morning while his new best friends whipped up breakfast.

When Grady peered into the pantry, he discovered Puzzle and Riddle sitting on the floor as they had sat on the sofa the previous evening, not like dogs or even like prairie dogs, but as if they were human children. Their legs were straight in front of them.

Between her thighs, Puzzle held an open family-size jar of Skippy peanut butter. Riddle took a cracker from the Ritz box and passed it to her.

Reaching into the jar with her right hand, Puzzle scooped out a gob of Skippy's finest. She smeared it on the cracker that she held in her left hand.

She returned the cracker to Riddle. He fed it to himself with his left hand while he plucked another cracker from the box with his right.

The fur around their black lips remained remarkably free of peanut butter; however, golden cracker crumbs littered their white coats.

"I'm surprised you're not having some grape jelly with that," Grady said.

The two astonishments looked up at him, smacking their lips with satisfaction.

"Sorry if you prefer chunky peanut butter. I'm afraid I only have smooth."

In unison, the pair cocked their heads, regarding him as though he was the most peculiar creature they had ever encountered.

Grady stepped past Merlin and into the big pantry. He bent down to take the cracker box from Riddle and the jar of Skippy from Puzzle.

Although they didn't attempt to hold fast to their treasures, they made soft sounds of dismay, a sort of warbling-mewling, and Riddle put a hand on Puzzle's shoulder as if to comfort her.

Grady said, "If you've really moved in, like Cammy thinks, I guess I'll have to monkeyproof the house."

He snared the lid of the Skippy jar and took everything into the kitchen. He put the lid on the peanut butter, closed the box of crackers, opened a lower cabinet door, and dropped both items into a small trash can.

When he turned around, the two were sitting in the middle of the floor, intently watching him. Riddle continued to smack his lips, and Puzzle had three fingers in her mouth at once, assiduously cleaning away every trace of Skippy. They appeared to have brushed the cracker crumbs from their chest fur.

In the open pantry, Merlin sniffed the floor with the enthusiasm of a bloodhound, licking up the debris.

"The cracker box is still nearly full," Grady said, "so I assume you only had a few. You still get kibble. But I'll have to look into fitting out the pantry with a titanium-steel vault door with a laser scanner that reads my palm print."

He rinsed the three drinking bowls and filled them with fresh cold water. Then he dished up three servings of kibble and placed them side by side on the floor.

As before, Puzzle and Riddle followed Merlin's lead, sitting in front of their bowls, waiting for the word from Grady—"Okay"—that formally announced **Breakfast is served**.

While the three pals ate as if they had never in their lives encountered peanut butter, Grady put a filter in the coffeemaker. From a can, he spooned enough Jamaican blend to make ten cups.

He heard a noise at the back door. Turning, he saw Merlin and Puzzle waiting while Riddle, standing on his hind legs, worked the knob with both hands.

Evidently, Riddle had already disengaged the deadbolt with the thumbturn. Now the latch bolt released and the door eased open.

Riddle dropped onto all fours and pushed the door out of his way. He scampered onto the porch, followed by Puzzle and Merlin.

Stepping to the window, Grady watched as the quick pair led the wolfhound across the yard to the taller meadow grass. Only the night before, Merlin had shown them that the meadow, rather than the lawn, was an appropriate toilet.

Grady went to the open back door and worked the thumbturn a few times, extending and retracting the deadbolt. The lock was simple to operate. No degree in engineering was required.

He couldn't remember for sure, but they probably had seen him use the thumbturn.

At the coffeemaker again, he poured ten cups of water into the reservoir, put the glass carafe on the warming plate, and twisted the brew switch.

Returning to the window, he saw the three pals chasing around the yard: bounding exuberantly this way and that, tumbling, rolling, up and running again.

"Maybe if you watch me do it at dinner tonight," Grady murmured, "you can have coffee ready for me in the morning."

Forty-four

Lamar Woolsey took an early-bird flight out of Las Vegas and landed in Denver in time for a late breakfast, which he did not get to order, let alone eat, because two men were waiting for him when he came off the enclosed jet bridge into the terminal. They were in the area from which, since September 2001, everyone except airport personnel and ticketed passengers was excluded.

The moment that he spotted them, Lamar knew they were waiting for him. They had a look with which he was familiar: fully ready but pretending weariness, vigilant but feigning indifference. One of them had a hands-off cell phone, shaped like an ocarina but hardly bigger than a peach pit, hooked over his right ear.

Out of courtesy, so they would feel that their plainclothes disguise was effective, Lamar looked away from them and continued walking until the one without the cell phone called his name. Then he halted, turned to them as they approached, and said, "Ah, you must be with the conference."

The one with the cell phone said, "No, sir," and with a gesture encouraged Lamar to step out of the flow of disembarking passengers.

Neither of them spoke the name of his agency, but when they flopped open their ID wallets, Lamar wasn't surprised to see that they were with the Department of Homeland Security: Derek Booker, Vincent Palumbo.

"I assume I won't be able to keep my commitment to speak at the conference."

Encouraging Lamar to walk with them, Palumbo said, "No, sir, you won't. The organizers have already been told you've got to withdraw from the program due to a sudden illness."

"What illness might that be?" Lamar asked.

"It's not been specified, sir. That's up to you."

"I'll use my imagination. I'm quite imaginative. Maybe it'll be a tropical parasite with outrageous symptoms." Lamar carried only his laptop. "I've got a suitcase coming through on the luggage carousel."

Booker said, "We don't have time for that now, sir. Feldstein will bring it to the site no more than an hour after we've gotten you there."

Lamar didn't bother to ask them the location of

the site. They wouldn't tell him in public, lest they be overheard.

They escorted him to a locked service door where someone waiting on the farther side opened it in answer to Palumbo's brisk knock.

Corridor, stairs down, corridor, corridor, exit door: On the concrete apron, a sedan waited for them. As Booker got in the front passenger seat, Lamar settled in back beside Palumbo. The waiting driver glanced back at Lamar and said, "Feldstein, sir."

"I've got a terrible tropical parasite, Mr. Feldstein, but not to worry. You can't be infected just by riding in a car with me."

"That's good to know, sir," Feldstein said as he popped the hand brake and tramped the accelerator.

"Is the site in the city?" Lamar asked Palumbo.

"No, sir. We're flying out from here."

"To where?"

"I'm not at liberty to say."

Palumbo's apparent discretion must mean that the agent hadn't been told the location. In Lamar's experience, that was unusual.

"What're we dealing with this time? Explosives, chemical, biological, nuclear . . . ?"

"Sorry, sir," Palumbo replied, "but I'm really not at liberty to disclose anything."

Extraordinary. The escorting agents always knew

the nature of the threat. Usually they presented a briefing en route.

Two airliners waited on a taxiway to use the runway that was being held clear for Feldstein.

Following the centerline stripe, the young agent drove at such high speed, he seemed to think he was expected to achieve flight velocity.

The executive helicopter was parked at the extreme end of the runway, on the chevrons marking the overrun area. As Lamar Woolsey, Palumbo, and Booker got out of the sedan, the chopper's rotors began to slice the air, casting scimitar shadows on the concrete.

The three men ducked under the blades, and the agents followed Lamar into the craft as Feldstein drove away.

Palumbo and Booker took the seats nearest the door, and Lamar made his way farther into the eight-passenger craft.

Another man was aboard, ensconced in one of the last two seats.

Lamar sat across the narrow aisle from Dr. Simon Northcott. "I've got a terribly vicious tropical parasite. What's your excuse, Northcott?"

"Food poisoning."

Belting in, Lamar said, "You lack imagination, my friend. As I've noted regarding other issues. Where are you coming from?"

"We took off from my hotel parking lot just

minutes ago. I was looking forward to this conference."

"Well, you never know," said Lamar. "Maybe
this time it's not just a plot to poison millions.
Maybe this time it's the end of the world, and you
wouldn't want to miss **that,** would you?"

Northcott's smile was indistinguishable from any
other man's grimace. He was a good enough fellow
and incredibly intelligent, but his sense of humor
had atrophied in the Paleozoic Era.

The whine of the engine escalated, and Lamar
looked out the window as the pavement fell away.

"How does a bankrupt government," Northcott
said, "pay to have all these cars and helicopters and
jets and field labs and swarms of mortician-faced
agents standing by 24/7, coast to coast?"

"I've heard the secretary of the treasury has
worked out a deal to sell the Chinese five
Midwestern states, where the people are just too
uncool, anyway."

Northcott didn't wince a smile, but stared at
Lamar as if he might be serious. Crane-tall, hawk-
faced, as lean as an anorexic stork, he hunched forward like a vulture on a tree limb. He really wasn't
an actively bad guy, and he truly was incredibly intelligent, but Lamar found him about as likeable
as an attack of gout.

"What do they want with you this time?"
Northcott asked. "Is it physics or maths?"

"You're a geneticist and physiologist, so you probably wouldn't be here if this had anything to do with explosives or chemicals. If they want me on a biological threat, my guess is it's not physics or maths so much as it is chaos theory."

If Northcott's smile looked like a grimace, then his grimace was more like the expression of a man who found a live cockroach swimming in his soup at the very moment he broke a tooth on a ball bearing spooned from the same bowl.

"The butterfly effect, fractals, strange attractors, nonlinear equations—it has a voodoo feel to me."

"Well," said Lamar, "the field hasn't been around half a century yet. When we've got a century and a half behind us, if we haven't piled up multiple irrefutable proofs of basic contentions, I'd agree with you that we should stop calling it science and start calling it religion. And of course we already have quite a lot of proofs we've built upon."

Northcott knew to what the century and a half referred, and he was about to skewer Lamar with pointed words when Agent Palumbo came along the aisle, holding on to the seats on both sides, and went down on one knee in front of them.

"ETA is fifty minutes. The pilot had a sealed directive for me. The site is in an unincorporated rural area in the higher foothills, a private residence belonging to someone named Grady Adams, and with him will be a veterinarian, Dr. Camillia

Rivers. Both are witnesses, not suspects at this time. It's a biological issue, but the decision has been made that decontamination and isolation protocols will not be necessary. The field lab needs only to approximate the sterility of a hospital operating room. Neither airtight nor positive-pressure antimicrobial suits will be required."

"Then what the hell kind of biological threat would it be?" asked Simon Northcott.

Palumbo corrected him: "Sir, the directive calls it a biological **issue**."

Northcott's face clenched, the high points of his cheekbones and his nose as white as tensed knuckles, the rest of it red. "I've been yanked from the conference to be flown off at high speed to consider an **issue**?"

"Sir," Palumbo said, "all I can say is, based on my experience, this might not be either a ticking-clock or a doomsday case, but it's big somehow. Something different and way big. It came up quick, and D.C. calls it a Priority One Incident, which until now has meant only one thing—nuclear detonation imminent. Paul Jardine is on his way to the site now."

Lamar had met Jardine a few times in the past six years. After the recent reorganization, he had been appointed deputy director of the Department of Homeland Security for the western half of the country, from the Mississippi to the Pacific.

Northcott said nothing more, but he looked neither mollified nor impressed.

Lamar said, "Agent Palumbo, I'm sorry. The engine noise, the rotors . . . I didn't get the owner of the residence, the site. What did you say his name was?"

"Adams, sir. Grady Adams. The veterinarian is Dr. Camillia Rivers."

"Within every chaos," Lamar said, "is an eerie order waiting to be revealed."

"Sir?"

Lamar said, "Just talking to myself, son."

"Sir, we're now in a communications blackout until the end of this. I have to impound your cell phone and laptop."

The laptop was at Lamar's feet, and he presented his cell phone to the agent.

"Sir, I also need any text-messaging devices you're carrying."

"Oh, son, I have too few years of life remaining to spend one minute text-messaging."

Northcott, on the other hand, proved to be a walking telecom store. Grumping, he shed two cell phones and an array of devices that filled Vincent Palumbo's available sport-coat pockets.

As the agent went forward again, carrying their laptops, Simon Northcott said, "They're all idiots at Homeland Security. This does it. I'm going to take my name off the volunteer specialists roster."

The more enlightened officials in the federal government were aware that the scientists directly in their employ were not generally speaking the most brilliant in their fields—with the exception of some people at NASA and a number in institutes completely funded by the Department of Defense. Consequently, specialists in numerous sciences were solicited to volunteer to be available to Homeland Security in crises, if called.

As one of many on the roster who had his skills, Lamar had been tapped only six times in seven years, and he imagined there had been as many as a hundred crisis responses during that period. He doubted that Simon Northcott was drafted as often, because only a fraction of terrorist plots involved biological weapons, whereas a specialist in probability analysis and chaos would be a valuable team member regardless of the threat scenario.

"Priority One Incident," Northcott said with a sarcastic note, "yet it's not a threat, it's an issue. A Priority One **Issue**—now there's an oxymoron if I ever heard one."

Lamar put his forehead against his window, looking down at the shadow of the helicopter racing over the landscape below them.

Grady Adams of Colorado. Marcus had no closer friend than Grady Adams, who had been with him when he died.

Carl Jung, the psychologist and philosopher, had

believed that coincidence—most of all that most extreme kind of coincidence called a synchronism—was an organizing principle of the universe as real as any of the laws of thermodynamics and of gravity. On issues such as culture and human exceptionalism, Lamar Woolsey had little in common with Jung, but there was certainly a place for the man in chaos theory, where hidden order could be found in even the most seemingly disordered and formless systems like the actions of wildly tossing storm waves and the furies of tornado winds.

Grady Adams. Lamar figured, drawing this card at this time was like being dealt the most meaningful card from a thousand-deck shoe.

Forty-five

Driving to Grady's place, Cammy's attention repeatedly strayed from the highway to her hands on the steering wheel.

Having resisted embracing victim status for so long and having lived with the scars for most of her life, she thought about this disfigurement hardly more often than she stopped to think that each of her hands had five fingers and fourteen knuckles. The scars were a fact of her hands that embarrassed her no more than the fact that she had fingernails. A survivor could not be embarrassed by proof of her resolute spirit and endurance.

She kept glancing at the scars now because she felt trapped for the first time since her fifteenth birthday, for the first time in more than twenty years.

*

The trap from which she escaped on that long-ago birthday had been one that she endured from the age of five. It began when her mother and her mother's boyfriend, Jake Horner, took Cammy across state lines to avoid abiding by a child-custody decision handed down by the divorce court in Texas.

The court gave both parents joint—and equal—custody. Cammy's mother, Zena, didn't like anyone telling her what to do.

Jake Horner had inherited some money. He used part of it to buy a boat, a fifty-six-foot coastal cruiser, which he named **Therapy**.

Jake, Zena, and Cammy cruised ceaselessly, from Vancouver south to Puerto Vallarta, Mexico, and back again. They were never in port more than two weeks at a time.

Mike Rivers, Cammy's dad, tracked them down at a marina in Northern California, eight months later. Because differences in the laws between California and Texas hampered him, he took matters into his own hands.

When Mike Rivers appeared on the dock, he was talked aboard **Therapy** by Zena, who expressed remorse and fear of the authorities, and by Jake, who said he was unaware that Mike either wanted custody of his daughter or was granted any such arrangement by a judge. Jake was angry with Zena and assured Mike that they could settle the issue quickly and to everyone's satisfaction.

The spacious main cabin included a galley with teak cabinets and a matching teak floor, a dining area, and a salon. There, Jake and Zena stabbed Mike Rivers to death.

In the aft stateroom, beyond a closed door, five-year-old Cammy heard the brutal assault. She didn't see the murder—except in her imagination.

Her father took a while to die. But he did not beg for his life. She never forgot that he refused to beg.

Jake and Zena wrapped the body in a tarp, then in chains. Later that day, more than two miles offshore, they added a spare anchor to the package and dropped it overboard.

Cammy was on deck when the bundled body went over the side. Near twilight, the green and purple sea opened as if it were a great dark maw, hungrily swallowed her father in an instant, and licked the hull of the boat, wanting more.

At the marina again, Jake found Mike's car, drove it elsewhere, and abandoned it. That night, he was in high spirits.

In the morning, they cruised south toward Mexico. As if nothing had changed, nothing at all, the sea rolled vast and bright, the air smelled fresh, the sky was blue, and white gulls soared with a grace they did not possess when on the land.

Jake Horner loved books. He read fiction and nonfiction, but he especially liked volumes about therapeutic psychologies. He called himself a "journeyer," as if it were a vocation, an avocation, and a faith. He said life was about one thing and one thing only: the next possibility.

Because Cammy never went to school, Jake taught her to read. After that, being a dedicated autodidact, she taught herself what else she needed to know.

Zena appreciated the mood-altering power of drugs, particularly ecstasy, and Jake liked to torment children. And burn them. Their arrangement was beneficial for them; it was a living hell for Cammy.

Her patient reading tutor, who cheered her on when she caught fish and who personally baked her birthday cake each year, was also her torturer.

For ten years they plied the sea, and Jake himself was a sea of contradictions. When Cammy sustained a cut or an abrasion, Jake dressed it tenderly and monitored her healing with concern. In less compassionate moods, he burned her with cigarettes, with objects like spoons and cast-metal religious medallions that he first heated with a butane lighter, and with melted candle wax.

Her mother, having dissolved moral conscience with the chemical bliss of ecstasy, told her to be grateful for the generosity with which Jake shared his wealth and for his restraint. He hurt Cammy like that only twice a month, after all, always on the first and third Sundays, so she did not, Zena counseled, have to be afraid every day. Besides, he didn't mar her face or body, restricting his attention to her hands, her feet. And although the threat of sexual assault was present, he never touched her that way. Her obsequious obedience, her abject capitulation even to torture, gave him a sense of power that he needed. Her pain was his ecstasy.

"The poor thing's had a hard life," Zena told young Cammy. "His father was a psychiatrist. His mother was his father's patient. She suffered spells of ennui and psychosomatic rashes. Neither could heal the other. They conceived Jake as their cause, but he fulfilled them no more than did fund-raising for the symphony and donating to the opera. At night, he sometimes cries in my arms, he's so sweet."

Cammy never knew the significance of first and third Sundays or why burning mattered to him. He treated every burn with ointment, and when the wound healed, he kissed the scar and wept.

When she was eleven and a half, she learned that he had a gun. He kept it always loaded in a locked metal box, in a locked cabinet, in the galley. The day after her twelfth birthday, she discovered where he kept the keys to the cabinet and the box.

Cammy didn't act for three years. Later, she was shamed by this failure to free herself when the means to do so existed. She could not reason her way to an explanation or intuit one that satisfied and exculpated her.

After seven years of slavery, after being abused and humiliated and terrorized for so long, she had known no other way to live. All memories of her father had been washed away by time and by the tides of chaos on which **Therapy** cruised.

Despair was an emotion too intense to sustain for long. Somehow, she had allowed her despair to mutate into despondency instead of into desperation. Desperation was **energized** despair; it would have much sooner led to action, heedless of consequences. Despondency was the dismal incapacity to hope, and hopelessness fostered apathy.

The cake he made for Cammy's fifteenth birthday, however, was one cake too many. Although she could not explain why despondence abruptly became desperation, she got the keys, opened the cabinet, opened the metal box, went topside, and shot Jake Horner to death as he stood at the stern railing, watching dolphins frolic in **Therapy**'s wake.

She had learned how to drive the boat and navigate by watching Jake over the years. She needed three hours to make port.

Throughout the journey, Zena lay on the deck, cradling Horner's body, alternately singing to him and laughing. She had no ability to weep because she was so high on ecstasy that neither grief nor fear could touch her.

So confused had Cammy become by that decade of journeying from one possibility to the next, port to port, outrage to outrage, that she expected to be arrested and imprisoned for murder. For three years, she lived instead with her father's sister, Janice, who kept three dogs, two cats, and a horse, and thereafter she attended the university.

Eventually Zena went to prison. So many years of taking ecstasy gravely and permanently diminished her body's ability to produce endorphins, those peptides that stimulated feelings of happiness and that raised the pain threshold in times of injury and illness. In fact, after ten years of continuous chemical bliss, she could not feel unassisted happiness at all. And she was acutely sensitive to every smallest injury, so that to her a minor scratch felt like a saber slash and every headache was a splitting migraine. She served four years of her sentence before finding a way to hang herself in her cell.

*

The hands on the steering wheel could steer well, and the scars did not affect their function, and the things they had done to heal the innocent had redeemed Cammy from the dishonor of her servile submission to intimidation and disfigurement.

As she approached Grady's house, Cammy felt trapped as she had not been in twenty years. She feared that she might have no choice but to do something more terrible than she had ever done or had ever allowed to be done to her while aboard Jake Horner's **Therapy**.

If she cooperated with Paul Jardine and surrendered Puzzle and Riddle to him, she would have taken their freedom and consigned them to imprisonment, inevitably to anguish, and possibly to torments that she couldn't know. She would have betrayed the innocent that she was sworn to serve.

On the other hand, the laws that compelled her to cooperate with the authorities in a matter like this were reasonable laws. They were enacted to protect public health and ensure civil order. Thwarting those who enforced the statutes might land her in prison, might at least result in the revocation of her license to practice veterinary medicine.

But insofar as these laws related to animals, they concerned laboratory subjects on which experiments had been performed: animals that might have been intentionally infected with disease and needed to be contained for that reason, or animals whose release would put in jeopardy thousands of hours of important research that would have come to nothing without further analysis of the subjects.

Yes, and the nub of it was **there:** Puzzle and Riddle were not lab animals. They weren't engineered. She couldn't prove that contention, but she knew in her mind and heart that it was true.

Regardless of glow-in-the-dark pigs, pigs with organs suitable for human transplant, and pigs with human brains, scientists' ability to manipulate genes and create whole new life forms was not so far advanced that wondrous creatures like these could be conjured out of test tubes and petri dishes.

Paul Jardine and Homeland Security were hot about this, but not for the stated reasons. They knew something they were not revealing. An additional factor drove their crisis response. As astonishing as Puzzle and Riddle were, they were but a part of something bigger.

When Cammy stopped in Grady's driveway, Merlin and his new friends were chasing one another around the yard with great energy and with a joy that, in less somber circumstances, she would have found contagious.

She got out of the Explorer, and the three raced to her. She dropped to her knees, and they swarmed her, three tails lashing, panting happily.

As she stroked all three, scratched them, and told them they were beautiful, Cammy Rivers knew that whatever integrity she might claim depended on continued commitment to animals, that what honor she had regained would be lost forever if she did the wrong thing this morning. She could have no virtue without duty, and her hard-won self-respect hung now by a filament as thin as spider silk.

Forty-six

Henry Rouvroy braced the back door with a dinette chair once more, left the chair under the knob of the cellar door, and threw the bloody leather gloves in the trash can under the sink. Overcoming his aversion to touching the notepad, using a carrot-shaped magnet, he fixed the sheet of notepaper with the haiku to the refrigerator door for later study.

After he braced the living-room door with another chair, there was no entrance where the tormentor could gain easy access to the house with just a key.

In the bedroom, Henry went to the window facing out on a side lawn. At the end of the mown grass, the forest rose, but the trees weren't as closely grown as elsewhere, and they provided few points of concealment for someone conducting surveillance. Anyway, Henry suspected that if an enemy was watching the house, the observation post of choice would be the barn.

He unlatched the window, raised the lower sash, and exited with his shotgun. As he pulled the window shut, he slipped a tiny piece of notepaper between the sash and the sill. If the scrap was gone when he returned or was in a different position from the way that he left it, he would know someone found the unlocked window and perhaps waited inside.

As he walked around the house to his car, he moved cautiously when approaching corners or when passing any shrubs or structures from the cover of which a man with two thrust-and-cut weapons might overwhelm him before he could use the shotgun. A sane adversary would shoot him down from a distance when he revealed himself, but judging by the evidence, his tormentor might well have seen the inside of a psychiatric ward more than once in his life. The haiku and the pair of missing knives argued strongly that, for some reason, this enemy wanted the pleasure of doing the deed up close, regardless of the risk.

The Land Rover stood in the driveway near the stump that Jim used as a chopping block, where Henry had parked the day before. It remained locked, and the contents of the cargo hold appeared undisturbed. Henry backed the Rover to the foot of the front-porch steps.

When he got out of the vehicle, he glanced toward the barn and noticed that high in the gable wall, one of the two loft doors hung open several inches. He didn't believe—but couldn't be certain—that it had been open when he arrived the previous day. Intuition told him that some prone observer watched him from the darkness of the hayloft.

At the back of the Rover, he put down the shotgun on the porch, equidistant from the vehicle and the front door of the house. He couldn't complete the task at hand and hold the 20-gauge at the same time.

Henry opened the tailgate and began to transfer the weapons, ammunition, and other materials to the porch, beside the front door. From time to time, he glanced surreptitiously at the partially open hay door, and on one occasion he was certain he glimpsed movement in the loft, a paler shadow in the gloom.

By the time he finished this heavy work and locked the Rover, he was sweating both from the labor and from an increasing sense of vulnerability. Even when he had a two-hand grip on the shotgun again, he felt no safer.

When he returned to the bedroom window, he found the telltale scrap of paper precisely as he had left it. He entered the house through the window and locked it behind him.

In the living room, he removed the tilted chair from under the doorknob, opened the door, and transferred the former contents of the Land Rover to the house. After locking the door and bracing it with the chair once more, he opened a rectangular metal case lined with sculpted-foam niches. In each niche nestled a hand grenade.

Forty-seven

When Cammy started toward the house, Merlin and his buddies romped ahead of her, across the back porch, and inside, as if to announce her arrival.

Barefoot, in a T-shirt and pajama bottoms, Grady sat at the kitchen table, drinking coffee. "Have a cup?"

"Better get more presentable," Cammy said. "We're going to have a lot of company soon." As she poured coffee into a mug for herself and settled at the table, she gave him a condensed version of events and said, "I'm so sorry, Grady. I didn't think either Eleanor or Sidney would do anything like this, certainly not without discussing the situation first."

The coffee tasted fine, but her news appeared to sour him on it. He pushed his mug aside. "It's obvious in retrospect. But you can't have seen it coming."

"We could turn them loose in the woods," she said, and knew it was a lame solution.

"They'd come right back," he said, as a noise caused him to look toward the pantry.

"Oh, my," Cammy said as she saw Riddle standing on his hind legs and turning the doorknob with both hands.

"Just watch," Grady said.

Merlin and Puzzle were standing behind Riddle, waiting for him to finish the task.

When the door came open, Riddle dropped to all fours, entered the pantry, rose on his hind legs again, and switched on the lights.

Cammy eased her chair away from the table, rose quietly, and moved into the kitchen for a better view through the doorway.

Merlin remained an observer, but Puzzle went into the pantry with Riddle. The two climbed different walls of shelves, peering at the boxes, cans, and jars.

"I only saw the aftermath of their foraging this morning," Grady murmured as he joined Cammy. "I want to see how they do it."

Puzzle descended to the floor with a box of Cheez-Its. She sat, turning the box this way and that, apparently intrigued by the bright colors and the picture of the tasty little crackers.

When Riddle returned to the pantry floor, he had a small jar, the contents of which Grady couldn't identify. The creature studied the lid only a moment, then twisted it off.

Cammy said, "Grady, he shouldn't have that!"

She started toward the pantry, but before she'd taken two steps, Riddle had put the jar aside and thrust a jalapeño into his mouth. He issued an **"Eeee"** of shock and spat out the pepper.

Apparently, the remaining juice was nonetheless offensive, for he spat on the floor, spat on Puzzle, spat on himself, and made a repetitive sound of disgust: **"Eck, eck, eck, eck."**

"I'll get a slice of bread," Grady said, hurrying to a loaf on the counter by the ovens. "It'll cool his tongue."

Perhaps because the heat of the pepper lingered, Riddle became more alarmed. He raced out of the pantry and into the kitchen, wove past Merlin and circled Cammy twice before dashing into the hallway.

Grady started after him with the bread, but Riddle returned at top speed, dropped to his drinking bowl, and splashed his entire face in the water.

"Bread is better, short stuff," Grady said—and then looked at Cammy in shock. "What did I just see?"

For a moment, she couldn't answer him. What

they had both seen was Riddle running upright like a man, as no animal that sprinted as fast as a cat on all fours should be able to run erect. When he had wanted to run tall, something had happened to his hips, to his knees and hocks and stifles, as if the joints had the capacity to shift from one configuration to another as required.

Riddle raised his dripping face out of the water dish, plopped backward onto his butt, and suffered a sneezing fit.

Forty-eight

As in the night, Tom Bigger felt accompanied in the light. No one shadowed him on either the golden hills to the east or in the seaside fields to the west. No coyotes slunk, no great blue herons stalked. Yet he sensed that he was not alone.

Traffic increased with sunrise, and some southbound cars slowed as the approaching drivers glimpsed his hulking form, his ravaged face. He was an also-ran Elephant Man, a walking third-rate sideshow worth a few minutes of dinner conversation, a self-made monster who hadn't needed Nature's assistance to discover his inner horror and manifest it in his flesh.

Having walked throughout the night, Tom could not walk all day. At ten o'clock, he came to a motel where the vacancy sign, lit even in daylight to give it punch, was made a laughable understatement by the empty parking lot. This establishment was not a unit in a lodging chain, but a mom-and-pop operation, a little too cute in its details but perfectly maintained.

In times not too far in the past, he would have been turned away with minimal courtesy or none, not primarily because he was a fright to see, perhaps not even because his beard stubble and tequila eyes and backpack made him a hobo variant, but certainly because he had no credit card, no ID, and wanted to pay cash up front. Suppose that in a drunken fit he trashed the room—how would they track him down to make him pay? He had been turned away from places worse than this one.

But these were harder times than people had known in a while. Cash ruled, and even more so in a downturn when few people were spending either greenbacks or plastic. He figured they would take his money, because if they were too picky about their clientele these days, they might as well burn the business down and collect the insurance.

At the door to the motel office, he hesitated. He turned away, retreated a few steps, but halted and then faced the entrance again.

For as long as he could remember, Tom disliked going inside places where he had never been before. Whether it was this place or any other, crossing a threshold for the first time made him nervous.

In fact, at all times he preferred the outdoors, because if he crossed the path of the wrong person, he could simply walk away in any direction. Without walls and with sky above instead of ceiling, he had choices. Inside, obstacles to flight and limited exits were always a concern.

The wrong person would not be one who merely giggled at him or made a rude remark about his looks or his condition. He feared a more profound encounter with someone who strongly affected him in ways for which he was not prepared.

He didn't want to be affected. What had an affect caused an effect. **Affect** was another word for **change,** and Tom Bigger didn't want to change.

He was what he was, and he didn't know how to be anything else. At forty-eight, he'd been this way twice as long as he had not.

In the motel office, behind the registration counter, a white-haired guy, maybe seventy-something, was sitting at a desk, engrossed in a book. Wearing a gray cardigan over a white shirt, sporting a red bow tie, with a pair of half-lens reading glasses halfway down his nose, he looked as if he had been born an old man.

"Good morning, sir," he said, setting his book aside and rising. "What may I do for you this glorious morning?"

"Need a room," Tom said.

"Used to be bustling this time of the day, folks

checking out, all in a hurry to settle up and hit the road. As you see, I'm not at risk of breaking a sweat this morning."

"Walked all night," Tom explained.

"That's the smart way. When it's cool. And when traffic's light, so you aren't breathing exhaust fumes every step of the way."

The old man put a pen and a registration form on the counter.

"Don't have a credit card, don't have ID," Tom said. "Cash in advance is how I do it."

"Saves us both some bother. I've been hearing for forty years how cash money will soon be obsolete. There's not much of it floating around these days, but it's sure not obsolete. Just go ahead and print your name on the top line, sign at the bottom."

Tom did as instructed. Then he counted out the cash.

Presenting a key, the old man said, "Number twenty-four. Out the door here, turn left, and go to the end. Twenty-four is the last room in the north wing, so your sleep won't be interrupted this afternoon when all the big movie stars are checking in with their entourages."

"You have soda and ice machines?" Tom asked.

"End of the south wing. Enjoy your stay, Mr. Bigger."

In his room, Tom took off his backpack, dropped it on the bed.

He stared out the window at the empty parking lot.

He watched the fast traffic on the coastal highway.

He shut the draperies.

He looked at the TV but didn't switch it on.

On the bed lay a complimentary copy of **USA Today**.

He didn't pick it up.

He stared at his big bony hands.

He went into the bathroom.

He looked at his face in the mirror.

The old man in the cardigan had been reading a book, so he couldn't be blind.

Forty-nine

For a preliminary interview with his potential client, Liddon Wallace wore a dark-blue Ralph Lauren Purple Label suit, a shirt and tie from Costume National, shoes from Gucci, a Rolex watch—and just a touch of Black by Kenneth Cole, a fragrance for men.

Although his primary offices were in San Francisco and he lived in Marin County, across the Golden Gate Bridge from the city, Liddon was also a member of the bar in three other states, including the state of Washington. The amount of wealth in Seattle and environs, crossed with the tendency of the high-tech rich in particular to think they were wizards of the Web and above all laws, could from time to time lead to the kind of trouble that allowed a stylish lawyer to expand his closet space to infinity.

The potential client lived in a 28,000-square-foot Georgian Revival–style house on six walled acres. The guard at the gatehouse admitted Liddon to the property. A doorkeeper came outside to wait for him while he parked in the two-lane driveway. Once inside, the doorkeeper took his Ralph Lauren topcoat and turned him over to a butler, who led him to a drawing room where the future defendant waited for him.

If Liddon accepted the case, he would be compensated for his services by the client's father, Bob Marlowe. The twenty-two-year-old son, Swithen, was still making his way through college at a measured pace that had brought him to his junior year, and of course he had no job. The young man waited alone in the drawing room because Liddon always conducted the initial interview one-on-one.

Swithen was entirely outfitted by Costume National, head to foot, which suggested that he lacked the imagination to have an eclectic taste or that he was supremely self-confident. He was a handsome lad with a slightly pouty face; his thick and naturally windswept hair would be the envy of any male model.

During their initial chitchat, it became clear that Swithen understood how exemplary manners could be useful for crafting a good first impression. Evident as well was that his careful deportment was based on no underlying philosophy, only on self-interest, and that in fact he had disdain for society's rules.

Getting down to business, Liddon said, "So the charge against you is assault with intent to kill. Tell me about this boy, Branden Jones."

"He's no boy, sir. We've been friends since we were both six. He's a man like me."

"Yes, of course. Why would anyone think you did this to him?"

"Do you want to know if I did it?"

"I believe you've told the police you didn't do it."

"But as my defense attorney, sir, don't you want to know?"

"It's immaterial to me whether you're innocent or guilty."

"Really?"

"The way I work, it would only complicate my job to know."

Swithen visibly relaxed, slumping in his chair. "How long is this interview going to take?"

"Usually an hour or two."

"Let's not dance. Let's be two guys here. It's all about a bit."

"Excuse me?"

"A bit, a piece."

"Elucidate."

"A piece, a bit, a bitch, this girl—Rain Fishman."

"Her name is Rain, like the weather?"

"Yes. So tight and right."

"Tight and right?"

"Rain. She's mine and everyone knows it."

"You're engaged to her?"

"Who does marriage anymore?"

"What does Branden have to do with Rain?"

"He's a notorious poacher."

"You mean he makes moves on other guys' women?"

"He's poached more than the egg cook at a country-club brunch."

"Do you think he poached Rain?"

"What do you think I think?" Swithen asked.

"If he's gone after a lot of women, a lot of men must hate him."

"Oh, he's well and widely hated."

"So someone assaults him. Why did the police come to you?"

"Branden told them I did it."

"The victim says he saw your face?"

"You'll demolish him in court."

"How will I do that?"

"He's brain-damaged."

"The brain damage came from the assault?"

"Funny how a lug wrench can muddle your thinking."

"The weapon was a lug wrench?"

Swithen blinked slowly. "Or maybe a fireplace poker."

"What do the police say the weapon was?"

"They don't say. They don't have it."

"They'll have pictures and measurements of the victim's blunt trauma."

"The police are very professional here," Swithen agreed.

"They find the lug wrench, they'll match it to the wounds."

"And there's the blood on it, too," Swithen said.

"Lug wrenches aren't porous. The assailant would wash it clean."

"What if it didn't belong to the assailant?"

"Are we playing what-if now?" Liddon asked.

"Like on a TV mystery," said Swithen. "What if this would-be killer used some poor innocent bastard's lug wrench?"

"You mean, what if he took it from Poor Bastard's car trunk and put it back with blood on it?"

"It could be like that. Poor Bastard might be someone whose bit Branden poached and he even threatened Branden publicly."

"What-ifs are tricky to think through," Liddon cautioned.

"Yeah, like then how does the **real** assailant get the police interested in Poor Bastard?"

"Especially if he's already a suspect himself."

"Right. They have to think he might've set up Poor Bastard."

"The tip on Poor Bastard has to come to the

cops from a third party who's paid a bundle to do it but has no connection whatsoever to the real assailant."

"What-ifs **are** tricky, though," Swithen said. "If the real assailant tries to pay somebody to blow the whistle on Poor Bastard, he's asking to be blackmailed."

"There are safe ways to do it," Liddon said. "Several ways."

Neither of them spoke for a while.

Then Liddon said, "In court, are you sure you'd never use a word like **bit, piece,** or **bitch**?"

"Sure I'm sure. This was two guys talking. Court is serious."

Liddon nodded. "You've hired yourself a defense attorney. You're pretty much my ideal client."

Sitting up straighter in his chair, grinning, Swithen said, "I can't wait to see justice done."

"Even as imperfect as justice often is."

Neither of them moved to shake the other's hand.

"My dad's waiting to see you. I'll take you to him."

They crossed the drawing room, but before Swithen could open the door, Liddon said, "Wait. I have a what-if of my own."

"I'm getting good at this."

Liddon said, "What if you experienced something so astounding that it could turn your concept of life upside down, blow apart your idea of how the world works."

"Astounding—how, what?"

"Doesn't matter. Just say there was something that happened, something so difficult to get your head around, you needed to think hard about it."

"You have a close encounter of the third kind or something?"

"No. Something more astounding. Just say it's something, once you experience it, you need to think hard about it. But suppose you saw that chances were, if you thought about it enough, you would have to change almost everything about yourself."

"What's everything?"

With a sweep of his hand, Liddon indicated the elegant room with its priceless antiques and by extension the house and the inheritance.

With a wry contempt for the very concept of being astounded by anything, Swithen said, "And if I **don't** think hard about this experience? If I just say 'Screw it, I don't care what it means,' and instead I just keep on keepin' on?"

"Then nothing changes for you. You lead the life you always wanted to live."

"Then why is this even a what-if? I'm not that big a fool, and for sure, you're not."

Liddon didn't reply.

Frowning as though having doubts about his defense counsel, Swithen said, "What does this have to do with me, you, and staying out of jail?"

"Nothing," Liddon said. "If I hadn't already decided to say 'Screw it,' I wouldn't have come here. We both know what we want, and there's no reason we can't have it."

Clearly puzzled by this entire exchange, Swithen said, "You sure you're all right?"

"I'm more than all right," Liddon assured him. "I'm the best there is in a courtroom. If I put my mind to it, damn if I might not convince a jury that Branden Jones is the one who ought to be on trial for assault with intent to kill himself."

Fifty

After recovering from the jalapeño, Riddle apparently decided that the pantry might contain additional dangerous items that made another snack too risky. He turned out the light, closed the door, and sat with his back to it.

On the floor with her veterinarian, Puzzle seemed to think that she was the recipient of a most relaxing massage, for she purred and sighed as Cammy pressed firmly on all the joints of her hind legs in search of some indication of how Riddle could have performed as he did.

The previous evening, when she'd first seen the creatures, they impressed her as sophisticated mammals with some of the qualities of primates. By the time she had gone home, she regarded them more as primates. The complex and sustained curiosity they displayed by so methodically examining the contents of the living-room desk, the reasoning they revealed in their raid on the pantry, and the upright running posture that Riddle exhibited in his reaction to the hot pepper argued that they were hominids. But the only hominids on Earth were human beings and the extinct races of ape-men from which it was thought they had evolved.

Except for their well-articulated hands, Puzzle and Riddle did not **look** much like hominids. In truth she didn't know enough about evolutionary biology and anthropology to adequately classify any unfamiliar species or to properly compare this one to human beings.

While Cammy was still on the kitchen floor with Puzzle, Merlin padded in from the hallway.

Grady followed him, having quickly showered and dressed in expectation of the authorities. "While I was out of the room, did they suddenly reveal they can fly?"

"No wings yet. And I can't find anything odd about their joints by palpating them. I'd love to get X-rays. But what would they show, anyway? It's just not possible what happened—pretty much a dog-form leg straightening into a leg with an entirely vertical humanlike line of extension—and then back again. It's not simply a matter of two different structures for each ankle, knee, and hip joint. Muscles and tendons serving one kind of joint wouldn't likely stretch or torque perfectly to serve another kind."

"You ever see one of those crazy movies about cars and trucks that turn into robots?"

"Transformers. The science, technology, and mechanics of those things are ridiculous, just fantasy, they'd never work in the real world. What Riddle did shouldn't work in the real world, either, but we saw it happen."

"Maybe we're not in the real world."

"It seems more unreal by the hour," she agreed.

Pointing to the memory stick from his camera, which Cammy had put on the table, Grady said, "I've thought about it, and I'm with you on the photos."

Before leaving the clinic, she had loaded the photographs from the memory stick into her office computer and then had copied them onto three diskettes. Two of the diskettes were well-hidden at the clinic, and the third was tucked under the cargo-hold mat in her Explorer.

If Homeland Security claimed permanent possession of Puzzle and Riddle and eventually took them away, the photos were going to be blown all over the Internet with Grady's and Cammy's testimony. They would mount as strong a campaign as they could to free the creatures, risking prosecution under the National Security Secrets Act.

Puzzle and Riddle were not engineered animals.

No scientist on the planet possessed the knowledge or the technology to create them. They were mysterious, and if their origin was ever known, it would not be a cliché like recombinant DNA or extraterrestrial visitation, but something unexpected. No reasonable person could arrive at any sane scenario in which they were a threat to a single human being, let alone to the entire nation.

If Eleanor Fortney and Sidney Shinseki hadn't reported Cammy to the feds, and if Homeland Security hadn't moved so quickly, she might have tried to run Puzzle and Riddle out of the immediate area and find a place to keep them for a while, crazy as it might be to go on the lam with two creatures that seemed to be a cross between furry cherubim and Looney Tunes characters. But the authorities were already inbound, they knew her vehicle, and they had the forces to seal off the entire state. To go on the run successfully, she would have needed to leave the previous evening.

As if reading her mind, Grady said, "Maybe there's still time to turn them loose in the woods."

Stroking Puzzle, Cammy said, "They'd come right back. I know they would. They're socialized. They relate to people. Essentially, we're now a pack. And if they didn't come back . . . I'm not so sure how they'd fare in the wild."

"That's where I found them."

"But they hadn't been there long. Remember— no ticks, no fleas, their fur so clean."

Merlin issued a low, protracted growl as Cammy had never heard from him before.

Getting to her feet, she said, "Why does this have to happen?"

Body tensed, ears pricked, Merlin growled again and looked at the ceiling.

Puzzle and Riddle were on all fours, poised to sprint, heads cocked, listening.

After a moment, Cammy heard a familiar but not yet identifiable sound in the distance. Then she knew it: the hard, low clatter of helicopters.

"From the east, out of the sun, low and fast," Grady said, and hurried toward the front of the house.

Merlin, Puzzle, Riddle moved in the same in- stant, not in a play mood this time, but with ur- gency.

As Cammy reached the living room, Grady threw open the front door and stepped outside.

She caught up with him on the porch. Puzzle and Riddle sat on the steps in their prairie-dog mode. Merlin stood in the yard.

To the east, where Cracker's Drive met the state road, a large helicopter descended.

At an altitude of less than a hundred feet, an- other chopper continued uphill, following the county road. As it approached, Cammy realized the aircraft was even bigger than she first thought, the largest helicopter she had ever seen close up.

The rotors were loud, but they also slammed concussion waves across the slope, and Cammy's heart began to slam, too, harder and faster as the helicopter drew nearer.

Suddenly she decided that Puzzle and Riddle should not be out here, not in the open where they could be snatched up in an instant. They needed to be inside, behind closed doors, so the federal agents would need to go inside to get them.

To go inside, the feds needed a search warrant, didn't they? They probably had one. They probably had a court order to blow up the house if they were in the mood for pyrotechnics.

Nevertheless, a closed door was at least some kind of barrier, a way to delay surrendering custody of the animals, however briefly.

Cammy moved onto the steps, between Puzzle and Riddle, pulled at them, tried to herd them onto the porch and inside, but they were transfixed by the incoming chopper.

Above the thunder of the immense rotors, she shouted, **"Merlin!"**

The wolfhound heard her, he looked back, he understood that she wanted him, and he loped across the lawn to the steps.

"Let's go!" She shouted, **"House!"** which was one of his commands.

He bounded up the steps ahead of her. Although Puzzle and Riddle had not been interested in following her, they at once followed the dog, as she had hoped they would. The three scrambled into the house.

Cammy pulled the front door shut and returned to Grady's side.

East of the house, the helicopter touched down in the meadow, just past the end of the deep front yard.

The rotor-slashed air shook the big paper birch at the northeast corner of the house. Cascades of golden leaves fluttered down upon the porch, the yard.

At the back of the enormous chopper's main body, a bay door dropped, forming a ramp. Heavily armed, uniformed men hurried down the ramp, under the tail section. So many of them.

PART TWO

Death in Life

Fifty-one

Standing on the front porch with Cammy, watching the crisis team arrive, Grady knew something must be wrong. The response seemed out of proportion to the threat, if indeed any threat existed.

The chopper looked like a new generation—or a modified version—of the Huey with which he was familiar. The dark-green fuselage did not bear any numbers or insignia, and there was no legend identifying the military service or federal agency to which it belonged. The craft sported only a two-by-three-foot painting of the United States flag aft of the pilot's-cabin windows and before the side-entry sliding door.

The armed men who came down the tail ramp were dressed in black, like members of a SWAT team. Each had a sidearm in a swivel holster hung from his utility belt, and each carried what appeared from a distance to be a fully automatic carbine with an extended magazine. Some of them surely had been military at one time. None of them were military now; they were paramilitary agents of Homeland Security or of one bureau or another under its control.

Grady counted eleven. Ten of them tramped out of the meadow, heading down-slope and east on the county road, Cracker's Drive, and the eleventh proceeded to the point where the road terminated and Grady's driveway began.

If the chopper at the farther end of the road had been carrying as many, and if three were stationed at that intersection, eighteen were left to visit the other nine houses on Cracker's Drive, coming in from both directions, to tell those residents what was happening and/or to confine them to their homes.

Immediately after the first eleven debarked, four more appeared, also dressed in black but without carbines. They worked in pairs, between them guiding large wheeled crates, about six feet by four by four, down the ramp and onto the meadow.

Rotor speed dropped precipitously on touch-down, and now the pilot cut the turbines. When the rotors stopped cycling, the quiet, though imperfect, seemed like a hush.

"I'm sick," Cammy said.

He knew she didn't mean physically ill. She meant heartsick.

If they had entertained any hope that, when all this had blown over, Puzzle and Riddle might remain in their care, that hope was swept away by the amount of manpower committed to this investigation.

"It's not just about those two animals," Grady said. "There's something more we don't know."

"I had the same thought driving here earlier. Puzzle and Riddle are part of something bigger."

The sound of powerful truck engines rose along the county road, and soon what appeared to be a customized Greyhound bus rolled into view. The unpainted, matte-finish stainless-steel exterior appeared satiny in the sun. It might have been a motor home, except that it lacked windows along its flank and its engine sounded far more powerful than that of the average private or commercial conveyance of similar size. The wraparound windshield was so heavily tinted that the driver could not be seen.

As the armed agent stationed at the end of the road began to direct the vehicle into Grady's driveway, a second appeared behind it. As the first entered the driveway, which leveled out from the county route, and rolled past the house toward the garage and the workshop, a third appeared behind the second.

Eventually, the convoy consisted of four identical stainless-steel behemoths. They parked one behind the other, with a few feet between, nearly filling the driveway from end to end.

Referring to the vehicles as their engines were shut off one after the other, Cammy said, "Do they **try** to make them look ominous?"

"It's probably just form following function," Grady said.

"And what's their function?"

"Damn if I know."

The four men who had brought wheeled crates out of the transport helicopter were unrolling bales of flexible plastic gridwork across the yard. This material, when in place and locked, would form a solid base on soft ground.

Out of the east, fast and at a low altitude, shrieked a four-man helicopter. It banked to circle the property. Through the Plexiglas bubble, Grady saw the pilot and another man as they checked out the progress of the operation.

After two complete circuits, the chopper set down on the county road. One passenger, apparently the only one, got out of the craft. Pants billowing and suit coat flapping in the rotors' downdraft, he hurried toward the house as the pilot at once took the helicopter up and arced toward the east, from which he had come.

The newcomer, his sandy hair in disarray, proceeded directly to the foot of the front-porch steps. His handsome but rubbery face was reminiscent of the face of any hero's wisecracking best buddy in hundreds of movies, selling likability with every freckle, with ears slightly too large, with a minimal but endearing overbite, with blue eyes that were wide and clear and direct and twinkling more than a ballroom chandelier.

"Ah, Dr. Rivers," he said to Cammy. "What a marvelous thing to be a veterinarian. When I was a kid, my family had a cocker spaniel named Pete, I loved him more than anything, he got ill, almost died, and would have if our vet hadn't been so dedicated, so brilliant. Dr. Lowry was the vet's name. He was a **god** to me after that."

Before Cammy could reply, the newcomer looked at Grady and said, "Mr. Adams, I've seen your furniture, and it's wonderful. I've only seen photos, of course, on your website, but pictures never do that kind of thing justice, so it must be even more splendid, I hope you might show me what's currently under way in your workshop sometime before we wrap this and get out of your hair."

Grady instantly disliked the man. "Who're you?"

"I believe," Cammy said, "this is Mr. Jardine."

"I'm so sorry," the deputy director said. "I've seen photographs of you both, but of course you haven't seen any of me. Paul Jardine with Homeland Security. Pleased to meet you. And I do regret you're being inconvenienced like this. I'm grateful for your cooperation, your patriotism."

Jardine ventured onto the steps, expecting them to admit him to the porch, but by mutual unspoken agreement, they stood their ground, looking down on him.

"What are those stainless-steel vehicles?" Grady asked.

"Three of them are mobile laboratories. The fourth contains two Cray supercomputers capable of separate or tandem operation, immense analytic capability. We'll be drawing power from the utility-company lines to run the operation, but on the street side of your meter, so don't worry about being billed. Though we will need to tap your well, as there aren't public water mains out here."

Grady said, "I didn't know Homeland Security maintained its own paramilitary force."

"Oh, we don't, Mr. Adams. Setting up a training academy would be quite a long project and expensive. We contract them from a private company with excellent screening procedures to be sure we're getting only agents devoted to America and to the safety of the American people."

"Maybe we should get our politicians from the same company," Grady said.

"That's good," said Paul Jardine. "I'll remember that one, I'll make good use of it."

The armed agent who had directed the mobile laboratories into the driveway now joined Jardine, and the deputy director said, "Dr. Rivers, where are the two animals? I'm very excited to be able to see them, they appear incredible in your photos, we must get to work on our little mystery."

"They're in the house," Cammy said. "Do you have a warrant?"

"Yes, thank you so much for reminding me," Jardine said.

From one inside coat pocket he withdrew two folded documents. He examined them for a moment, then handed one to Grady.

"This is a facsimile of a warrant signed by a federal judge with jurisdiction in this district. The original will be here by courier shortly. You are herewith instructed by the court to give us full and immediate access to every building on the property as well as to the grounds in their entirety."

He handed the second document to Grady, as well. "The original warrant also gives us the right to impound any property we find that might be related to the commission of a crime or to a threat to the security of the American people. The second document I've just given you is a further and specific instruction from the court requiring you to relinquish custody of the two animals to us upon request, a request that I am at this time making. Mr. Adams, Dr. Rivers, will you please show me to these amazing creatures?"

Fifty-two

Cammy half hoped that Puzzle and Riddle had slipped out the back door and hightailed it into the mountains, regardless of their chances of survival in the wilds.

They were, however, in the kitchen. They weren't chowing down again, but were instead going through drawers in search of gadgets and other items that struck them as curious and appealing. Puzzle was standing on a chair positioned to allow her to look down into a drawer, holding out each discovery for Riddle's evaluation. When they found one they liked the looks of—an egg timer, a wine-bottle cork extractor of elaborate design, a packet of bright yellow cocktail napkins, ceramic-penguin salt and pepper shakers—they added it to an eclectic collection they were building on the floor in front of the dishwasher.

Perhaps anticipating trouble akin to the jalapeño episode, Merlin had retreated under the kitchen table. He lay there, peering out warily at his new friends as they ransacked the drawers.

When Jardine saw the wolfhound, he said, "Mr. Adams, please collar your dog."

"He's harmless," Grady assured the deputy director.

"Correct me if I'm wrong, but a couple of centuries ago, his kind hunted wolves virtually to extinction in Ireland. **Wolves,** for God's sake. I won't risk an attack by a dog that big. I'm ordering you to collar him."

"Good idea," said the armed agent. "I concur."

Cammy could see that the word **order** was not well received by Grady. Always surprised that the rough quality about him pleased her, she took particular pleasure from the menace in the glare that he directed at Jardine.

"You won't find a more peaceable breed or one with a gentler disposition," Grady said. "But I'll collar him to spare you the need to change your underwear."

Very nice, Cammy thought approvingly—and almost said it aloud.

Grady took a collar and leash from a Peg-Board, and Merlin crawled on his belly from under the table to submit to restraint.

Uninvited, another and particularly hulking

black-uniformed agent appeared from the hallway, carrying two pet crates. He put them on the floor and opened them.

"That one seems to be the male," Jardine said. "He might be agitated if you grab the female. So cage him first, Carter."

To this point, the golden-eyed individuals remained obsessed with exploring the kitchen drawers. Riddle startled but didn't resist when the most recently arrived agent, Carter, seized him by the scruff of the neck and by the tail, and manhandled him into a crate.

Merlin's restrained growl would not have frightened a wolf, but the disconcerted weasel said to Grady, "Keep that leash short."

"I'll kennel the other one," Cammy said.

"Please stay back," Jardine said, and in spite of the **please,** it was a warning. "These animals belong to us now, and we'll deal with them."

"But there's no need to handle them so crudely," she protested.

"For the record," Jardine said, "the animal didn't cry out or indicate in any way either that it was caused pain or even that it was frightened."

"They don't seem to know they should fear anything," Cammy said. "Maybe now they're going to learn."

Carter snared Puzzle from the chair and shoved her into the second crate.

Again Merlin growled, but he was too well-behaved to test his leash.

Infuriated by their insensitivity, Cammy said, "What's the matter with you? Look at them, look how beautiful they are, how amazing."

"Yes," Jardine replied, "they're pretty, they're very pretty, just like in their pictures. But whether they're pretty or not, we have a job to do, and we have to get on with it."

The spaces between the crossbars in the crate door would not allow Riddle to reach through and disengage the latch, but he tried.

From imprisonment, the animals regarded Cammy with bewilderment, as each of the uniformed agents carried a crate out of the kitchen.

No sooner had those two men cleared the doorway than another two entered the room, one after the other. Each of them carried an empty black duffel bag.

Jardine said, "Mr. Adams, officially you have five firearms in this house, but I'm sure you're in possession of others purchased before background-check applications were required. These gentlemen will accompany you room by room to collect those weapons."

"You have no right to confiscate my guns," Grady declared.

"We're not confiscating them, Mr. Adams. We're impounding them for the duration of this investigation, which is not only within our rights but is also our duty. You'll be given a receipt for them, and when we leave, the weapons will be returned to you."

Once Jardine had served the warrants and crossed the threshold, the movie-hero's-best-buddy persona had been stripped off and folded away in the costume trunk. Now he was who he had always been. His slight overbite no longer endeared him but was merely the better to gnaw at a bone. The blue eyes no longer twinkled, but darkled.

To Grady, he said, "Don't you think I would be a fool to leave such weapons in the hands of a marksman who has killed so many people at distances beyond a thousand yards?"

Although the marksman label came as news to Cammy, she found it strangely heartening instead of ominous.

Evidently mistaking the character of her surprise for shock, Jardine said, "So, Dr. Rivers, it unsettles you to know Mr. Adams was a sniper in the Army Rangers?"

"I'm not entirely sure why," Cammy said, "but it actually gives me a lovely sort of comfort."

"Every one of the men I took down," Grady said, "was as bad as a man can be. If you fear me having a gun, Mr. Jardine, then you must know something about your own character that I only suspect."

This time, Cammy could not keep it to herself: "Very nice."

The men with the duffel bags worked at being stone-faced, and they were reasonably successful, although they would never make it as guards at Buckingham Palace.

As if the deputy director had found Riddle's jar of jalapeño peppers and had tossed back its contents, his face appeared to swell tight, his lips paled, his cheeks flushed, and his eyes phased out of focus for a moment.

When he dared to speak, his voice was tight: "Your house phone and Internet connection have been disabled. These gentlemen will collect your cell phones and text-messaging devices. For the duration of this operation, any attempt to communicate with anyone beyond this property is a federal offense punishable by up to seven years in prison. Scientists on the team will be arriving over the next few hours. During these two days, you will from time to time be asked to answer questions about the two animals, their behavior, their demeanor. You're free to go to and from the labs to meet with them. At one o'clock this afternoon, I will debrief you here, in this room, Dr. Rivers. We will need two hours. At three-thirty, Mr. Adams, I will need two hours to debrief you. I am punctual. Please also be."

When Jardine turned his back on them to leave,

Merlin issued a single bark so loud it rattled the windows as much as it rattled the deputy director. He jumped, blasphemed, but wouldn't give the wolfhound the satisfaction of looking back at him.

While Grady went through the house, surrendering his guns to the agents with duffel bags, Cammy sat on the kitchen floor, telling Merlin that he was excellent, noble, true of heart, and wise.

As the agents departed, Cammy accompanied them and Grady onto the front porch. Several inflatable tentlike structures swelled into shape across the yard and in the meadow, the interlocking plastic grids serving as their floors and as the walkways between them.

"Sleeping quarters, mess hall, latrine, communications center, conference space," one of the agents explained as they descended the porch steps.

Cammy stood at the railing with the wolfhound and with the sniper who shot words and bullets with equal marksmanship.

He said, "It's like some circus from Hell is setting up for a two-day stand. They don't have any elephants, their acts are boring, and their clown isn't funny."

"Vivisection. Dissection of a living animal. What if **that's** on their agenda? What's going to happen to Puzzle and Riddle?"

"Nothing."

"But they're already gone."

"They're not gone. They're here."

"I don't see us getting them back."

"I do," he said.

"How?"

"Somehow."

Fifty-three

The grenades made Henry Rouvroy happy. He had worried that the haiku-writing sonofabitch had looted the Land Rover. If the grenades had fallen into the mysterious poet's hands, the balance of power would have shifted dramatically against Henry.

He enjoyed sitting on the living-room floor, staring at the grenades, handling the grenades, and even kissing them. The casing of a hand grenade was actually a steel waffle of shrapnel waiting to be blown apart and rip savagely through the bodies of everyone within range. It was a beautiful thing.

The senator, whom Henry had served as chief aide and political strategist, had acquired considerably more ordnance than Henry could have dreamed of getting his hands on, but right now the grenades and his cache of firearms were enough.

When civil order collapsed, the senator would be at a specially prepared retreat, one of many that were well-concealed and protected for the highest of high government officials. He expected Henry to come with him and his family to ride out the half year or year of blood in the streets. But Henry knew in his bones that the social tension in a remote and fortified compound with a slew of politicians and their kin could lead only to paranoid suspicion, ferocious infighting, and eventually cannibalism. While allowing the senator to think he was in for the plan, he made plans of his own. Henry didn't want to be eaten alive.

Now he began to distribute the grenades throughout the house, hiding them under cushions, in drawers, under chairs. If his enemy launched an assault on the place, Henry wanted to have a grenade always within arm's reach, so he could open a window and surprise the hell out of the bastard, blow his booty off and put an end to this game. He hid twenty-nine grenades and decided to carry the last one with him everywhere he went until he killed his tormentor.

When he finished, he noticed the disgusting filth under his fingernails. He didn't know how he could have gotten so grimy just unloading the Rover. Manual labor was such dirty work, it was amazing that the blue-collar class didn't lose millions a year to pestilence and disease.

He returned to the bathroom, drew a sinkful of hot water, and set to work with cheaply scented soap and with the clever brush that he had discovered the previous night. He scrubbed diligently for forty minutes before his hands were clean enough to satisfy him. His nails were white and shiny.

As he dried his hands, he wondered if something more than a desire for cleanliness drove him to wash his hands until they were fiery red from hot water and bristle abrasion. Having graduated from Harvard, he knew quite a lot about psychology. Excessive washing of the hands could be a subconscious acknowledgment of guilt. Perhaps murdering his brother had affected him more deeply than he thought.

Well, what was done could not be undone. One thing you learned from a good education was to face the reality of existence and not live with the illusion that wrong was always wrong and right was always right. Sometimes wrong was right, and sometimes right was wrong, and most of the time neither word applied. Think, do, accept, move on.

In the kitchen, as he was preparing an inadequate lunch from the pathetic provisions left to him by his departed kin, he heard noises in the attic. Someone was crawling around up there.

Fifty-four

Monday morning, less than two hours after his meeting with Liddon Wallace on the eighteenth green, Rudy Neems flew out of Seattle to San Francisco.

He had told the attorney that he would make the trip that afternoon. He also promised to kill the wife and son Tuesday night.

In both instances, Rudy lied.

He didn't trust Liddon Wallace. A guy who hired you to kill his family couldn't be relied on to treat you with fairness and respect.

Wallace admitted having other guys like Rudy on tap. Say one of them was named Burt.

Say Burt's job was to be waiting in Rudy's hotel room when Rudy got back from killing Kirsten and her little boy.

Say Burt killed Rudy and made it look like suicide.

The suicide note, composed by Burt in a perfect imitation of Rudy's handwriting, might say Rudy killed a lot of girls over the years and hated himself and hated Liddon Wallace for getting him acquitted in the Hardy case when what he really wanted was for someone to stop him before he killed again.

Alive, Rudy was a loose end. Dead, he couldn't rat on Wallace.

With Rudy dead, you wouldn't want to be Burt.

Say one of Liddon Wallace's other guys was named Ralph—or it could be Kenny or anything. When Burt returned to his **own** room in the hotel, maybe Ralph would be waiting for him.

Ralph wouldn't know that Burt just killed Rudy, so when Burt was dead, no one survived who could link the attorney with the murders of his wife and child. No more loose ends.

Or maybe when Ralph returned to **his** room in the hotel, Kenny—or maybe his name might be Fred—was waiting to kill him. Maybe it just went on and on until the hotel filled up with dead people.

Rudy Neems possessed sufficient self-awareness to know he was paranoid. That was one of the reasons why he killed people. Although not the primary one, of course, because if it had been the primary reason, he would have been insane.

Rudy was as sane as anyone. He did not kill in mad rages. He knew exactly why he killed. His motivation was complex and arrived at by reason: masterless freedom.

So he lied to Liddon Wallace. He flew out of Seattle eight hours before he said he would. And Rudy intended to kill Kirsten and Benny that same night rather than on the following night, when Burt would be waiting to kill Rudy.

The flight from Seattle could not have been more pleasant. They encountered no turbulence, and they didn't crash.

Rudy chatted all the way with Pauline, an elderly woman en route to San Francisco for the birth of her great-great-grandson.

She carried a little album of snapshots of her family. She had pictures of her two cats, as well. They were cuter than her family.

Rudy had no desire to kill Pauline. Because he didn't have sex with elderly women, he never killed elderly women.

At the baggage carousel, Pauline's daughter and son-in-law were waiting for her. Their names were Don and Jennifer.

Pauline introduced Rudy as "the angel who made me forget all about my fear of flying."

In fact, Rudy chatted with seatmates on airplanes because he, too, feared flying. He needed to distract himself from thinking about all the things that could go wrong in the air. Like, say, an engine might fall off, probably because a mechanic sabotaged it.

At the airport, he picked up a rental SUV and headed for the Golden Gate Bridge and Marin County.

Rudy disliked cities. They were chaotic.

Being a golf-course groundskeeper might be the best job in the world. The golf environment remained at all times quiet, serene, orderly, manicured.

And the work didn't require constant thinking. While you did your job, you could let your mind roam.

On the job, Rudy mostly replayed in memory all the murders that he committed. Indulging in hours of nostalgic recollection seemed to be one reason he could restrain himself for so long between killings.

Another reason that he killed no more than two people a year was because he only killed people whom he found attractive, and very few people met his standards.

There were guys who could do any halfway-appealing woman they met. Rudy would never be one of them. They were transgressing on the installment plan, rebelling against moral order in a tedious series of minor skirmishes. By contrast, Rudy launched only powerful and profound attacks.

Fifty-five

After arriving by executive helicopter at the site, logging in, and signing nondisclosure agreements customized to the unusual nature of this incident, Lamar Woolsey and Simon Northcott were presented with laminated holographic photo-ID cards on lengths of cord, which they had to wear around their necks at all times.

Following an in-depth background presentation on the situation, they were told where to find Specimen 1 and Specimen 2. Already, the names given to them by the veterinarian, Camillia Rivers, were being used by both the uniformed security agents and the Homeland Security bureaucrats: Puzzle and Riddle.

The animals were confined in an inflatable tent in the backyard, only steps from the line of four mobile laboratories. Blood, urine, and other tissue samples would be collected here and taken to the labs. When needed for an MRI or other test, the animals would be conveyed to the laboratory containing that specific equipment. By keeping Puzzle and Riddle primarily in a structure accessible to the personnel in all four labs, several scientists could observe and examine them at the same time.

The twenty-foot-square tent had been anchored to forty pitons. Each eighteen-inch-long piton measured an inch in diameter and had been driven into the earth with a pneumatic hammer.

Access to the tent was through an uninflated flap, next to which stood an armed agent. They flashed their photo ID and went inside.

Interlocking panels of tight plastic grid made a stable floor. Four free-standing racks of adjustable lamps provided illumination.

A nine-foot-long, seven-foot-wide, four-foot-high platform occupied the center of the tent. The platform held an eight-by-six steel cage that the Colorado crisis-response team acquired somehow before leaving their home base in Colorado Springs.

In the cage were a bowl of water, a dog bed—and two creatures who were inexpressibly more beautiful than the photos of them that Lamar had seen during the background briefing. They came at once to the wall of the cage and reached out en-treatingly, between the bars, with their small black hands.

The sight of them affected Simon Northcott as nothing and no one ever had before: He was stunned silent.

As Lamar approached the cage, he reached out to hold one hand of Puzzle's, one of Riddle's.

The feeling that came over him must have been different from the one that rendered Northcott speechless, for he would have ranted his enchant-ment in whatever humble poetic language he could summon—if anyone had been present who would understand this most human of all yearn-ings for mystery and meaning.

These animals had about them an aura of inno-cence and purity that he found almost palpable, that he had never before encountered nor imag-ined he ever would. He approached them rapt with wonder, but then found himself surrendering to an unexpected veneration for which he had no explanation. He came to tears.

Moving slowly around the cage, intently study-ing the animals and oblivious to Lamar's emotion, Northcott broke his uncharacteristic silence and spoke of things that didn't matter, of things that Lamar could not compute.

When at last Lamar could speak, he said, "Their

eyes. Isn't it ironic, Northcott, that perhaps the principal challenge they offer you is the impossible nature of their eyes?"

Northcott understood his reference and was not pleased.

Fifty-six

On the kitchen table stood a two-foot-square multilayered pane of sandwiched glass, held in a steel frame between two three-inch-diameter steel cylinders. Red light shown within a penny-size hole near the top of each cylinder. The device plugged into a wall outlet but also into Paul Jardine's laptop.

Cammy had been told that lasers scanned her eyes for responses of the irises, recording a continuous measurement of the dilation of her pupils, which assisted in determining the truthfulness of her answers because the pupil involuntarily opened wider when a lie was told. Other changes in the eye, unspecified by Jardine, were also evidently analyzed.

At the start of the session, the lasers also mapped her face as expressionless as she could make it.

Thereafter, a continuous record of her facial to-pography detected the subtlest nuances of expression that researchers had found to be associated with either truth-telling or prevarication.

This laser polygraph had been developed exclusively for Homeland Security. Jardine used it in conjunction with a tightly fitted glove woven full of electronic sensors that measured changes in the body activities that were of interest to more traditional polygraphers: pulse, blood pressure, perspiration.

Before being subjected to the session, she had been provided with a statement signed by Jardine in the presence of a witness, stating that no information obtained herein could be used against her in any court of law and that she was immune from prosecution for any matters touched upon by his questions and her replies.

"We are more determined to get the full truth of all this than we are interested in prosecuting anyone for anything," Jardine had said.

On the other hand, once she had been granted immunity, if she still declined to be polygraphed, she could be prosecuted under two statutes that, upon conviction, allowed for consecutive sentences totaling as much as four years in prison.

When Cammy had still hesitated, Jardine said, "Look at it this way. If you want to lie your head off, you can do so with no fear of punishment. You've got immunity. But if you lie, it's still worth my time to conduct this debriefing, because I'll see when you're lying and I'll have some hope of deducing **why**."

"I have no intention of lying to you."

"By the time we've gotten this far," Jardine had said, "no one ever intends to lie."

Now, an hour into the interrogation—which Jardine insisted on calling a **debriefing**—the blinds were closed over the kitchen window and door. Light came only from the soffit lamp over the sink and the screen of the deputy director's laptop.

Cammy couldn't see the low-intensity lasers. They were of a single specific wavelength of light or a narrow band of wavelengths, and all the crests of the individual waves coincided. Although the beams were invisible to her, she sometimes thought she saw shadows tremble or leap in her peripheral vision, where in fact nothing moved.

She had not once lied to him. His questioning was meticulous but unimaginative, therefore tedious. Then one of two moments came that were different from all the rest of the session.

He looked up from his laptop and regarded her through the pane of sandwiched glass. "Dr. Rivers, have you been to the state of Michigan in the past two years?"

"No."

He returned his attention to the laptop. "Have you **ever** been to the state of Michigan?"

"No."

"Have you ever heard of Cross Village, Michigan?"

"No. Never."

"Have you ever heard of Petoskey, Michigan?"

"No."

"Have you ever known anyone from Michigan?"

She thought for a moment. "In college, veterinary college, there was this woman from Michigan."

"Where in Michigan was she from?"

"I don't remember. We weren't close friends or anything."

"What was her name?"

"Allison Givens. We called her Ally."

"Is she in veterinary practice in Michigan?"

"I assume so. I don't know. I didn't stay in touch with her."

"Have you stayed in touch with anyone from vet school?"

"Yes. A few."

"Have any of them stayed in touch with Ally Givens?"

"I don't know. I don't think so. They've never said anything. What's all this about Michigan?"

"Please remember, as we discussed, I ask the

questions, you answer them, not the other way around."

Either he had come to the end of that subject or he did not want to pursue it with her curiosity raised. He moved on to her experiences with Puzzle and Riddle.

Almost an hour later, as the session was drawing to a close, he asked a question that was a verbal punch.

"Dr. Rivers, have you ever killed anyone?"

Stunned, she met his eyes through the glass.

He repeated the question. "**Cammy,** have you ever killed anyone?"

"Yes."

"Who did you kill?"

"My mother's boyfriend."

"What was his name?"

"Jake Horner. Jacob Horner."

Jardine didn't bother consulting the graphics on his laptop screen. He knew that she was telling the truth.

"That was on your fifteenth birthday, wasn't it?"

"Those police records, the court hearing—that's all sealed."

"That was on your fifteenth birthday, wasn't it?"

"Sealed. It's all sealed. I was a juvenile. Nobody has the right to know about that."

Jardine's eyes gave out no light in the gloom, but

in the glow of the computer screen, Cammy could see them well enough to recognize his contempt.

He said, "Was it ten years aboard **Therapy**? Ten years? Was it ten years, Cammy?"

In addition to his contempt, she saw his rich satisfaction in her reaction, her distress.

He had the power to reveal her ten-year ordeal and thereby to ensure that, ever after, when people looked at her, they would see her past in her present and would disdain her or, worse, pity her.

This was his way of guaranteeing her perpetual silence about Puzzle and Riddle, and her meek cooperation.

She stripped off the glove woven full of electronic sensors and threw it on the table.

"That's it," she said. "I'm finished."

"Yes," Jardine said. "I believe you are completely finished."

Fifty-seven

The noise in the attic came and went, came and went. Sometimes it was a crawling sound, like someone shuffling from eave to eave on hands and knees. At other times, someone softly rapped out rhythms on a ceiling beam.

Henry walked through the house, back and forth, gazing at the ceiling, tracking the sounds. Wondering.

Standing in the bedroom closet, staring at the attic trapdoor, listening to the rapping, rapping, rapping on the back of that panel, which was bolted from below, he began to think of the sound as being more precise than mere rhythm. This was measured rhythm divided into stanzas. This was **meter,** as if some poet living in the garret above was composing new lines and rapping out the meter as he wrote.

When this thought fully flowered in his mind, Henry decided not to listen to the rapping anymore. He returned to the kitchen to continue preparing his lunch.

Later, as he ate, he wondered what the secret retreats were like where the senator and the other power elites would hide out when the social order had been purposefully pushed into collapse. He supposed they would be far more comfortable and better-provisioned quarters than any Henry could arrange for himself.

Of the many hundreds of billions of dollars that had gone out the treasury door, not all had been wastefully spent. Fully a third of it had been cleverly and secretly transferred into the accounts of those who had devised this strategy for the remaking of the world, which included numerous politicians but also many private-sector entrepreneurs.

The senator and those with whom he ran had panicked just once, when an investigative journalist with the **Post** reported that seventy billion of funds were gone and unaccounted for from just one package of the economic stimulus. But the public seemed indifferent. And considering that the **Post**'s number was woefully short of the true figure, the reporter's sources could not be inside the circle of the conspiracy.

It was during that crisis-that-never-was that Henry decided not to throw in with the senator but to make his own preparations. Now, as he listened to the rapping in the attic, to the rapping that he was **not listening to,** he wondered if he had made a serious mistake when he had come west to become his brother.

Fifty-eight

For the first time in memory, Tom Bigger slept deeply and peacefully. The trouble began when he woke.

Usually, dreams poured from a reservoir of venom and flooded sleep. In the murk of sunken cities and drowned countryside, he moved ceaselessly, going nowhere and seeking nothing, but going and seeking with quiet desperation nonetheless. Out of submerged streets, down from fathomless hills, along lonely airless roads came half-seen figures to menace him. In perpetual flight, he breathed water with increasing panic, until he woke and breathed air. Awake and sometimes while asleep, he suspected that every one of those who menaced him was only a shrouded aspect of himself.

At 4:15 Monday afternoon, after a uniquely

dreamless sleep, Tom woke, and the real world felt as airless as his usual dreams. A suffocating need oppressed him. In this condition, he found relief only and always in one thing: spirits of the bottled kind.

Having been unable to still his restless mind, which had circled incessantly around the memory of the incident on the bluff above the sea, Tom had stretched out on the bed with no expectation of sleep, still wearing his clothes. Now he sat up, stood, moved toward the motel-room door, hoping that fresh air might relieve his sense of suffocation.

One step short of the door, he turned from it and went to his backpack. The previous night, from a bridge, he threw an unsampled pint of tequila into a dry creek. Five pints remained in his supply.

He extracted a stuffsack from the backpack, a bottle from the sack. The glass was smooth in his rough hands, smooth and cool.

The journey ahead and the task at its end required commitment, focus, sobriety. He had spent his life fleeing from all three.

Smooth and cool.

Considering that he was forty-eight, still alive, and not in jail, an argument might be mounted that he had fared better than some who made more responsible decisions than he did. Fundamental change at his age might bring the opposite of what he desired; he might be trading failure and sorrow **not** for hope and peace, but for worse misery and despair.

One incident, one moment of recognition in decades of barren existence, did not justify a revolution of the mind and heart. At the time, his head and stomach turning in spirals of vertigo, he had been vomiting into a barrel, not a situation in which his perceptions or his judgment were necessarily reliable.

The pint bottle of tequila felt smooth, cool, full of power, full of promise, the power of forgetfulness, the promise of death by incremental self-destruction. The power of the tequila passed through the glass container and into his clutching fingers, causing his hand to shake, then his arm, then his entire body. The tremors shivered cold sweat from his palms, and he gripped the suddenly slippery bottle with both hands.

Although he needed a drink, a long one, he intended instead to empty the bottle into the bathroom sink.

He stood no more than six steps from the bathroom door. The sink lay one or two steps beyond that threshold. Eight steps. During the previous night, he walked mile after mile. Now eight steps seemed to be a greater distance than he traveled from his cave to this room.

Except for the shakes, Tom Bigger couldn't move. He trembled so violently that his teeth chattered and each exhalation stuttered from him, but he could not uproot either of his feet.

He must have been in a brief fugue when he twisted the cap off the bottle, for he had no memory of cracking the seal. Suddenly the cap lay on the floor between his feet, and with the mouth of the bottle to his nose, he inhaled the fumes of death in life.

Another fugue—how long?—and somehow the familiar taste was in his mouth, and the fragrant toxin dripped from his chin. Held in both hands, the bottle revealed the weakness of his will, for the level of the tequila was an inch lower than before.

Inch by inch, he would lose the future, the world, the hope that he had so recently allowed himself, and he knew what he must do. He must slam the bottle against his face, slam it and slam it until it shattered, puncturing and slashing his face, perhaps this time bleeding so much, so fast, he would be done with life at last.

But he was a coward, gutless, not energized by self-hatred but paralyzed by it.

The motel-room door opened, and with the flood of daylight came screaming. Screaming and sobbing simultaneously, the most wretched and despairing cries that Tom had ever heard.

In the sunlight, on the threshold, stood the

seventy-something man in the cardigan, the front-desk clerk who had told him to enjoy his stay. Beyond the man stood an old woman with a cell phone in her hand.

Neither of them was screaming or sobbing, and then Tom realized that **he** was the source of these terrible lamentations, a howling siren of anguish and grief and self-loathing.

Tom tried to warn off the desk clerk, for fear his rage would at last turn outward. In another fugue he might smash the bottle against that kindly face and slash the old man's jugular with a shard of glass.

Indeed, another fugue took him. But the next thing he knew, he was sitting on the edge of the bed, no longer clutching the pint of tequila.

The old man held the bottle, twisting shut the cap. He set it on the dresser.

No screaming anymore. Just the sobbing.

The old man returned to Tom and put a hand on his shoulder. "I've never been in your place, son. But maybe if we talk about it, I can help you find a way back from where you are."

Fifty-nine

Paul Jardine wanted two hours for the debriefing, but after five minutes, Grady said, "This is bogus. I'll give you half an hour. Keep it tight, get it done. If half an hour isn't enough, bring charges against me, and I'll fight for full disclosure in an open court."

When Jardine began reciting the statutes under which a citizen could be prosecuted for failure to cooperate in a national-security matter after being granted immunity, Grady closed his left eye and slightly squinted his right, as if sighting a target. He whispered, "CheyTac M200," the name of the favored sniper rifle in the services.

Jardine understood. For a moment he considered Grady's skills and reputation. The deputy director proceeded with less arrogance, in a more succinct style of interrogation.

When they were done, Grady took two bottles of beer from the refrigerator and joined Cammy—and a subdued Merlin—on the front porch. She sat in one of the rockers, watching four more scientists disembarking from yet another executive helicopter at the end of Cracker's Drive.

"Thanks," she said, taking a beer. "Done already?"

He sat in another rocker. "People think power makes them big, but it brings out their inner bratty child and makes them small."

"You ever been to Michigan?" she asked.

"Yes. And that sure did interest him."

"What do you think's happening in Michigan?"

"Something. We knew this was bigger than Puzzle and Riddle."

After a silence, she said, "You told me you were in the army. You've never said much more."

"Joined up when I was eighteen, after my mom died of cancer. I thought there must be something better than these mountains."

"Some reason you don't want to talk about it?"

"No. Except it makes me bitter. I don't like being bitter."

"Can you really target someone at a thousand yards, like Jardine said?"

"Much farther. All the way out to twenty-five hundred yards. The rifle comes with various sighting aids. With the CheyTac, you use a .408-caliber, 419- or 305-grain round. One of those tends to do the job."

"Where was this?"

"Mostly Afghanistan. Some Iraq. Terrorists, mass murderers. They don't even know they're spotted. Scope them out, take them down. As far as war goes, it's about as humane as it gets. Snipers don't cause collateral damage among civilians."

"It's a long way from that to making furniture," she said.

"It's a long way from that to anything."

"Where's the bitterness come in?"

"My best friend. Marcus Pipp. He was on my sniper team. The other side has snipers, too. They look for us looking for them. Marcus took one in the neck. It didn't need to happen."

"Then why did it?"

"This grandstanding senator back home holds up a photo of dead women and children in an Afghan village. Marcus—he's in the picture with his rifle. Senator is so sure we kill for the thrill of it, he doesn't even try to get his facts straight. He names Marcus for the press, demands a court-martial. The Taliban killed those people, and all we did was find the bodies."

"Surely Marcus wasn't court-martialed."

"No. Army set the senator straight, though he

never apologized. Marcus saw his photo on the Internet, newspaper stories with captions all but calling him a baby-killer. It upset him."

"But it wasn't true."

"You had to know Marcus. Sounds funny—he was like my mom in some ways. It wasn't he never lied—he **couldn't** lie. And the army mattered to him. He believed in the use of righteous force. He knew what the world would be like without it. The lie wasn't just about him, it was about the **army,** about this country and its people. The injustice ate at him, distracted him. You can't be distracted on a sniper team. Your focus is your fate. I saw how he was. I thought he'd get over it. I should have done a lot more to get him centered again. I didn't, he was careless, and he died two feet from me."

"You can't blame yourself."

"If we aren't here for one another, why are we here?"

Beyond the porch, the bureaucrats and the armed agents of the Department of High Anxiety bustled this way and that through their inflated settlement, saving the nation from the threat of wonder and joy.

Lying beside Grady's chair, the wolfhound raised his noble head occasionally to watch one passing individual or another. None of them inspired him to wag his tail.

After a while, Cammy said, "What're we going to do about Puzzle and Riddle?"

"Stay focused. Be ready to act when the opportunity arises."

"What if the opportunity doesn't arise?"

"It always does, if you stay focused."

Sixty

Having changed from shoes to slippers but still in cardigan and red bow tie, Josef Yurashalmi shuffled around the table, finishing the place settings with white linen napkins precisely folded to display the single, small embroidered bouquet of colorful flowers on each.

Hannah, Josef's wife, was busy testing the tenderness of the vegetables in a soup pot on the stove. Tom had first seen her outside his motel room, holding a cell phone, on which she had been ready to call an ambulance or the police.

The couple owned the motel and lived in a tidy apartment that constituted the small second floor above the office. There was a dining room, but Josef said, "The older I get—and nobody's getting older faster than me—the more I prefer cozy. The kitchen table is cozier."

Moving through their quarters and then sitting at the table as the elderly couple prepared dinner, Tom felt clumsy in build, awkward in motion, gauche, and out of place. He was bewildered to be there, unable to explain to himself why he had not taken up his backpack and fled. Josef and Hannah were together a force of nature, a wind both gentle yet powerful enough to sweep him to the place they wished him to be.

Although he had washed his face and hands in their guest bath, Tom felt grimy compared to their meticulously clean apartment. He had combed his unruly hair as best he could with his fingers, and buttoned the collar of his denim shirt.

Hannah filled bowls with beef noodle soup, and Josef put them on the table. Potatoes, carrots, and lima beans enriched the soup. Tom had eaten nothing as tasty as this in many years.

The second course was a slice of a molded gelatin salad full of finely chopped carrots and celery. Tom expected not to like it, but he did.

Fried fish patties followed, made from flaked halibut, mashed potatoes, eggs, and minced onions. On the side were succotash and sweet-and-sour beets.

Tom Bigger had not eaten home cooking like this in longer than thirty years. Considering that he drank more calories than he ate every day, he was surprised that his shrunken stomach suddenly had the capacity for everything that was put before him.

Josef and Hannah did most of the talking, or so it seemed to Tom, yet more surprising than the capacity of his stomach was the fact that he told them where he was going and what he hoped to do when he got there. He never revealed himself to people—until now.

He didn't tell them about the incident on the bluff above the sea or about the coyotes. Those things were his to keep until he proved that he could make the journey and complete the task.

Over dessert—lemon-cream pie—Josef offered to drive Tom to his destination after dinner. Tom gratefully declined six different ways. In spite of his failure to accept the favor of a ride, his hosts began to talk about the best route and estimated driving time—two hours—as though Josef and Tom would be leaving shortly.

When Tom expressed concern about Hannah being alone, the couple explained that the evening-shift clerk, Francisco, now manned the front desk downstairs. And in an emergency, Rebecca, their daughter, and her family lived only fifteen minutes away.

Tom found a seventh reason why he must politely decline, and he insisted that their offer was too generous, but at the conclusion of dessert, Hannah encouraged Josef to "say **bentshen** and

hit the road." **Bentshen** proved to be a benedic-
tion, a grace said following dinner, after which
Josef went to the master bathroom to "say hello to
Mother Nature," and Tom used the guest bath.
Hannah waited at the apartment door and hugged
each of them, and Tom followed Josef down the
stairs, through the motel office, outside to a thirty-
year-old Mercedes sedan idling in front, where it
had been brought by Francisco. The evening clerk
also fetched Tom's backpack from his room, put it
in the trunk, provided four bottles of cold water in
an insulated carrier in case they got thirsty during
the trip, and stood waving at them as they drove
out of the motel parking lot and north on the
highway.

Tom had long been afraid of crossing the threshold of a new place for the first time, lest he have an
encounter with the wrong person, one who profoundly affected him and forced in him a change.
In his gray cardigan and bow tie, still wearing slippers because "they're comfier than shoes to drive,
and when you get to be my age, which is a number
Methuselah would envy, comfy matters more than
style," Josef Yurashalmi was that wrong person, the
embodiment of Tom Bigger's fear.

Although Tom had long been all but humor-
less, the realization that the dreaded agent of
Apocalypse turned out to be this sweet old man
might have inspired a laugh under other circum-

stances. But he was no longer a ten-day walk from the task that he must perform; only two hours would bring him to it. He lived for decades as a coward, and now with an onerous confrontation rapidly approaching, he had no well of courage to tap.

Sixty-one

In the room, all day the people come and go, excitement high but voices often low.

The light is bright but not as bright as the light of their becoming. Still, the night would be nicer, the big full moon and all the shining stars.

Men and women come and go, and some return, and later yet return again, and always they appear and disappear through the same drapery, which falls shut behind them.

Directly opposite that entrance in the western wall is another entrance in the east. There the drapery is fixed, zippered shut, and no one comes and no one goes by that portal.

Some people stand close and stare, and accept an offered hand, while others sit in chairs to watch, record their notes or take them down by hand.

Sometimes they confer with one another, usually

in murmurs and hushed voices. Now and then, they speak louder and with passionate intent, but it is always an angerless argument.

In their cage, Puzzle and Riddle listen with interest to the voices of their visitors, to the music of the voices, to the rhythm of the voices, voices, voices.

They have water, and food is given twice. All is well, and all will be well, as it has been well since their becoming.

This is a time of waiting, and the two wait well, for waiting is only an acceptance of the ways of time. Occasionally slow and on other occasions faster, yet in truth always at the same pace, time flows forward toward one shining moment or another, toward the place where they will fully belong then, as they fully belong in this place now.

In the room, the people come and go, and in time they only go, until dust motes float in the bright light, in the stilled air.

In the night beyond the drapery waits the one who admits all the others. His scent is a scent of weariness, loneliness, and yearning.

Quietly in the quietness, Puzzle works the zipper on the cover of the mattress, and the divider softly clicks as it makes the teeth unclench.

Inside the cover, under the mattress, her probing hand locates what earlier she had hidden. The blade is short, not sharp, rounded without a point.

When she saw it while standing on a chair and searching kitchen drawers for new treasures, her eyes were drawn not to the plain blade but to the pretty handle. It was shiny, full of color, and its contours pleasing.

She plucked it from among other items of interest at the moment that she was lifted from the chair and pressed into the dog crate.

When a thing is provided, the provision is for a reason. This she knows.

After their transferal to the large cage here in the room, as they explore their new quarters, the reason for the thing with the pretty handle becomes clear. The reason is not the handle, but the blade.

The ceiling and the floor of the cage are large pans. The bars of the cage are in framed panels. The panels are bolted to the walls of the floor pan and the ceiling pan. Each panel is held by two bolts at the top, two at the bottom.

Now Puzzle looks at Riddle, and Riddle looks at Puzzle, and by unspoken agreement, they choose a panel and begin.

Holding the tool, she reaches between the bars and bends her wrist severely, inserting the curved head of the blade into the slot in the round head of the bolt.

Between thumb and forefinger, Riddle pinches the square nut in which the bolt is seated, inside the pan of the cage. His small black hands are strong, and strong they need to be as Puzzle begins to turn the bolt.

The revolving bolt, the stable nut, the threads unthreading now and then produce a scraping, a brief squeak, but the soft sounds are only a whisper short of silence, and the man on guard outside will never hear.

After setting the blade aside, Puzzle turns the bolt the last few times with her fingers, the better to capture it when it comes loose, so that it will not fall and clatter against the platform on which the cage stands.

The nut releases the bolt, and freedom is a quarter won.

Hurriedly but without any concern, they engage the second bolt, which begins to turn. Puzzle's calm—and Riddle's—is a grace of their condition, their unique position. She relies—he relies—on the highest knowledge that precedes all learning, and they know that whatever will be will be for the best.

And now their freedom is half won.

Sixty-two

Shortly after seven o'clock, Grady and Cammy were reviewing the contents of the refrigerator and freezer, deciding what to have for dinner: salads and frozen pizza or salads and frozen fettuccine Alfredo, or salads and frozen homemade meatloaf, or just beer and chips.

Usually, Merlin would be at the refrigerator door, alert to the discussion, hoping to discern what kind of scraps he might be able to wheedle from them at the end of the meal. Instead, he prowled the room, sniffing here and there, and Grady had no doubt that the scents he ceaselessly reviewed were those left by Puzzle and Riddle.

As the dinner decision seemed to be sliding toward grilled-cheese sandwiches, cole slaw, and frozen waffle-cut french fries, a knock came at the door. For privacy from the Homeland horde, they had not raised the blinds at either the window or the French door, which Paul Jardine had lowered during the laser-polygraph sessions.

When he answered the knock, Grady expected to find someone with an agenda that would make him want to throw a punch, but the identity of the visitor surprised him. "Dr. Woolsey. Come in, come in. What brings you here?"

"The fate of the nation," said Lamar Woolsey with a sly smile. He closed the door behind him, and nodded to Cammy. "Dr. Rivers, I have the advantage. I'm Lamar Woolsey, but please call me Lamar."

Grady said, "He's Marcus Pipp's father."

"Stepfather," Lamar corrected. "Mr. Pipp died when Marcus was three. I married Estelle, his mother, when he was seven, raised him from then."

"I'm pleased to meet you, Lamar. Grady speaks so highly of your son."

"He had a great heart," Lamar said, "and a mind to match it. I don't go a day without thinking of him."

Abruptly tumbling to the truth, Grady said, "You're part of the crisis team."

"Now don't hold that against me, son. Often, Homeland Security does good and necessary work. This just isn't one of those times."

Merlin came to stand before Lamar, gazing up at

him solemnly before breaking into a grin and wagging his tail.

Pulling a chair from the table and sitting down, the better to rub the dog's head, Lamar said, "This one could eat the hound of the Baskervilles in a single bite."

Grady had met Lamar only once, eleven years before, between overseas tours of duty, when he had gone home with Marcus for a week while on leave.

"What do they have you doing in something like this?" Grady asked.

"There's never been something like this. Previously, in a crisis response, I've had two roles. Probability analysis—such as reviewing a planned response to a terrorist event that's still under way and developing a best-guess report on the likelihood that the proposed response would work as intended, work at all, or exacerbate the crisis. And pattern recognition in apparent chaos."

Cammy swung a chair away from the table, positioned it behind Merlin, and sat facing the mathematician, with the dog between them. "You said there's never been something like this. That's been obvious to Grady and me since we first saw Puzzle and Riddle. But what is it, Lamar? What's happening?"

"The end of one thing and the beginning of another."

"Lamar is a mathematician and a physicist, but he can go mystical on you," Grady warned.

"When a scientist tells you that 'the science is settled' in regard to **any** subject," Lamar said, "he's ceased to be a scientist, and he's become an evangelist for one cult or another. The entire history of science is that nothing in science is **ever** settled. New discoveries are continuously made, and they upend old certainties."

"Isn't that obvious?" Cammy asked.

"Most people tend to believe that the scientific theories of their time are the right ones, and that what remains for scientists to do is find ways to develop wondrous new technologies from their absolute understanding of nature's laws, structures, and mechanisms. Even many scientists succumb to the illusion that they live in the age of ultimate enlightenment. They become so committed to a theory that they spend entire careers ever more desperately defending it as new discoveries ever more rapidly undermine it."

Receiving the attentions of both Lamar and Cammy, the wolfhound sighed with contentment, but in the context of their conversation, he seemed to be expressing exasperation with the scientists of whom Lamar spoke.

"Aristotle's theory that the universe was not created in a singular event, that it had eternally existed, was the unanimous scientific view for twenty-three hundred years. Then in the early 1950s, we discovered the universe is expanding, driven ever outward by the force of the big bang that created it. What was **known** for twenty-three hundred years was wrong. Even in the latter part of the nineteenth century, it was believed that living organisms could spontaneously generate from inert matter—insects from rotting vegetables or dung, for example. How ludicrous that sounds now. And much of what we believe we know now will appear equally ludicrous in a hundred or two hundred years."

"If Puzzle and Riddle signify the end of one thing and the beginning of another," Grady said, "what's ending?"

"Darwinian evolution."

"But that's been proven. The fossil record."

"There isn't one," Lamar said. "Darwin knew it. He accounted for it by saying paleontologists hadn't yet looked in the right places. He predicted that in a hundred years, they would have found thousands of the dead-end versions of species against which nature selected. More than a hundred fifty years later, not one has been found."

As Grady pulled up a chair to a third side of Merlin and got in the game, stroking the wolfhound's broad back, Cammy said, "But evolution itself, a species adapting to its environment, changing over time—there's a fossil record in a couple of cases. At least with the horse, the whale."

Lamar shook his head. "They say—here are fossils showing the horse in stages of its evolution. But they're only **assuming** the fossils are related. These fossils may more likely be of different species instead of stages of the same one. They prove nothing. The other species became extinct. The horse didn't. And the assumption that those fossils are arranged in the correct order, showing progression in certain features, can't be supported with evidence. Neither carbon dating nor any method of fixing the period of a fossil is precise enough to support that arranged order. Again, they've been assumed to belong in that order, but mere assumptions do not qualify as science. Understand, I'm not making a case for God."

"Then what are you making a case for?" Grady asked.

"I believe what I believe about God," Lamar said, "but that has nothing to do with my opinion here. Darwinian evolution offends me simply as a mathematician, as it does virtually every mathematician who has ever seriously thought about it."

"Just remember," Grady said, "we're **not** mathematicians."

"I'll keep it simple. The tiniest measure of time

isn't the seconds shown on a clock face. The smallest measure of time is how long a ray of light takes, traveling at the speed of light, to cross the smallest distance on the molecular level of the universe. For argument's sake, let's just say it's a millionth of a second. The Earth is four billion years old. If you multiply four billion by the number of millionths of a second in a single year, you get a staggeringly large figure, arguably greater than the number of grains of sand on all the beaches around the Pacific Ocean."

"With you so far," Grady said.

"Now think about the complexity of a single gene. It contains so many features—thousands of bits of data—each of which had to be acquired by mutation. But the tiniest worm on Earth could not have evolved from a one-cell organism in four billion years even if there had been a mutation **in every one of those millionths of a second**."

Playing devil's advocate, Cammy said, "Maybe Earth is older than we think."

"It isn't older by much. By observing and measuring the rate of the universe's expansion and calculating backward to the big bang, we can date Earth's creation in the process. The entire universe is only twenty billion years old. So let's be irrational and say Earth was formed an instant after the big bang, though it couldn't have been. That doesn't help our little worm. There still wouldn't be enough time in twenty billion years for him to evolve from a single-cell organism at the rate of one mutation per millionth of a second."

Amazed, Grady said, "So it's not exactly a closed case."

"It's why evolutionists hate mathematicians. Here's another thing to think about. The minimal number of genes required to support cell function and reproduction in the simplest form of life is two hundred fifty-six. Our little worm may have a couple of thousand. It's estimated that the **human** genome contains anywhere from thirty thousand to a hundred fifty thousand genes. If the worm couldn't have evolved during the entire existence of the universe, how many hundreds of billions of more years would have been required for us to evolve?"

Cammy said, "Puzzle and Riddle. They weren't made in some lab."

"No," Lamar agreed. "Humankind has never created a new life form and will never have the knowledge to do so. We can selectively breed, modify, but not create. And your Puzzle and Riddle . . . they're **new**."

Perhaps sensing that he was no longer the wonder at the center of their attention, Merlin wandered off, sniffing the floor for the scents of his missing pals.

"Then where did they come from?" Cammy pressed.

Lamar shrugged. "Taking a strictly materialist point of view, their sudden appearance suggests some mechanism entirely different from evolution through natural selection. In the Cambrian period, at some point during a five-million-year window, which is as close as we can calculate it, a hundred new phyla appeared, thousands of species. They could have appeared steadily throughout that period—or in an instant, for all we know. No phyla have appeared since. No new phyla have **evolved**. Today, only thirty phyla remain, the rest having become extinct. Now maybe we have thirty-one."

"So what are you saying?" Cammy asked. "That one minute, Puzzle and Riddle didn't exist—and the next minute they did?"

"I'm a mathematician and a scientist, and from that materialist perspective, I've told you what there is to tell about the origins of those two stunning creatures. To give you an answer that makes any practical sense, I have to turn away from materialism and turn to intuition, to that knowledge with which we're born and from which we seem to flee most of our lives. T. S. Eliot wrote, 'What you do not know is the only thing you know.' What I do not know is where Puzzle and Riddle came from or how they got from there to here. But what

I believe is that one moment they were inert matter or perhaps not even matter but only concepts, existed only as thought—one moment breathless, the next moment breathing."

A noise drew their attention to the back door, which opened.

Sixty-three

From the cage to the table to the floor, Puzzle and Riddle descend, fearing neither capture nor harm of any kind. They trust in the wit they have been given and in the covenant that has been made with them.

They cross to the closed portal in the eastern wall of the room, through which no one ever enters and no one ever leaves. The way out is zippered shut, the pull-tab resting on the floor. Puzzle pulls the tab up, and the wall becomes a door.

She steps with Riddle out of strong light into night, into early moonlight, as only the previous day they had stepped out of infinity into the finite, from out of time into time. She has no memory of her creation, but of suddenly existing and filled with elation. She is here for a reason, and her life in time must be well-lived to ensure that she lives again outside of time. This she knows.

On all fours, they hurry around the place in which they were caged, across the grass on which so recently they played, to the steps and to the door.

They would rap, but the door is unlocked. They enter from the dark into the light, where the fearless gentle good dog greets them with delight. And the three people abruptly rise from chairs, Cammy and Grady, and the one who cried when he took their hands through the cage bars.

Puzzle approaches Cammy to return the short blade she used to extract the cage bolts, and Cammy drops to her knees. She is full of grace, it shines in her, and yet somewhere she is sad inside. This Puzzle knows.

As Cammy takes the offered blade, Grady says, "Mom's old cheese spreader. She loved that Santa Claus handle."

Having listened to many people talking, having listened well and closely, Puzzle believes that time has brought them to the next path, to the next step, as time always will. She looks at Riddle, and Riddle looks at her—and, yes, the time has come.

To Cammy, Puzzle says, "You are clear, so clear, and good and beautiful. You are a strong, strong light."

PART THREE

Life in Death

Sixty-four

A turning point in the history of science and of humanity, the passing of one great theory and eventually the devising of another: That was one thing, that was a major event, but the moment Puzzle spoke, **major event** became an inadequate description, and even the word **singularity,** used as scientists used it, would not suffice.

Cammy was no less shaken by what Puzzle said to her than by the fact that Puzzle spoke in the first place. The creature's voice was mellifluous, the sweet voice of a child, and with her strange eyes, she seemed to see to the heart of Cammy, as a child sometimes can see a truth to which adults have willfully blinded themselves.

When Riddle spoke to Grady in the equally musical voice of a young boy—"Please don't be afraid. We would never devour you in your sleep"—the clock began ticking and their course was set. No discussion was necessary between her, Grady, and Lamar; they knew in the instant that they could not allow Paul Jardine and Homeland Security to keep these creatures secret from the world.

This was not merely the event of the century. This was perhaps the most significant event of a millennium. The future of humanity, the paths that mankind followed and the choices it made, would be affected by this event in more ways than she could imagine. No one, no bureaucrat or king, no institution, no government, had the right to deny this news to the world.

They couldn't hide the two anywhere here and hope to ride out the search, for the search would not end until Puzzle and Riddle were found. Jardine had considerable manpower at his disposal, and he had as well the laser polygraph.

"The scientific team's at dinner in the mess tent," Lamar said. "Then they're scheduled to stay there for at least an hour to blue-sky this as a group. As long as the guard at the tent doesn't glance inside and see the cage empty, we've got a couple hours before the alarm bells."

"We can't drive out, no way," Grady said. "Two guards at every house on Cracker's Drive, to see us going past. And then an entire contingent, a roadblock most likely, at the intersection with the state route. If we didn't stop, if we tried to run it, I think they'd shoot the tires out, **at least** the tires. If we use four-wheel drive, go overland, they'll hear us, even see us in this moon, and cut us off."

No phones, no text-messaging devices, no computers with Internet access were available to get a message out. Besides, there was no way to describe Puzzle and Riddle that would convince and energize anyone who hadn't seen them.

"Going overland in any direction, I mean on foot," Cammy said, "where's the nearest house? The MacDermotts'?"

Grady shook his head. "That's over two miles through some rough territory, ravines and rock-slides."

Sitting prairie-dog style, Puzzle and Riddle flanked Merlin, each with an arm across his back. The three of them listened to the big furless folks, heads cocked one way and then the other.

Grady said, "The Carlyle place is a mile and a half, and that way is all deer paths through easy woods and a meadow or two, before you come to their open fields."

"Jim and Nora Carlyle? I take care of their horses. They're good people, and they're smart. When they see Puzzle and Riddle, they'll understand what's at stake, they'll let us use one of their vehicles. Then we drive out from there, and we're past all the guards, the roadblocks."

Lamar said, "I should stay here, do what I can to

delay them from discovering you've gone, then confuse and misdirect them. Chaos is what I do."

"No," Grady said. "Jardine knows about me in the army, so he knows about me and Marcus, so he probably knows about the connection between you and me by now. You'll grow old and die in the slammer. Your best hope is to stay with us all the way until we can present Puzzle and Riddle to the TV cameras, when and wherever we're able to do that."

"What about these shoes? Will I make it in these shoes, maybe slow you down?"

"Aren't those Rockports? Sure, you'll be fine. We aren't rock climbing, just walking in the woods."

"I've never been a walking-in-the-woods kind of guy, but I'll do my best, I'll keep up with you."

"Will there be guards between us and the woods?"

"Yes," said Lamar. "Definitely."

"We'll know," Puzzle said. "We see everything in the dark, all the way to the bottom of the night."

To Cammy, Grady said, "I'll grab a jacket. Collar Merlin for me. We can use flashlights when we're so far into the woods no one here can see them, but for some distance, when the branches are too thick to let the moonlight in, we might need Merlin on a leash to lead us. He knows the paths that way, it's one of our favorite walks."

Cammy slipped into her jacket, collared Merlin, and clipped the leash to the collar.

Standing at the door, ready to open it, Lamar Woolsey said, "Too bad I don't have time to run a probability analysis on this plan of yours. I have a nasty feeling, there's chaos brewing in it."

Puzzle said, "What is leads to what will be, and all will be well if we do what is right."

Lamar nodded. "If you say so."

"She did," Riddle told him. "She said so. And she's right. Never fear the future. Whatever happens, the future is the only way back."

The novelty of hearing them talk was probably years away from wearing off, and Cammy listened, rapt. "The only way back to what?"

"Back to where we belong forever," said Riddle. "The future is the one path out of time into eternity."

Grady returned with three flashlights. "Are we ready?"

"Absolutely," Lamar said. "The coach just gave us a pep talk, and we're in gear for action. I'll scout the way."

Lamar stepped onto the back porch, leaving the door open, and after a moment motioned for them to follow him.

Sixty-five

In Jim's cramped study, Henry Rouvroy put down the hand grenade, looked over the books on the shelves, and removed the volume of his brother's haiku.

The noise in the attic faded away. He took no comfort in the silence. He knew the rapping-out of meter on a ceiling beam would soon resume.

Or the torment would take another form. His tormentor had not finished with him yet; and would not be finished until he thrust in the knives, thrust again and again.

Restless, Henry walked the house, back and forth, around and around, carrying the hand grenade in one hand and the book in the other, reading haiku, thumbing pages.

He didn't know why he felt compelled to read

Jim's haiku. But intuition told him that he might be rewarded for doing so.

When he found the harrier poem, his breath caught in his throat:

Swooping harrier—
calligraphy on the sky,
talons, then the beak.

Henry's keen intuition served him well, and his classes in logic at Harvard prepared him to reason his way quickly to the meaning of this discovery.

The poem left on the kitchen notepad was not a new composition. Jim had written it long before Henry's arrival, not just hours ago.

Therefore, the poem could not possibly refer to the harriers in the sky moments before Henry murdered Jim. The poem had nothing to do with Jim's murder and nothing to do with Henry's, either.

Not that he had believed for a minute that Jim had returned from the dead to compose verse and threaten him with it. Henry was not a superstitious person, and even immersion in the primitive culture of these rural hills could not so quickly wash away the education and, indeed, enlightenment that he received in those hallowed halls in Cambridge. But at least finding the haiku in this book **confirmed** his certainty that his tormentor must be someone **pretending** to be Jim.

Or did it?

Jim didn't need to copy a haiku out of a book. Having written it, he would remember it. Remembering, he would see how useful it could be in the current circumstances.

No. Jim was not alive and was not one of the living dead. Jim was, damn it, as dead as—

In the attic, someone rapped out a few lines of iambic pentameter, then a few lines of dactylic heptameter.

Sixty-six

After more than thirty-one years, Tom Bigger remembered the way home as clearly as though he had left it only a month before. The street canopied with alders that were old even when he'd been a boy, the cast-iron streetlamps with the beveled panes, the grand old houses behind deep lawns all stirred in him a time when he was a boy, preadolescence, before he became so angry, before he was made angry by ideologies that now seemed insane to him and alien.

Like some others, his parents' house had not been restored so much as remade into a greater grandeur than it originally possessed. Nevertheless, he could recognize it, and the sight of it thrilled as much as it saddened him.

The time had arrived to say good-bye to Josef

Yurashalmi, and Tom fumbled for words to adequately express his gratitude.

But as the old man parked in front of the house, he said, "You don't know they still live there, Tom. All these years . . . And though it pains me to say it, the way you look, you won't inspire the confidence of whoever might live there now. If maybe your folks have moved and if maybe the people here know where they've gone, you'll be more likely to learn their whereabouts if I'm at your side when you ring the bell."

"You've done too much already. You should be heading home to Hannah, she's not—"

"Hush, Tom. I'm an old man trying to do a **gemilut chesed,** and if you care about my soul, you'll stop arguing with me and let me get it done."

"**Gemilut chesed?** What is that?"

"An act of loving kindness, which I guess you haven't seen much of in your years of rambling. At this time in his life, any old Jew like me starts wondering if he's done enough of them."

Humbled, Tom said, "I don't think I've done any."

"You're young, you have time. I'm sorry if my slippers might embarrass you, but let's go see if your **tata-mama** are waiting for you."

The street was quiet, but Tom's heart was not. Walking with Josef toward the front door, he lost courage step by step. He had rejected them, had spoken of despising them and their values, and after all this time, they would be justified in despising him.

"You can do it," Josef said. "You need to do it. I'll stay as long as it takes for the three of you to be comfortable. But your folks are my age, Tom, so I probably know how they think better than you know. And how they'll think about this—they'll thank God you came back, and they'll kiss you and cry and kiss you some more, and it'll be like none of it ever happened."

On the veranda, Tom took a deep breath and pressed the doorbell.

Sixty-seven

With Puzzle and Riddle looking into the very bottom of the night, they found ways around three guards at different stations. The escapees made their way boldly toward the line of mobile laboratories, between two of them, south and then west toward the end of the yard, into the meadow.

From there they had to double back toward the north to find the entrance to the woods and the path that Merlin knew as well as any dray horse, in older times, knew and could follow its route without its driver's direction.

Under the interlaced branches of the trees, the moonlight flickered and eventually went out. The way before them became black and forbidding. But Cammy knew that Merlin saw well in darkness, and his two new friends apparently saw even more clearly than he did.

Halfway to the Carlyle house, Puzzle halted them with a single word, **"Bear,"** and they waited for a while in silence. Perhaps the bear had paused to listen to them, for after four or five minutes, Cammy heard it moving off, through the woods.

After the bear, they used flashlights, and progressed more quickly, with less stumbling and thrashing through the brush that here and there intruded on the trail.

When they left the forest and entered the fields farmed by the Carlyles, the lights of Jim and Nora's house were a welcome sight.

At the front-porch steps, on the lawn, someone had parked a Land Rover that Cammy had never seen before. She was prepared to reveal Puzzle and Riddle to the Carlyles, but she wasn't pleased about taking the risk of bringing someone unknown into the picture.

When her flashlight revealed Virginia license plates on the vehicle, her concern grew, and she whispered to Grady, "Better take them to the garage back of the barn. Jim's Mountaineer is there, and I think he keeps the keys under the floor mat on the driver's side. Load everybody and drift down here as quiet as you can."

"Come with us," Grady urged.

"Tell you what—I'll wait on the porch until I see you coasting down this way. Then I'll knock on the door. If I get Jim and Nora's okay, we'll be able to go legally, and that's a lot better, nobody looking for a stolen Mountaineer. But if something's wrong here, we'll go any way we can."

Sixty-eight

Earlier, in the late afternoon, Rudy Neems parked the rented SUV a block from Liddon Wallace's house. In the cargo hold stood ten two-gallon cans that he bought at a Pep Boys and filled at a Mobil station. Because the cans featured safety vents, the interior of the vehicle smelled of gasoline, but there weren't sufficient fumes to cause an explosion. When he had finished with Kirsten Wallace and the boy, he would return for the SUV, drive it into their garage, and prepare for the burning.

He approached the house openly, carrying a clipboard and a small toolbox that he also bought at Pep Boys, as bold as anyone would be who belonged there. He might have been a meter reader or a repairman of some kind.

No one saw him, no one crossed his path, and

he used a key that the attorney had provided to let himself into the side garage door.

During the day, the alarm system was not engaged. When Kirsten Wallace switched on the system later, Rudy would already be inside and comfortable in his hidey-hole, contemplating his enjoyment of her.

Because two housekeepers were in the residence, one until six o'clock and the other until nine, Rudy was cautious when he entered from the garage and through the laundry room.

He was prepared to kill the housekeepers if he encountered them, even if he was not attracted to them, so much did he want Kirsten. But if Kirsten came home shortly before six, as per her schedule, she would know something was wrong when she found the housekeepers gone. Rudy would have lost the advantage of surprise, and he would have to take her the moment that she came through the door, before her suspicion was aroused.

Happily, he found the mechanical room across the hall from the laundry. Here were water heaters, one of the furnaces, the water softener, and other equipment.

According to Wallace, the two maids cleaned the mechanical room on the first Friday of the month and otherwise never entered it. Nevertheless, Rudy crawled into a space behind the furnace and sat there in the dark, where he would not be seen even if someone turned on a light and came in here for some reason.

In his mind, he rehearsed all the things he intended to do to Kirsten. The afternoon and early evening passed so quickly that he was surprised when the authoritative digital voice of the security system announced, **"Alarmed to night mode,"** so loud that he could hear it clearly through the closed door, from the speaker in the hallway.

Just before the second housekeeper left at nine, she brought dinner to the table. At that point the boy, Benny, was in bed and asleep, and Kirsten could enjoy her meal uninterrupted.

Except that Rudy Neems would interrupt her tonight as she had never in her life been interrupted.

He waited five minutes before easing open the hallway door, just to be sure she would be sitting at dinner in the dining room. Even dining alone, she preferred to eat there, where she could spread out her newspaper on the big table.

Rudy Neems intended to spread out her newspaper as she had never had it spread out in her life.

Between the butler's pantry and the dining room, one of the two swinging doors stood open. Kirsten sat at the table, her back to him.

She wore her blond hair short. So elegant was her neck that it entranced him.

When he had done her as much as he wanted,

then part of the way he would kill her would be by strangulation. That neck.

He watched her turn a page of the newspaper. Her hands were slender, long-fingered, beautifully shaped.

Before strangling her, he could break her fingers one by one.

As he crossed the threshold of the butler's pantry, a floorboard creaked underfoot.

She turned her head, more gorgeous than her photos suggested, and she screamed.

Rudy rushed her as she came up from her chair. She had a fork in her hand, raising it like a dagger, but he didn't care about that. She was fast, but Rudy was immeasurably faster. He seized her wrist and almost broke it, she cried out in pain, the fork fell, he pushed the chair out of the way, he shoved her back onto the table, onto her dinner, and—

He heard the window shattering an instant before the alarm went off. Startled, Rudy relented from his assault just enough to allow Kirsten to get her breath.

She screamed again, she threw a wineglass at his face, Rudy dodged it. As the glass shattered on the floor, this guy appeared in an archway on the right, this big strange guy coming in from the hall, his face a ruin, a guy so bizarre that Rudy was for a fatal moment paralyzed.

When he subdued a woman, Rudy liked to force

her into submission with nothing more than his hands, his body. He didn't use a gun, a knife, a sap. He was a solid block, and he liked to start their time together with a fun demonstration of his great strength and his delight in using it.

The sight of this charging fury, this Frankenstein thing, shocked Kirsten's scream out of her. Gasping, she backed away from both of them.

Rudy snared her knife off the table, but it was not a steak knife, just a regular dinner knife, and he didn't get to slash with it anyway, because this giant hand closed around his wrist the way his hand had closed around Kirsten's wrist, the biggest damn hand in the universe. In the broken face were the most terrifying eyes Rudy had ever seen either in a horror movie or in a mirror, eyes full of **wrath**. Now the broken-faced man had Rudy in a two-hand grip, twisting Rudy's wrist, bending his hand backward. Everything had happened so fast that maybe six seconds after this thing burst into the room, Rudy was screaming instead of Kirsten, and when his wrist snapped like the wrist of a little girl, the pain was a white flash, as sharp and bright as lightning behind his eyes, and the monster threw him down out of the blinding white light into blackness and silence.

Rudy Neems was unconscious only a couple of minutes. When he came around, his assailant loomed over him, stared down at him, and he didn't want to meet those eyes. He looked away from those eyes for the same reason he would have looked away from the challenging stare of a rabid wolf.

He did not see Kirsten, but a white-haired old man in slippers was shuffling around, gathering up the debris from the struggle: the fork, the dinner knife, pieces of the broken wineglass. He returned the silverware to the table and dropped the shards of glass in a plastic trash bag.

"Good thing she hadn't poured wine yet," the old man said to the monster. "What a mess that would've been. Oh, no, look at that—some fava beans smashed in the carpet." He clucked his tongue. "Now, Tom, I'm not sure an act that violent qualifies as a **gemilut chesed,** even if I think it was loving kindness that motivated you. But who am I to say, one way or the other, I'm just an old fart trying to run a business and do what's right in a time when neither of those things pays."

The pain in the shattered wrist was so bad and the old man was so blurred through his tears that Rudy wondered if he might be hallucinating.

Sirens rose in the distance.

Sixty-nine

Henry Rouvroy could do nothing to keep Jim out of the house, because the poet would come in through the attic if he wasn't able to enter through a door, because next he would **walk through a wall,** with no regard for the opinions of the enlightened professors and elite power brokers who would dismiss the idea of ghosts with a sneer or a laugh. He was in control now, the dead brother, and there was nothing to be done about it.

Consequently, because a grenade would be useless against a man who was already dead, Henry put it in the refrigerator. The choice of the refrigerator puzzled him for a moment, but then he decided he must be reacting to a subconscious awareness that the hand grenade resembled a pineapple.

In a despairing mood of resignation, he removed all the bracing chairs from the doors and returned them to the dinette table. When he opened the cellar door, he stood at the head of the stairs, peering down into the lower room, where the lights had been on for more than twenty-four hours. He heard nothing down there, but he said, "Jim?" When he received no reply, he said, "I shouldn't have killed you myself, not my own brother. I should have hired someone to kill you and then killed him."

He went from window to window, opening the draperies and raising the blinds. He was finished hiding. He couldn't endure another night of waiting for retribution.

At one of the front windows, he saw a woman on the porch. At first he assumed that she must be Nora, joining Jim for the next phase of the haunting, but when she became aware of him and turned, she proved to be a stranger. And an attractive one.

If an attractive woman came to him, rather than Henry having to go stalk and capture her, perhaps his fate wasn't sealed, after all. Perhaps this was a sign that the Hour of Dead Jim was over, that the worst of the haunting lay behind him, that he had passed this initiation rite into the pagan reality of rural life, had won the approval of the earth spirits and fertility gods that ruled this world of farms and logging operations. If so, he could now establish his retreat and dig in to ride out the chaos that the senator and his friends were engineering.

He opened the door to her and smiled.

She frowned and said, "Jim?"

"I've tried to be," he said.

"What did you say?"

"A little joke. It's been a long day." Evidently she knew the Carlyles, which encouraged him to step back from the threshold and say, "Nora and I were just going to start dinner. Can you join us?"

After a hesitation, she stepped inside. "I can't, Jim. The most incredible wonderful thing has happened."

Closing the door, he said, "I sure could use a wonderful thing. A day like this, I need a lift. Come tell me and Nora about it."

"It's going to be better to show than tell," she said, following him toward the kitchen.

"Nora's in the potato cellar. I'm supposed to go down and help her carry up some spuds."

The door stood open. The light glowed below. He was pleased at how plausible the story sounded.

"The thing is, Jim, I really need to borrow your Mountaineer."

"Sure. No problem. How about helping Nora

bring up some baskets of potatoes, and I'll get my car-insurance card for you just in case there might be an accident or something."

"I don't need the card," she said.

"Oh, I know, I know. But the law does say you have to carry proof of insurance, and you know how I am, living by the law."

In fact, Jim had written a poem titled "Living by the Law," about the beauty of law, though it was about natural law, not the laws written by men.

The reference to the poem worked. The woman bought it and smiled. "All right, sure, get the insurance card. Straight-arrow Jim. I'll help Nora."

He watched her descend the stairs, and when she reached the bottom, he called out, "I just had a senior moment **way** before my time." He hurried down after her, adding, "Forgot the insurance card is right here in my wallet."

As Henry reached the lower room, the woman arrived at the potato-cellar door, which stood ajar. The light was on in there.

A pang of terror pierced Henry, and for a moment, he did not know why—and then he knew.

The woman opened the door and stepped inside, and on the floor lay Nora, the first woman in his planned harem.

"I was being Jim, after all," Henry said.

In his mind's eye, he saw himself wearing Jim's gloves, moving Nora from the barn in the wheelbarrow. After dinner the previous night. Being Jim. Really into the role. Well, he **had** taken some drama classes at Harvard.

His visitor, the nameless woman, turned to stare at him from the trap of the potato cellar, her eyes wide.

As he moved to the doorway, Henry said, "And Jim. Jim's in the chicken house. Stripped and thrown in the chicken house. I didn't have time to feed them. Let them peck the meat off his bones. A smaller grave to dig."

"Jim, what's the matter with you?"

He looked at his hands, at his clean nails, remembering the grime, the filth, the gummy blood under his fingernails from wearing the gloves and being Jim.

"Henry," came the dreaded whisper, **"Henry . . . Henry,"** and he dared not look to see what stood behind him.

The woman, who could see what stood behind him, only said, "Who is Henry?"

"Henry," Henry said, and knew chicken-pecked Jim did not stand behind him, after all.

"Jim," the woman said, "back away from the door, I'm coming out of here, Jim."

He had worn the gloves to copy the poem from the book, and then had to wash his hands again.

"I'm not quite sure of my exact condition," he told the woman in the potato cellar. "I never had the time to take as many psychology courses as I wanted to."

She came to the doorway, but he did not back off.

He said, "Do you hear that? Do you hear iambic pentameter? The rapping, rapping, rap-rap-rapping."

"No," she said.

"Oh, I do. I hear it all the time. This is so sad. You would have been such an exciting woman to keep in the potato cellar. Then I could have had it all. But look what this rustic world has made of me in just one day. This isn't who I am or want to be, and clearly there can be no going back for me in any sense."

"Move, Jim," she said, and tried to push him backward.

"I've got to go upstairs now," he said, "and get the hand grenade from the refrigerator."

He went to the stairs. After ascending three, he glanced back at her. "Do you want to come with me to get the hand grenade?"

"No, Jim. I'll wait here."

"Okay. Thank you for waiting. I'll bring a

grenade for you, and we'll pull the pins in the potato cellar."

He continued up the stairs. He was sorry to hear the outside cellar door open, and the rain doors over the stairs. He really didn't want to go out alone in the potato cellar. Oh, right. Not alone. There was Nora.

Seventy

The Mountaineer coasted through the moonlight. Not daring to look back, Cammy ran around the front of it as Grady pulled to a stop. She yanked open the passenger door, clambered into the SUV, and couldn't find her voice.

Lamar was in the backseat. In the cargo area with Merlin, Puzzle and Riddle were giggling.

Cammy had never heard them giggle before. Under the circumstances, their sweet childlike voices sounded sinister.

Her cry at last broke free of her throat: "Move, move, **move**!"

Grady accelerated away from the house before he asked, "What? What's wrong?"

"Hell if I know. Jim . . . he . . . I don't know, I think he killed Nora, she's dead in the potato cellar."

This announcement put the damper on what-ever fun the three pals were having, and left Grady gaping.

After a moment, she turned to Lamar and said, "You predicted chaos, and you were right. Was that it? What's ahead of us?"

"Just the future," Puzzle said from behind Lamar. "Just where we're meant to be."

*

Henry Rouvroy, alias Jim Carlyle, descended the cellar stairs, a grenade in each hand.

Nora remained on the floor, eyes open, in the potato cellar.

He sat on the floor beside his sister-in-law, his wife.

He pulled the ring from the first grenade but kept the safety lever depressed.

For reasons he could not imagine, in his mind's eye he saw not Jim's naked corpse in the chicken house, among the cackling hens, but instead the senator at a press conference, waving the photo of Marcus Pipp and demanding a court-martial. Henry had advised him on that strategy, but he'd done so based on misinformation, and it had not gone well.

The senator didn't fire him because the senator thought the episode achieved exactly what he wanted it to achieve. The senator was an idiot.

Henry couldn't get Marcus Pipp's face out of his mind. He didn't want to die while thinking about Marcus Pipp. That's how he died, anyway.

＊

Grady drove as fast as the winding road would allow, heading south out of the county, into a somewhat more settled area, where the dark hills were speckled with house lights. They were a long way still from a small city with its own TV station, but if their escape had not yet been noticed, the odds were in their favor.

They passed a roadhouse where the parking lot was packed with pickups and the marquee advertised a country band.

A quarter of a mile later, when they topped a hill and saw the roadblock at the intersection below, Grady braked and slid into a turn, and Cammy said, "The roadhouse. All those people. It's some kind of chance."

As he crested the hill he had topped from the other direction a moment earlier, Grady glanced at the rearview mirror and saw that the pursuit was already under way.

Bailing from the Mountaineer in the roadhouse parking lot, Cammy sprinted to the back, opened the tailgate. "Out, out, hurry!"

Merlin leaped from the vehicle, and the lantern-eyed duo sprang after him.

As the six of them ran toward the roadhouse entrance, Lamar said, "Where's the music? Never heard a country crowd this quiet."

Inside, the joint was packed, as the herd of pickups indicated that it ought to be, but the band played no music, no dancers danced, and people were gathered in peculiar configurations at the bar, at an area to the left of the stage, and in a separate raised lounge area near the rest rooms.

"Must be a hundred people here," Cammy said. "Maybe a hundred fifty. Homeland Security can't arrest them all, can't shut up all these people. Come on. It's time. Come on, Puzzle, Riddle, it's time for your debut."

"The stage," Grady suggested. "The microphone."

Behind them, Lamar said, "Oh, my God," but Cammy didn't look back, just kept on moving through the mostly abandoned tables, with the wolfhound and the two amazements rushing ahead of her.

She mounted the stage, took the microphone from the stand, and said, "Please, may I have your attention!"

Joining her, Grady said, "It's not turned on."

She fumbled for a switch, found one, and her voice boomed out—"Folks, everyone, hey, I've got an announcement!"—and as she spoke, the black-clad legions, carrying fully automatic carbines at the ready, burst through the front doors, an instant later through a back entrance.

The patrons turned toward her. But half the armed agents spread through the room, intimidating the crowd, while the other half came toward the stage.

Clambering onto the stage, one of them said, "You're under arrest," and she heard another one telling Grady that he had the right to remain silent, and she said, "But you have no right to **make us be silent**!"

In the chaos, she heard Lamar shouting at her from among the tables, and just as she was about to start clubbing one of the agents with the microphone, she understood what he was saying: **"Cammy, Grady, look at the TVs!"**

In the distant lounge was a big flat screen, a smaller screen behind the bar, another to one side of the stage. The music had stopped, the dancing, the drinking, because people had been drawn to something on television.

On the screens were Puzzle and Riddle.

Cammy stared uncomprehending.

Someone cranked up the sound on the flat screen as an anchorman appeared in place of Puzzle and Riddle. "We've got breaking news now, something big is happening out there tonight. Whatever this event in Michigan means, and the pair in western Pennsylvania, apparently they aren't alone." He spoke to someone off screen, off mike, and turned again to the camera. "I'm being told we've got a live report coming right now from an affiliate in Marietta, Georgia, and three more to follow, and I think somebody's saying the same thing's happening in Italy . . . France, I think I heard Italy and France. We're going now to Marietta."

In Georgia, a pair like Puzzle and Riddle were capering on a lawn around which forty or fifty people had gathered, for once not to be seen on camera but to see more directly what the camera saw.

In confusion, the armed agents in the roadhouse backed off the stage. Cammy heard a squad leader on a cell phone nearby, but the TVs interested her more than Homeland Security.

The roadhouse crowd, however, appeared less drawn to the TVs now than to the two wonders here among them.

Cammy carried Puzzle, and Grady carried Riddle, down from the stage, into the room, to allow these citizens of Colorado to meet the new creations with which they now shared the world.

Puzzle whispered in her ear, "You're so clear, you shine so bright, and there's no sadness in you anymore."

Seventy-one

Bald and hunched, his mustache white, the old man sat on a bench in the park across from the retirement home. He wore sunglasses on an overcast day. Hooked to the bench was a white cane.

Tom Bigger sat beside the blind man and said, "What do you think of all the news?"

"I've heard their voices. They sound like angels. The sound of them makes me happy. I wish I could see them. Are they beautiful?"

"They are. They're the most beautiful things I've ever seen."

"The news last evening said seventy thousand pair counted so far, worldwide."

"You hear the news this morning?" Tom asked.

"No. What now? Mirna, my wife, she says the

next thing we'll discover they can fly like birds. What do you think it means?"

"Another chance," Tom said.

"That's how it feels to me, too. You know what I think?"

"What do you think?" Tom asked.

"One of us ever kills one of them, then that's the end for us, for all of us. That's the end, right there."

"You could be right," Tom said. "On the news this morning, they say scientists have sequenced their genome. Know what they found?"

"Something amazing," the blind man said. "That's what I hope. I've been waiting all my life for something amazing."

"First," Tom said, "they don't look anything like us. Not like us at all. But what the scientists say is their genome matches ours in every detail."

The blind man laughed. He couldn't stop laughing for a while. The character of his laughter was sheer delight, and Tom found it infectious.

When they had stopped laughing together, the old man said, "Have you seen one for real or just on TV?"

"I not only saw two for real, sir, but I saw them come through—from wherever they came."

The blind man reached out, found his shoulder,

pressed a hand to his arm. "Is this true? You were a witness?"

"On a bluff above the sea, farther down the coast from here. It changed my life, seeing it happen."

"Tell me about it. Tell me all about it, please."

"The first thing I need to tell you is, there were squirrels on the bluff, and a dozen birds, and they all became very still when it happened. But it wasn't the appearance of the pair that transfixed them. It was something else. I sensed something was with us that I couldn't see, something that maybe the birds and squirrels could see, something that brought the two animals or passed them through from wherever. I don't know. I was very afraid, but at the same time . . . more alive inside than I had been for a long, long time. And . . . I was changed."

The blind man considered this in silence for a while, and then he said, "Are you my Tom?"

"Yes, Dad. I'm your Tom."

"Oh, I want to touch your face."

"It's not a good face, Dad. I'm afraid for Mom to see it."

From behind the bench, a woman said, "I've seen it, my love. You passed me on the way to sit with your father. You didn't know me, but I knew you."

Tom allowed his father to touch his face, and his

father wept, not only at his son's suffering, but also with joy.

When Tom rose and turned to see his mother, she said, "You are so beautiful, Tom. No, look at me. You are beautiful. Your face is a face of transcendence."

Seventy-two

Cammy watched them from the kitchen window as they frolicked in the new snow with Merlin. But for their black hands, black feet, and black noses, they might have been invisible.

The coffeemaker began to gurgle, and the sudden aroma of fresh Jamaica blend flooded the kitchen.

Grady said, "Already, I'm inadequate to home-school them. Their minds leap ahead of mine. Think you could help?"

"I'd like nothing more. But they'll probably leap ahead of me too, in no time."

He joined her at the window, a hand on her shoulder. "Do you lie awake some nights, wondering where this is going—I mean the world now, with them in it and everything so changed?"

She shook her head. "No. Wherever they're going, they're taking the world with them, and I know beyond doubt that wherever they want us to be, that's where we'll belong."

About the Author

DEAN KOONTZ is the author of many #1 **New York Times** bestsellers. He lives in Southern California with his wife, Gerda, their golden retriever, Anna, and the enduring spirit of their golden, Trixie.

Correspondence for the author should be addressed to:

Dean Koontz
P.O. Box 9529
Newport Beach, California 92658